Cover design by Daniel Castlewrite

This book is a work of fiction. Names, characters, places, and incidents either are products of the author's imagination or are used fictitiously. Any resemblance to actual persons, living or dead, events, or locales is entirely coincidental.

Printed in the United States of America

First Printing: August, 2022

ISBN-979-8-9867455-0-3

D0901500

This book is dedicated to all the amazing people in my life who have stuck by me through the toughest times.

A special thanks to everyone who helped make this book special. Thank you for reading all the variants, providing invaluable input, and <u>constructive criticism</u>.

I could not have done this without all of you.

Thank you and enjoy!

HELIX

MYSTERIES

THE FIRST CHANGE

By: Daniel Castlewrite

PROLOGUE

"I have a clean shot," a voice rings out over the radio.

"Hold, do not fire." The response in the sniper's earpiece is calm but calculated and alert.

In the darkness of night, men and women in black suits scramble to get into positions that would provide some cover just in case a firefight were to break out. Their weapons drawn and at the ready. Another group, outfitted with tactical gear and heavy weapons, comes sprinting out of a heavily reinforced door, on the side of a stone building. All of them moving in unison, as though they had rehearsed for this moment hundreds of times.

Everyone settles into their own predesignated, defensive position surrounding the main entrance to the massive structure. Each, taking aim at a dark figure that is casually strolling towards them, along a well-manicured lawn.

"Stop right there!" A voice says sternly over a loudspeaker. "You are trespassing on government property."

The figure pauses briefly to look back at a decimated steel gate through which it passed. Almost as if to taunt the two dozen or so men and women now taking aim at it.

"Put your hands up and lay down on the ground with your arms extended!" Is the next set of instructions from the loudspeaker. "If you do not comply, we will open fire!"

The figure turns its gaze back to the front entrance of the building and continues to walk calmly, as though there is nothing out of the ordinary. A radio click resounds in the earpiece of a sniper, who is perched on top of the massive building.

"Eagle one, give him a warning," the voice says firmly.

Instantly, the silence of the night is broken by a sharp, echoing pop. A bullet lodges itself into the ground just in front and to the right of the figure. Sending up a small cloud of dust and debris.

"I said stop! Put your hands up and lie down on the ground!" The voice from the loudspeaker reiterates the instructions.

Unfazed, the figure continues to stroll forward as though nothing happened. The sniper's earpiece clicks again.

"Eagle One, take out his knee, over," the voice commands.

"Eagle One, copy, out," the sniper responds with affirmation.

The crosshair of the sniper scope pans down the torso of his target. Although the men and women on the ground struggle to identify the dark figure's features from a distance, the magnification of the Eagle One's scope allows him to see every detail. The man's white hair is pulled back in a clean ponytail. His blue eyes appear to almost glow in the dark. White stubble covers his face…

He must be in his mid-fifties. A leather duster fits snugly around his chest and waist, held tight with thin straps that run across and around his body. Black riding boots come up almost to his knees, with loose-fitting pants tucked in neatly. He looks like a pirate that should be hijacking a spaceship in a sci-fi adventure film.

Although he does not appear to have any firearms, a long sword handle protrudes from behind his right shoulder. Perhaps a katana or something similar. The sniper's crosshair stops at the man's knee. Exhaling to steady his aim, the sniper pulls the trigger with expertise and another pop shatters the silence, echoing through the cold night.

Although what happens next only takes a fraction of a second, the story of a bullet being fired is quite fascinating – The trigger pull releases the hammer, which hits the firing pin. The pin then impacts the primer, creating a tiny spark, which ignites the gunpowder. The resulting explosion, inside the bullet casing, forces the tip to separate and begin its journey down the barrel.

As the bullet moves along it is compressed and spun up. The bullet then emerges with incredible force, accompanied by flames from the explosion. Now, charged with all that energy and perfect spin, it flies towards its target. Ready to penetrate whatever it hits and expend all its energy instantly upon impact. Without protection, such as armor, a bullet like this is absolutely devastating to the human body... but not this time.

Within an inch or two of the pirate's knee, the bullet simply dissipates into a blue ball. That, in turn, releases a bolt of lightning, which extends from the pirate to where the bullet originated. The bolt's energy travels instantly through the rifle and the sniper. The remainder of the bullets explode in the magazine and the sniper's heart explodes in his chest... All in less than half of a second.

The beauty of the lightning bolt, followed by the sound of a small explosion on the roof, takes even the most seasoned security team members by surprise. However, they quickly shift their gaze back to their target.

"Open fire! Fire at will!" The voice yells over the loudspeaker.

The quiet night instantly explodes with the chatter of assault rifles and pistols firing in near unison. But, from a distance, it sounds like only one or two shots had been fired. In less than two seconds, fifteen of the twenty-seven ground team members, along with every sharpshooter and sniper on the roof, are all dead. Just like Eagle One, the moment their bullets came within an inch or two of the dark figure they dissolved. For every bullet, a bolt of lightning arced back to each and every shooter, simultaneously.

Those still standing either missed or never discharged their weapons. Now paralyzed by the image of smoke slowly rising from the bodies and weapons of their teammates, they stand frozen with shock and disbelief. The mysterious stranger doesn't stop. His pace remains constant, as though he is oblivious to what transpired just moments ago.

As he nears the main entrance, he stops to take in the carnage and terror that now surrounds him. Looking over the horrified, incredulous expressions of the ones still standing, he begins to speak.

"What a waste…" He says in a tone that is both calm and matter-of-fact. "They did not need to die, and neither do any of you. Do not get in my way and show me to the President."

CHAPTER I

FRIEND IN THE DARKNESS

Darkness… Total darkness. My eyes struggle to pick up some outline in the emptiness. I need a glimmer of light, something, anything! I begin to wonder if I'm blind, but that's not it. Yet, there is definitely something different about my vision. It's like I'm in a void, enveloped by it. I cannot tell if I am standing on solid ground or floating in mid-air. Nothing makes sense… I must be dreaming.

I blink repeatedly to try to adjust, but it's of no use. Suddenly, two hands lunge at me from the dark. I see them clearly, almost as if they're emitting their own light. In typical dream fashion, time slows to a crawl. The hands move toward me slowly enough to analyze and even observe specific details about them, but I cannot react.

As the hands move closer, I notice dry, cracked skin. I can see blisters and cuts. There is a tint to them as if they had been exposed to the sun for far too long. Perhaps I am in a desert? But I don't feel hot… or cold for that matter.

Short fingernails, with jagged corners, as if the owner has been biting them incessantly. There is dirt under the fingernails, and the knuckles have dried blood, from cuts that weren't properly dressed. These are the hands of a laborer - perhaps a mechanic, a construction worker, or maybe a battle-hardened soldier.

As the hands stretch further toward me, my instincts begin to kick in. I should be jumping backward, sideways, or at least edging away. Yet, I feel no malice or threat. I stand frozen in time, almost as if the hands were moving in so quickly and unexpectedly that my body did not have time to react. Though in my mind, I seem to have all the time in the world.

The hands grab onto my clothes. I feel a tug and my shirt pulls tighter around my shoulders. It seems I am being drawn into the darkness or perhaps being held onto by someone who is being pulled away. I desperately try to focus my vision in an effort to discern what is happening – whose hands are these? Why are they holding onto me?

A part of me feels compelled to reach back and reciprocate, to help this person out there in the darkness... Then, just as the hands first appeared, a face begins to take shape. I know it is someone familiar but cannot make out who. The vast darkness begins to fill with an air of chaos. Try as I might, I cannot discern the individual's face, not even to determine whether it is a man or a woman.

The grasp tightens and the gap between myself and the familiar stranger closes fast. I do not fight back, not that I could, even if I wanted to. I am being pulled with intent, but still, I feel no fear. The face gets closer, but like a photo with a filter, it is too blurry to make out the person's identity.

Suddenly, the lips become clear, and all my focus shifts to them. Like the hands, the lips show signs of wear from the elements. They are chapped and cracked. They part as if yelling something, but just as the darkness obscures my vision, the deafening silence makes it impossible to hear.

Whatever words escape the stranger's lips, come out muffled and unintelligible. In trying to decipher the words, I lose track of the proximity of the stranger's face. Then, I feel the mysterious lips press against my own.

A kiss? It feels like being kissed for the first time. All the confusion, fear, and concern melt away. Replaced by a mix of longing and desire, excitement and thrill. The kind of emotions you experience when you get something you've been waiting for forever!

Is this someone I've been attracted to for a long time? I try to think - to picture the faces of people I know... but my mind draws a blank. I am too stunned to do anything but return the affection.

For a brief moment, time grinds to a halt. Any second now, the darkness will dissipate, and all will be made clear. Yet, it seems that I have stopped caring about this as well. Passion consumes me and I no longer want this perfect moment to end.

Alas, the kiss ends as abruptly as it began. My friend in the darkness pulls away. The grasp on my shirt is released, and the hands fade back into the gloom from which they emerged. I am once again alone, all alone in the darkness.

As I reel from the kiss, my void fills with a familiar tune. It is distant and soft. A melody that I have heard many times over. It is telling me something, reminding me of something I must do.

The feeling is akin to being carried in by a tide. I gradually float back into consciousness and my world turns from darkness to blackness. The tune gets louder, closer almost… I open my eyes.

This feeling is not new to me. It happens often, several times a week actually. I know exactly what time it is - 5:13AM. Five days a week I awake to this tune. For some reason, I still try to verify this fact with my sleek smartphone. Hoping that perhaps a coworker pulled a prank and changed my alarm to 2AM, and I have another three hours to sleep...

The alarm always starts out softly and gradually becomes louder. I am still amazed at how long it took engineers to implement the ingenious concept of bringing someone out of their sleep with a melody that increases in volume. Rather than startling and snapping people awake with a loud, obnoxious car horn. That beats redundantly against the eardrum, like a baseball bat to the head.

It is Monday. Unlike many, I do not dread Mondays. In fact, I kind of embrace them. They imply that yet another week has begun. I get excited about the potential changes that I can bring to the company where I work. I have always known that I am destined to bring something great to the table. At one time I thought it would be the world, but for now, I will settle for a medium-sized business."

Over the years, people have told me that monumental change takes time. That it may seem difficult, especially if I am the one driving it. Of course, there are the natural disasters, wars, and a few other catalysts that can change the world almost instantly; but otherwise change, real, lasting change, does not come overnight...

At least that's what I remind myself, each and every Monday. I am aware that I am not much of a motivational speaker, but I am an awesome realist. The alarm's melody starts again, as the snooze timer runs out... I don't even remember having pressed 'snooze.'

"Ok, ok, I am awake!" I yell at my phone, as though it will make a difference.

The default snooze setting on my phone allows me a five-minute reprieve. Then, just as I begin falling back into a dream state, it smashes my eardrum at full volume!

"I've got to change that setting," I mumble to myself knowing full well that I will forget. Just like the last hundred times, I told myself to change it. As I prepare to get up, I realize that something isn't right. My body feels as though I was hit by a train. The bed is so comfy and warm... It beckons me to stay.

"No!" I yell out loud. "I am getting up. It's time to get ready for work, get some breakfast, and head out." After all, this is what I wanted, isn't it? Independence, self-reliance, and the ability to make my own way. To be the captain of my own ship and all that other empowerment stuff.

During the winter months, my room is especially dark. Sunlight does not penetrate the windows for another two hours. Yet, somehow today it seems even darker. The sole source of illumination is ambient lighting from the buildings and streets of the city. It permeates and reflects off the cheap, plastic blinds. Other than this, the darkness is almost palpable. There is little I need to see though. Especially, since I don't really have anything to stub my toe on in this place.

Some might call it 'living out of a box,' but I prefer the term 'minimalistic lifestyle.' There's an inflatable mattress, a cardboard box for a nightstand, and a seldom-watched television that sits on the floor. My greatest concern is avoiding stepping on my phone or punting it across the room, as I get out of bed.

The downstairs neighbors are still asleep when I get up. I often wonder if the periodic squeaking of the floor beneath my feet is enough to make them curse the day they rented an apartment that was not on the top floor. Maybe they've become accustomed to it? Perhaps the sounds of my creaking floorboards just blend into the general hum of the city. Along with the horns, sirens, and car alarms that incessantly pierce what would otherwise be calm, quiet nights.

I make my way to the kitchen and visualize myself taking that first sip of coffee. It's made in what may very well be my most prized possession - my Keurig. That little, magical, black and silver appliance has saved many innocent bystanders from experiencing my wrath. I may not do drugs, but I imagine there is little difference between a heroin addict fiending for his next fix and me without my morning coffee.

That first sip is always so hot! I can imagine it scorching my poor unsuspecting tongue. No matter how many thousands of cups I've consumed over the years, I can never get used to it... However, once the heat dissipates throughout my mouth and gradually makes its way into my stomach, I will awake. For that brief moment, my life will be sheer bliss. Until then, I will just enjoy the aroma that fills my tiny apartment, while I try to make myself look like a person again.

Chapter II

Change doesn't come overnight…

OR MAYBE IT DOES

I dread turning on the lights and seeing myself in the bathroom mirror. I look like a train wreck every morning, especially on Mondays. However, today feels even more unique. I feel weirder than usual… Less of a train wreck and more like a plane crash…

Stumbling into the bathroom, I search for the light switch. Yup, still there. Here we go again…

"Shit!" The word escapes my lips as the lights flicker to life and nearly blind me... again. My vision slowly comes into focus.

"Fuck me sideways!" I blurt out, realizing just how awful I feel! I approach the mirror and inspect my face as if expecting something different. Nope, still there, still the same. I reach for my toothbrush.

"Holy shit! What the fuck?" I scream.

My hand! It's… I don't even know how to react as I inspect my nails. They are long, probably half an inch longer than they were when I went to bed. I know, because everyone tells me to stop biting my nails. They don't even look normal, more like the talons of some exotic bird. This is surreal.

"Black nails, why?" I mumble out loud in utter frustration, as I examine my manicure! I didn't even drink last night.

Is this a prank? Did someone knock me out and take me to some fucked up nail salon? I think as I try to come up with some rational explanation for this absurdity.

"Fuck!" I blurt out loud, as I realize that it's not just the nails. The skin on my fingers, it is…

"Scales?" I fumble for words, now that my eyes have adjusted to the bathroom light. I come closer to the mirror. Compelled to make sure that I didn't just wake up in the body of someone auditioning to be the main act in a circus freak show.

Nope, still me… same as ever. I think to myself with a hint of relief, as the reflection of my face comes into focus.

At least that hasn't changed. The relieving thought passes through my mind, as I grin to inspect my teeth.

"Holy shit! That's new!" The words come out weird because I say them while opening my mouth as wide as I

17

can. Then take a moment to run my tongue along my teeth. Taking extra care as I pass it over a set of sharp new fangs!

What in the world is going on? I think as panic begins to set in. Suddenly, a wave of relief washes over me, and I calm down...

"Shit! This is just one of those lucid dreams." I say out loud, to make it so. I remember waking up and everything feels normal, but I know that I'm still dreaming.

I turn off the lights and close my eyes. So that I can 'will' myself to wake up for real, this time around. Everything goes dark. I take a few deep breaths, imagine myself lying in bed, and slowly open my eyes...

"Son of a bitch!" I yell, realizing that I'm still in the bathroom.

"Cold water, that'll do it!" I say out loud, like a crazy person. I pull the stick behind my faucet to plug the drain and run the cold water for a minute to allow the sink to fill up.

If I'm asleep, this will definitely wake me up! I submerge my face up to my ears in the seemingly icy depths. The water is so cold that it hurts. I endure... I can feel the air bubbles form at my nostrils and float up my cheekbones. Finally, my breath starts to run out, and I yank my face from the numbing liquid. A chill runs down my spine and I know that I am fully awake. I grin at the mirror, preparing for that sigh of relief, but my shiny new fangs are still there.

"Oh god! What is happening to me?" I mutter, as though there might possibly be a logical explanation for this insanity. A million thoughts begin to surge through my mind: *I need to go to the emergency room! Maybe this is the side effect of some terrorist chemical attack?* I run to my window and open the shitty plastic blinds, that have a permanent yellowish tint to them, from the decades of dust, baked in by the sun. No… there are no sirens and I don't see any hazmat teams.

I grab the remote and turn on the TV, which is so humbly sitting on the bare floor. The dark screen slowly illuminates the room. That seven seconds it takes to power up and tune into the last channel feels like an eternity! Finally, the morning news brings a twisted glimmer of hope for some answers:

"Fighting in Syria has taken a major toll –"

No! This can't be right! I think as I change the channel...

"We have a special guest with us toda –" I press the 'Channel Up' button in frustration before the host can finish her sentence.

"Damn it!" I blurt out loud.

Maybe the next network…

The hosts are laughing: "I know Tom, I cannot believe how silly those –" I press the power button on the remote with such ferocity that the remote cracks in my hand, as the TV screen fades to black.

"Shit! Fuck! What is happening?" I feel the rage turning into paralyzing fear. I am alone in the dark. College may have prepared me for real life, but not this. This isn't real, it can't be. I grasp for an explanation - something, anything - but my thoughts are so scrambled that nothing comes to mind other than the resounding yet silent - *What the fuck?*

I suppose the next step is to go to the hospital. Get them to run a blood analysis or something. But what the hell does modern medicine know about fangs and claws on humans? I've seen the movies and shows. They'll just lock me up in some white, sterile room. Where assholes with big-ass needles will poke, prod, and scan me. Until the day that the government takes me away and erases any trace of my existence.

Hell no! I think in anger. *That won't be me!*

I turn to my phone, press the unlock button, and the screen comes to life. Its soft glow illuminates my face and hand. I stare in disbelief. The nails are thick, each one seemingly razor-sharp. I lower the tips into the old floorboards and my nails sink into the wood like a hot steak knife into butter.

As I draw my hand back, deep scratches form in the wood. Like some monstrous cat was sharpening its claws. I suppose that on the bright side, I don't have to worry about getting jumped by some asshole with a knife. If this is what I can do to the floorboards, I cannot fathom the damage I could cause to the human body.

The scales on my fingers do not resemble anything I've ever seen. Though they look simple from afar, upon closer inspection I realize that they have a diamond shape to them and they fit together ever so perfectly. They are like gunmetal, a bluish-grey color. Reflecting the light from my phone as if they were made of polished aluminum.

Staring at the scales proves a great distraction from the panic. My eyes grow tired.

"I… should… call into… work…" I say through a yawn, as I relax onto my mattress. Then, darkness…

My eyes open slowly as sunlight begins to permeate the room. I lay still, afraid of what I will see when I look at my hands. The fear is similar to what I felt as a child when I imagined the monster lurking under my bed. Waiting to jump out or grab my foot as I lowered it onto the floor.

This time is different, however. I have no fear of anything under my bed. Partly, because my mattress is on the floor, but mainly because I am terrified of the monster I truly can't escape. Like a shitty gif, images of my scales, talons, and fangs are coursing through my mind on an endless loop.

Suddenly, my phone beeps in that familiar chirp, reminding me in the sweetest way that I am an idiot who forgot to plug it in. That can't be right, it was charging all night, and I've only fallen asleep a couple of hours ago. I need to focus.

I feel like I'm trying to process thousands of thoughts a minute. It's like standing in one of those machines that blow game tickets around in a tornado, and I'm supposed to grab as many as I can. Only instead of tickets they are thoughts, memories, and images of my life, my friends, my job.

My job! Everything I was thinking about comes to a grinding halt and is replaced by panic about being late.

I'll probably get written up or fired! How will I pay rent? I need to call in and tell them… What the fuck can I possibly say? Oh god! I'm so screwed! Emily, I'll call Emily first. She always has great ideas.

The moment I think of her name, everything else melts away. Her blue-green eyes, partially covered by jet-black bangs. The contrast makes them appear as though they glow, toying with the light like crystals. But Emily is far more than just a pretty face.

Since we were children, it made no sense as to why she was friends with me. We went to the same school, but that's where the similarities ended. Everyone liked Emily. She was pretty, smart, funny… Hell, she made class President without campaigning! What made her so unique was that in spite of all the popularity and admiration, she not only remained humble, she remained my best friend.

Even after her family moved to Europe, where she picked up the accent that made her sound all proper, she would still call me at every opportunity. It is crazy to think how quickly the years flew by. Alas, my trip down memory lane ends abruptly as my phone chirps. Reminding me that I have a missed call.

Again, I reach for my trusty friend - the smartphone. At present, it is probably the only 'friend' who won't judge my new look. I catch a glimpse of my reflection in the phone screen, and all my hopes of this morning being a terrible nightmare are shattered. The scales that had started on my fingers have made their way to cover my face. What is scarier, is that I can no longer see the whites of my eyes. Perhaps it's just the distorted reflection playing tricks on me, but right now, I don't even want to look.

With the push of a familiar button, the black mirror comes to life and my reflection is replaced by the blurry background of my phone, along with the date and time.

"Fuck my life, that can't be right! It's Sunday?" I say quite audibly.

This makes no sense! I think in confusion. *It can't be... It would mean that I have been asleep for six days!*

Twenty-seven missed calls, forty-eight text messages, and nine voicemails. One name accounts for most of them: EM. Emily and I still talk all the time. Not a day goes by without at least a brief text message, letting the other know that everything is all right... and it's been six.

She's going to kill me, I think to myself as I play the first voicemail:

Monday 9:05 pm: "Hey Sam," Emily's voice sounds cheerful as usual. "I sent you a couple of texts, but you haven't responded. Just making sure you're all good. Talk to you later."

Monday 10:13 am: Good morning Sam, this is John from the office. I noticed you weren't at the meeting and I have not heard from you. This is your first no-call, no-show, so I just hope everything is all right. Please call me as soon as possible so we can avoid any serious impacts to your personnel file.

Wednesday 1:48 pm: "Congratulations! You have been selected for -" I hit the delete button before the robocall can finish. I am sure that all they need is my credit card and all my personal information to 'confirm' that I am indeed the lucky winner of some amazing prize. Does anyone really fall for that bullshit anymore?

Wednesday 8:09 pm: "Hey! What the fuck?" The next message begins playing. Emily's voice is now frustrated and worried. "Did you lose your phone or something? You know where I live, come by and let me know you're ok, or call from a neighbor's phone. Something!"

Thursday 11:07 pm: "Hey asshole, open the door! I drove all the way across town, just to make sure you're ok, and you won't even let me in!" Although she moved back to the U.S. as an adult, the accent she picked up while living in the U.K. has never faded. Perhaps it is because all her coworkers are overseas... What's fascinating is that even though she's obviously pissed, she still sounds more eloquent than I do on my best days.

The next voicemail in the chain begins to play. Thursday 11:20 pm: "Sam! What the fuck is your deal? I know you didn't lose your phone! I had your neighbor let me into the building. I can fucking hear it ringing in your apartment! Stop acting like a little bitch and talk to me… Come on! Are you really just going to make me stand out here?"

Friday 4:00 pm: "Hey Sam, it's John again. I sincerely hope that you're all right. Tom in security asked me to call and let you know that they have been told to get all your stuff out. I really didn't want to do this via voicemail, but you haven't come to work nor called anyone at the office all week. I imagine you understand the repercussions of that. Security will hold your stuff for another hour before they have to dispose of it. Give me a call and let me know if you need a little extra time, maybe I can hold onto it for you. Again, I hope you're okay and I am very sorry to see you go."

Saturday 5:30 am: "Sam, whatever your problem is, you know I've always been there." The concern in Emily's voice is evident. "I called your work yesterday, and they said you no longer work there. Please, just talk to me. You know I will not judge, no matter what it is… I just need to know that you're ok. I haven't slept in two days… Please, just call me…" Her voice sounds like she has been crying for hours.

I feel like a total jerk…

I need to call her, I think to myself. *What the hell do I say? "Hey EM, sorry. Had a rough week. Look like a monstrosity. You get it, right? Hee Hee…"*

I stand up and walk to the bathroom mirror, dreading what I am about to see… I turn and gasp. The monstrous face staring back at me from the mirror is something that can only exist in myth and fantasy. Seems that my phone wasn't playing any tricks. My eyes are completely black and scales

25

cover every inch of my face. My ears have become long and pointed. I've read my share of fantasy books, but I have never heard of a scale-covered, black-eyed, elf with fangs and talons.

What the fuck is happening? The thought is now etched into my mind, playing over and over like nails on a chalkboard. *I have to focus... I need to call Em. If nothing else, at least let her know that I'm still alive. She has always been there for me... If there's a single person in this world who may not run away, screaming in terror, it's her.*

I can't imagine sharing this with anyone else...

CHAPTER III

DISCOVERY

"**H**ome Three, Home Three, this is Explorer 13," a male voice comes through a speaker. We are entering sector ten-thirteen-oscar-six, do you copy?" A blue indicator light blinks on a massive display board, in a room filled with transparent screens. Each one displaying extensive data about various stars, planets, and moons.

A small overlay window, with the tab "10-13-06," expands on screen number 13. Covering up the previous window labeled "Ten-one-A1."

"Explorer 13, what is your code?" An officer asks as she turns to face screen 13.

The blinking, blue indicator turns white, and a countdown clock appears above it, displaying "0:00:27.7." The officer knows that her transmission was sent and that it will take 27.7 seconds to reach the vessel claiming to be Explorer 13... The counter hits zero, turns green, and begins to count up. This time, with a minus sign in front of the timer, indicating the amount of time that has elapsed since her transmission reached the ship in sector 10-13-06.

She knows that if Explorer 13 takes longer than 5 seconds to hear her request and send their authentication, the counter will turn orange. At 7 seconds, the counter turns red and Explorer 13 will be considered compromised.

A wave of relief flushes over her as the counter stops at "32.1."

"Security code Alpha-eight-five-two-six-eight-four-seven." A wave pattern appears on the screen and is contrasted against a prerecorded version. The blinking light turns a solid green color.

"Code accepted, access to direct channel granted, proceed with transmission." The officer replies in a monotonous voice.

"Home 3, we are on approach to planet Echo-Victor-one-two-two-one. Planetary scan report is negative for lifeforms, negative for tech, negative for unique resources. Requesting permission to land."

"Explorer 13, clarify request for permission." The officer replies, sounding confused.

"Home 3, our empath is assured that scans are insufficient. Requesting eyes-on."

"Explorer 13, confirm scans. Empath, reading requires at least one positive scan."

Several minutes pass prior to the next transmission... "Home 3, rescan complete. Confirms negative on all three. Empath insists on eyes-on assessment."

"Explorer 13, wait 5."

The female officer touches a section of the holographic dashboard in front of her. The entire conversation is condensed, the transmission times are removed, and the packet is sent up for authorization. Within minutes, a new overlay appears on the screen. An older woman, obviously displeased with the situation, begins speaking directly with Explorer 13.

"Explorer 13, this is Admiral Bree. Why the fuck are you in ten-thirteen-Oscar-six? We are months away from that sector! You have no support there!"

"Admiral, with all due respect, I have one of the best Empaths in the fleet, on my ship. Everyone aboard has learned to trust him. My team is aware of the risks and..."

"Captain, I am in command of three fleets! In case you forgot how to count, that is six home ships! I trust you know how many hundreds of Explorer vessels that adds up to... If every Captain ran off to unknown sectors because their damn Empath 'felt' something, our mission would drag on for decades. More importantly, we would lose countless ships! Perhaps you forgot, but space is literally infinite, and I can't risk abandoning 50 Explorer vessels to go recover your crayon-eating team!"

"My apologies, Admiral. Respectfully, I maintain my request to explore the planet."

"You have wasted quite a massive portion of your time to get to this planet, Captain. I will allow you 12 hours to follow your Empath's hunch. However, if your 'detour' yields nothing, you will be subject to disciplinary action and your team will get a Captain who can follow procedure. So, for your sake, I sincerely hope I am wrong. Home 3, out…"

"Secured Connection: Terminated" The indicator on the communications array inside Explorer 13, flashes red. Although their faces are covered with black visors, the tension among the team is blatantly evident.

"Well," the Captain says with a sarcastic pep in his voice, turning to his team, "that's what I call a 'win, win' situation! Either we find something worthwhile and come home heroes, or you guys get a new Captain."

The icebreaker works to dissipate the tension and everyone chuckles, despite their concern for the Captain.

"I wouldn't have told all of you to gear up if I wasn't planning on exploring this rock. Get to your stations, we're going in!" The certainty in the Captain's voice makes it clear that this is an order.

As each team member sits down, clasps automatically extend from various sections of their exoskeleton suits, to secure each individual to his or her respective seat. Ensuring his team is secured, the Captain sits down last. As the last clasp engages, he is drawn tightly into the command chair.

"All team members are secured." An autonomous voice echoes through everyone's intercom, as Explorer 13 pivots towards the planet and begins its rapid descent. Despite the seemingly turbulent ride, the seats in the vessel are stable. Mounted on multi-directional shock absorbers, which work in synchrony to eliminate nearly all vibration and discomfort.

Hidden wings extend and retract from multiple sections of the vessel as it enters the lower portions of the atmosphere. As Explorer 13 levels out, the clasps securing the crew release automatically. The panel in front of the Captain displays various controls which had been disabled during the descent.

"Stable flight achieved; manual controls enabled; movement restrictions disengaged." The autonomous voice announces through the intercom.

"All right boys, girls, and other species," the Captain exclaims jokingly. "Another successful joyride! We've got 11 hours to get back into orbit and tell everyone on Home 3 why team Atlantis is fucking awesome and that Max is the best Empath in the damn fleet!"

"Hell yeah!" The team exclaims in almost perfect unity.

"Get up here, Max, the controls are yours." The Captain exclaims as he jumps up and walks away from his station.

Max, ironically the smallest member of the Atlantis team, takes the Captain's seat and positions his hands on the control console. He closes his eyes and the heads-up display inside his helmet's visor turns off completely. His audio channels are silenced and he begins moving his hands across the ship's controls. Guiding Explorer 13 to whatever mysterious force that called him here from across the far reaches of space.

The team sits in their chairs, taking in the breathtaking beauty of the planet. Their visors displaying feeds from Explorer 13's external cameras and complex sensor arrays, as it coasts through the magenta sky.

"Hell," one of the team members breaks the silence, "if this is our last run together, at least it's a pretty one."

As the team members laugh and chat about their past adventures, Max brings Explorer 13 to an abrupt halt. He opens his eyes and his visor and comms come back online.

"We're here," he states calmly.

"Ummm… Hey buddy," one of the female crew members responds incredulously. "Are you sure that your abilities are ok? I am not getting anything on the sensors. I am running -"

"Ether," the Captain cuts her off mid-sentence. "Switch from your sensors to live video."

As the obvious tech guru of the team, Ether normally views nothing but sensor feeds. They may not be as pretty as the live view, but they provide a staggering amount of information that is not visible to the eye. In the past, her preference for the unseen has saved the crew from countless perils.

"Fuck my life!" Ether exclaims as the live camera feed takes over inside her visor. "That thing didn't register on any sensors... That's not possible! It's massive!"

"Set us down," the Captain says in a decisive voice.

Explorer 13 slowly descends, until its body is nearly flat against the metallic-blue grass. A side panel slides open, and the crew wastes no time. One by one, they jump onto the field. Their exoskeleton boots absorbing the majority of the impact.

"Ember and Thile," the Captain begins, "you're on guard. Everyone else, fall in on me and keep comms open. If this mountain is invisible to all our instruments, I'd hate to find out the hard way that our scans missed something else. Especially if that something else decides that we're a tasty snack."

As the team moves away from Explorer 13, they and the ship are dwarfed by what appears to be a mountain. However, unlike a normal mountain, its faces are not jagged and rough. If anything, it resembles a massive, black crystal, randomly protruding from the ground.

"Well Max," Ether's blatantly astonished voice fills the comms, "you've definitely outdone yourself this time! What the hell called you to this?"

"Ember, Thile," the Captain cuts in "I am not sure what we're walking into. If I was to place a bet, I would guess that it's some kind of really complex hologram. After all, how can a 5000-meter-tall crystal not show up on any of our systems?"

"All due respect Captain," Ether responds, "if this was a hologram, it would still emit energy. Explorer 13's sensors would've registered inorganic power readings. It would take quite a lot to generate something of this magnitude."

"Then, perhaps it is an illusion." Ember, responds over the comms.

"Max," the Captain interjects. "Do you have anything for us? We're entertaining all ideas at this point."

"No sir," Max responds quietly. "I don't know of any species who would be able to project an illusion or hallucination this grand. More importantly, I felt like I needed to come here from another solar system. It would take an incredible being to be able to do that."

"Should we notify Home 3?" Ember asks.

"Not yet," The Captain says decisively. "I think I am in enough trouble as it is. If they end up rerouting a home ship for a hallucination, I might spend the rest of my days mopping landing decks with a toothbrush... Let's figure this out first. We have another 10 hours."

CHAPTER IV

WHAT AM I?

plug in my dying phone and hit the call button. There is a single ring and the call connects.

"Sam?" Emily asks with trepidation in her voice.

"Hey Em, I am so sorr-" she cuts me off before I can finish responding.

"Your story better start with 'I got hit by a truck and was in a coma this whole time!' I swear, Sam! How could you fucking do this to me?" She wants to sound livid, but the angry tone fails to hide the underlying concern and relief.

I can visualize Emily wiping tears from her cheeks. What I can't imagine is what she must've been through these last few days. I disappeared. After six days, she must've thought I had to be dead. She probably came up with a couple of hundred gruesome ways in which I had been killed, dismembered, or worse... She composes herself, clears her throat, and says:

"Well? Start talking."

"I'm so sorry Em," I respond with the utmost sincerity. "Really, I haven't been ignoring you. I was literally out cold."

"Bullshit! For six days?" She interrupts, incredulously.

"I can't explain it, I am at a loss myself," I reply, maintaining my sincere tone.

"Stop!" Emily's voice is filled with frustration and disbelief. "I came by your place! I even called your office. They said you didn't work there anymore! What the hell? Did you start doing drugs or something? You loved that job!"

"Em, I swear to you, no drugs, no parties, nothing like that at all."

Silence fills the phone...

"Em?" I ask quietly.

"Are you sick?" She asks after a few moments.

"I... I don't know," I respond almost inaudibly.

"Well, I'm coming to -"

"I don't know that it would be a good idea right now," I cut her off before she can finish her sentence. "Em, I'm truly not sure what's happening to me."

"Then why aren't you on your way to the hospital?" Her voice once again filled with frustration.

"I… I am afraid to… If you saw me, you would probably faint," I say quietly.

Her next few sentences remind me of just how great her grammar really is. She never misses a comma. I am able to hear them clearly because she replaces each one with some variant of the word 'fuck.'

"I am serious Em," I interrupt her rant sternly. "I look like some damn monster."

"Did a fucking dick sprout from your forehead? Did you turn into a fucking werewolf? Maybe you got tentacles growing out of your god-damn ears?" Emily continues tearing into me.

"No dicks on my forehead and no tentacles. Though the werewolf piece may not be too far off," I reply jokingly.

"Well, I'm sure fucking glad that you still have your sense of humor, Sam! Because I've been losing my fucking mind over here! Do you kno-"

"I really wish that I was joking," I cut her off again, this time in a somber tone.

"Seriously, is your body somehow deformed or something?" She asks. The calm in my voice must have caught her off guard. Her tone is suddenly compassionate and filled with concern.

"It's like I'm changing physically. My skin is covered with…" As I start thinking of the words to describe the changes, I begin to feel dizzy and nauseous. I didn't even realize that I paused mid-sentence.

"Sam?" Her voice snaps me back.

"Sorry, I am just having a hard time... I'm still processing all of it... It's a bit much," I say candidly.

"Can we meet? I'll come over," she says reassuringly.

"I don't know..." I say sounding uncertain of what I want. "What if I'm contagious? I know you probably think that I'm full of shit. But I promise that if there is one of us who wishes that this was all some fucking nightmare or an elaborate ruse, it is definitely me."

"Look, Sam," her voice surprisingly collected, "I haven't heard anything on the news or social media about any outbreaks. We live in a city where if some disease broke out, thousands of people would get sick within a day or two. I don't know what's up with you, but if you're that concerned, I will wear one of those germ masks or something."

"And if that doesn't help?" I ask.

"Sam, you're like family... I'm coming over," she responds decisively.

"Ok, but not to my apartment... just in case. I'll meet you at the park. Around eleven pm," I agree with hesitation.

"Why not now? Why are we waiting till it's that late?" She asks impatiently.

"I'm sorry Em. I can't have anyone else see me. I will be there waiting. When you see what is going on, you'll understand. I promise," I say sincerely.

"Ok, yeah," she concedes "Eleven it is. But you better fucking be there!"

"I promise Em... I'm truly sorry! I promise I'll be there."

As night falls, I get ready to meet Emily. I realize that since hanging up with her, I literally sat there staring at my lifeless television screen for hours. My mind playing that image of my face in the mirror, over and over again. Like a bad TikTok video. It starts with my hand. Then, skips to the reflection of a monster, staring at me through the mirror. I just see my eyes – black as night – it is so surreal, that I cannot come to terms with the fact that they are my own.

The only breaks from this loop come in the form of realizations that my life, as I know it, is over. I can't even begin to imagine how Emily will react. Her lifelong friend is now a beast from the most horrendous fairy tale of all – real life.

The endless neurotic cycle is finally broken by a familiar tune coming from my phone. I glance over to read the notification. It is from Emily:

"On my way. You better be there."

"Yes," is all I respond.

I bring myself to stand up. My legs feel shaky and unsteady. I want to believe that they 'fell asleep' from lack of circulation, but I know it's my nerves. They're completely shot... As the floorboards squeak under my feet, I make my way to the closet and find an old college hoodie. It might be dark outside, but if anyone sees me as I go downstairs, they'll probably scream and at best call the police. At worst they might have a heart attack or try to shoot me... Hell, I wouldn't even blame them. The hoodie should cover my face enough to where most people won't notice.

It feels tight as I pull my arms through. Which is odd, because I ordered a size larger, just in case it shrank in the wash. I always felt like I was swimming in it, but now it feels small. *Cheap-ass junk...* I think to myself in frustration as I struggle to get it over my head. It doesn't matter right now. I just need it to cover my face, and this is the least conspicuous way to do it. *Keys, check; phone, check. All right... time to face the music.*

I haven't been this nervous to unlock my door, since that one time I received a notice that several people in my building had been assaulted and robbed as they walked out of their apartments. I check the wide-angle peephole to make sure that no one is outside the door.

Unlocking the deadbolt, I take a deep breath and turn the doorknob. As the door opens, my nostrils fill with more smells than I can bare. I stagger a little, trying to process everything - pizza, curry, and most of all that stupid garbage shoot.

These smells are always there but they are never this vivid, especially not right at my door. The garbage shoot is down the hall and behind a closed door. It usually doesn't smell until I walk into that little trash room. I can also smell old cigarette butts and a faint hint of marijuana that the potheads smoke in the stairwell... but how? That's at the other end of the hall...

Maybe I'm turning into a dog? That would explain the heightened sense of smell. I think to myself... *Doesn't explain the scales and razor-sharp talons though.*

I step over the threshold into the hallway and close the door behind me, as quietly as I can. The deadbolt clicks into the locked position and I quickly make my way to the stairwell. Normally, I would've taken the elevator which has cameras and is well-lit, but this time these are all things that I am trying to avoid.

I sprint down several flights of stairs, paying attention to how loud my footsteps are, so as not to attract any unnecessary attention. As I hit the last landing and enter the lobby, I feel a sense of relief - *I am home free.* However, that feeling quickly fades away when I approach the back door, only to realize that three teenagers are hanging out, taking selfies with their smartphones.

Unlike many, I have never had the desire to become an internet sensation. With my new look, that feeling is exponentially greater. I would storm by them, but one of them is leaning up against the door. Well, I suppose that means the back door is not an option.

Going to the front door means crossing the lobby, which has better lighting and a security camera. I begin to take into account the angle of the camera. Along with considering my options for what I would do if someone was walking into the building as I am walking out.

I process how well the hood actually hides my face and whether or not the hall lights might expose me. Fuck my life, I feel like a damn prisoner or an assassin trying to escape some kind of weird fort. One that is crawling with oblivious security guards and countermeasures at every corner. However, waiting for the teens to leave could take hours... *Fuck it, I'm going through the front,* I think to myself decisively.

My heart begins to race and the front door appears to move further and further away. This distance of a couple of hundred feet might as well be a mile-long stretch of rough terrain, covered in barbed wire and littered with landmines. As I compose myself, I see a family walking up to the door. Two young children and their parents laughing and smiling...

Shit... I can't let them see me. I step back into the stairwell, where I can wait while they take the elevator. Then, I'm making a break for it!

How did it come to this? From upstanding citizen to lurking in the shadows, seemingly overnight. My thoughts are suddenly shattered as I hear echoes of voices and footsteps resounding throughout my hiding place...

"Shit!" The word slips out. *Who the hell takes the stairs these days? Doesn't matter, I can't let them see me.*

I hear the family chatting about their evening as they wait for the elevator. I imagine their gleeful expressions, turning to shock, horror, and screams if they catch even a single glimpse of me. The footsteps and voices are getting closer. For a brief moment, time seems to slow to a halt. I can picture the family, the foot hitting the step mid-stride, and the teens playing on their phones outside. The world is closing in.

Suddenly, my instincts take over. After a brief calculation in my head, I conclude that the teens are likely oblivious to the world. Therefore, I can probably push my way through and run past them before they can get a good picture. That is if they even take their eyes off their phones. Perhaps more importantly, the teen who is leaning on the door should be taught a lesson in being more considerate of others.

With my mind made up, I step out from the safety of the stairwell. My head angled down, hopefully enough for the hood to conceal my face. The hallway stretches out in front of me. I feel like I have to cover the length of a football field, rather than a few short steps. I turn from a frozen, terrified statue into a freight train. Full steam ahead for the backdoor.

As I slam into the door with both hands, the teenage boy leaning against it doesn't just get pushed aside, he is thrown! His phone is ejected from his hands. It impacts the concrete, emitting the ubiquitous sound that all phones make as they hit a hard surface. The sound that puts your entire body in a state of panic, which grips you until you can check and make sure the phone still works.

The boy hits a patch of manicured grass, with a soft thud. By the time he and his friends realize what just happened, I am already twenty feet away.

"What the fuck, asshole?" I hear their confused and frustrated voices behind me.

I ignore them and walk briskly, trying to put more distance between us. Alas, their tones change and I hear them say something that I was really hoping to avoid:

"Hey! Asshole! You're going to pay for my phone!" One of them yells assertively.

The teenagers start running after me. My stride increases and I break into a run. Desperately hoping that they are not on the track team. I cross the street and run a few more blocks for good measure. Their profanity fades, either because I am outrunning them or because they can't run and curse at the same time.

I turn my head for a quick glance. Much to my relief, I see the pursuers give up the chase, one by one. I can barely make out their evident exhaustion and confusion. Each one doubling over, trying to catch his breath and scratching his head in disbelief at their inability to catch me.

I guess there is a perk to my transformation - I can now outrun a bunch of punks. I think to myself as I turn the corner.

I get to the park and find a bench, next to a light pole with a burnt-out bulb. It only feels like a moment into my solitude that my phone begins to vibrate with an incoming call. I answer, and Emily's voice fills the silence:

"I am pulling up. You better be there." She says as though she had expected me to back out at the last minute.

"I am," I respond. "Far bench, under the tree. Next to the light post that is out."

"You know, we were told to avoid dark areas when we were kids," Emily says lightheartedly.

"I know Em," I say in a somber tone, "but trust me, it's for the best."

I see her car pull up and park by the curb. Emily steps out and locks the doors. She walks briskly and looks over her shoulder. Despite this, there is a confidence in her stride. Unfortunately, what she doesn't realize is that the monster is actually right in front of her...

CHAPTER V

FIRST CONTACT...

As Emily approaches, my heart feels like it is about to stop. I can envision her screaming in horror when she sees my face and claws... I feel like turning and running away. She has no idea of what she is about to see. My mind is once again flooded with panicked thoughts:

What choice do I have? Where could I possibly go? I have no one else to turn to...

I turn on my phone screen and wave it at her. Emily waves back and within a few moments, she is standing in front of me. She rears back and punches me in the arm.

"You deserved that!" She says sternly.

"I know, I'm sorry," I respond. Hanging my head, still trying to conceal my face.

"It's so dark, I can barely see shit. And why the hell are you wearing that hoodie?" Emily demands.

"Promise you won't scream?" I ask.

"What? Jesus Sam, you're freaking me out a bit."

"Just promise..." I repeat solemnly.

"All right, I won't scream... promise." She says with trepidation.

I stand up from the bench and Emily takes several steps back. After a few seconds, she finally mumbles:

"Did you hit a growth spurt or something? You're taller... Like noticeably taller and your shoulders are broader!"

"I suppose... I haven't had much time to assess it." I respond trying to buy myself a few more moments to prepare. "This is all quite new. Please, don't ask me to take the hood off." I request, knowing full well that she won't let it go until I show her.

"Oh no! You're not backing out on me now, Sam. You promised!"

I sigh and slowly pull the hood off my head.

"Shit..." The word falls from Emily's lips involuntarily.

I see the expression on her face turn from frustration to horror. Even in the dark, it is evident that she just turned several shades paler. She slowly lowers herself onto the park bench and stares at me silently. I sit down next to her gently, ensuring to keep my distance. As the color returns to

Emily's face, her expression changes to that of someone who just realized that a person they cared for had died.

We stare at one another in utter silence for a few minutes, though it feels like an eternity. I decide that it would be better to show her everything up front.

"That's not all," I say in a trite and quiet tone.

I part my lips in a grimace to reveal my fangs. Emily gasps but remains seated. Which is probably the opposite of what I would be doing. I half expected her to bolt back to her car and call animal control or start Googling a local vampire hunter.

"Ok, what the hell? How did this happen, Sam?" She asks in a concerned tone, after gathering her thoughts.

"I have no idea," I respond candidly. "I woke up Monday, saw this, tried to watch TV, to see if there was some weird epidemic, chemical spill, a portal to another dimension, anything that could remotely explain it. Then I just passed out..."

"Passed out?" She asks incredulously. "Then what, just woke up almost a week later? No food, no water, didn't even wake up to go to the bathroom?"

"Not that I know of..." I sigh in response. "Maybe I was sleepwalking for those things. All I know is that I woke up and realized that I was living a nightmare. Rather, that I became the nightmare."

"Are you ok? You must be starving!" Emily exclaims sounding like a concerned mother.

"Nothing hurts if that's what you're asking. I am not sure why I am not hungry. I know I should be, I'm just not."

"Do you want me to take you to the hospital?" She continues, with concern in her voice.

"Come on, Em... What the hell do you think they're going to do? These doctors can't figure out what's wrong with someone when the person's throat hurts. Not without running a battery of tests first. They'll get one look at me and turn my happy ass into a guinea pig for sure! No, no hospitals," I say sternly.

Emily finally breaks eye contact. Her gaze shifts to something, no, more like to a different time. A smile tugs gently at her lips and she says:

"All right. How about Dr. Mavro?"

"Dr. Mavro? What would he know about this?" I ask.

"I don't know," Emily retorts, "but he is one of the most amazing theoretical physicists of our time. Plus, he has always been an amazing teacher. I don't know that he will have all the answers, but he wouldn't turn you in. He never even yelled at that one girl who used to doodle flowers throughout all his lectures, and would ask the most absurd questions because she didn't pay attention."

We both laugh, as we visualize the look on Dr. Mavro's face whenever Sarah would raise her hand. She had the

49

uncanny ability to ask questions that were either so pointless or ignorant, that it just made you scratch your head.

"More importantly," Emily continues "his access to the scientific community would allow him to find something or someone who might help you make sense of it all."

"I suppose he always did encourage his students to think for themselves and dig deeper. To never just accept the obvious answer... Still, I don't know, Em." I say with hesitation.

We sit in silence for a while. Despite the fact that I refrain from making eye contact, hoping that it would somehow make me invisible, I can sense that Emily is studying my new appearance with intensity. I still don't get why she hasn't run away, like one of those people who just saw a magic trick that can't possibly be real.

I can feel her gaze locked on my face, as though she is staring at someone who was disfigured in a horrible accident. It is one of those things that you don't want to stare at but simultaneously cannot look away from. Suddenly, she breaks the silence.

"You know, it's kind of cool."

"What the fuck are you talking about, Em?"

"I mean it. Once you get past the initial shock, you look like one of those aliens in a movie..." She sounds like a comic book fan who just ran into the main antagonist - scared but filled with admiration. "... or like some sort of mythological creature… Different, unique, but beautiful in your own way."

"Shock is right, Em. I think you might be going into it."

"I'm serious!" She fires back. "There is a certain elegance to your appearance. You aren't disfigured, just... transformed somehow. I cannot put my finger on it. Either way, my mind is made up, I am taking you to see Dr. Mavro, that is final!" The certainty in her voice is unquestionable.

She would get like this whenever one of her ideas made sense to her. It didn't matter what anyone told her after that point. Even if I objected, she would drag me wherever she intended to go.

"I don't suppose that I have much of a say in this, huh?" I ask, but it's too late. Without another word, Emily stands up and takes on the assertive posture that accompanies that tone. She begins walking back to her car, without even glancing back.

"Come on, or do I need to hold your hand?" She asks in a belittling tone.

"You're crazy!" I shout back in protest.

"You know it, Sam, that's why you love me!"

She's the furthest from 'crazy' of anyone I know. Yet, her firm demeanor is unquestionable. I've never met another woman with so much confidence. She should be terrified, but instead, she is assertive and unwavering.

"Let's go Sam!" She shouts back with impatience.

Reluctantly, I stand up and follow her to the car. The streetlights reflect off the deep gun-metal, blue paint. I grab the passenger side handle with extreme caution, careful not to scratch it like I did my floor. As I sit down and shut the door, I realize that Emily is already making a phone call.

"Wait! Who are -" I begin to ask.

"Hi Dr. Mavro!" She says with excitement, cutting me off.

The moment of silence that follows definitively means that he answered…

Damn, I was really hoping for a disappointed voice mail message, I think to myself.

"I realize it is very late and am extremely sorry to bother you at this hour. Unfortunately, you're the only person I know who may have some answers or at least an idea about what is going on," Emily says. Knowing that to a caring, inquisitive individual those words are like a laser pointer to a cat.

Silence… "No, I am not in trouble…" she responds, "it's Sam."

"Yes, the one from your intro class," she continues.

"I can try to explain, but I am sure you realize that I would not bother you on your personal number, especially close to midnight if it wasn't life or death."

"No, Sam isn't hurt, just… transformed." Her voice finally sounds like she is realizing how crazy it is to say those words out loud.

"We can't go to a hospital or anywhere public. You know me, at least well enough to know that I would never try to do something like this as a prank." Her tone softens and fills with sincerity. "Sam, lost almost an entire week and now looks like something out of a sci-fi movie… Please, you're the only person I can think of who might be able to make sense of this. More importantly, you're the only one who I can trust not to contact the authorities."

Another moment of silence... Then, her facial expression changes to that of relief. Surprisingly, similar to when she got an A+ on a paper that she had been stressing over for weeks.

"Thank you, Dr. Mavro!" She exclaims. "We will be there in twenty minutes."

CHAPTER VI

DON'T JUDGE ME!

A s we drive, I catch glimpses of my reflection in the passenger side window. Emily must be able to tell that I am deep in thought and allows me my peace. She knows that I do not have any answers, so asking me anything would be a moot point. She only glances over in my direction occasionally, as if to make sure that I am still there.

We pull up behind Dr. Mavro's garage. Emily sends a one-word text and the door opens almost immediately. It feels like we're in a movie about a car heist and just pulled up to our safe house. An outline of a man is standing in the wide doorway of the garage. He is holding a cup, with steam rising slowly into the cool evening air. Emily pulls up into the driveway and stops a few feet short of the door.

"Give me a minute Sam... I want to explain the situation to him." Her tone is cautious, as though she thinks I might get offended.

I glance at her and raise an eyebrow. Although I don't need to say it out loud, I know that Emily understood what I meant. In her head, she probably interpreted it as something like: 'Are you serious right now? I look like a fucking demon! And you're worried that I might get my feelings hurt?'

Emily responds with a knowing smile, steps out of the car, walks up to Dr. Mavro, and gives him a big hug. As they talk, all I hear are the periodic words 'What?' and 'How?' Then Emily turns to me and waves. Gesturing for me to join them.

My heart starts to race as I reach for the door handle. I open the door and slowly get out of the car. I can almost feel Dr. Mavro's curious glance, trying to get a glimpse of what I look like.

I walk towards them with a guttural fear coursing through my body. Trying to imagine what thoughts must be going through his mind. Finally, I step into the light emanating from the garage. His gaze intensifies.

"Fascinating!" Says Dr. Mavro.

His tone reminds me of a scientist in a sci-fi movie, who just observed some crazy virus under a microscope. Though that is definitely not the word I would have used if I were in his shoes. If nothing else, I am certainly not in a petri dish. He comes closer and begins to study my new appearance.

"Please, step into the garage. I need more light," he says with a modicum of excitement.

Emily walks in without hesitation. I, on the other hand, am still leery of the idea of anyone else seeing me. Noticing my reluctance, she swiftly turns around, grabs my arm, and drags me inside.

The moment I clear the door, Dr. Mavro quickly walks up to the button on the wall and closes the garage door behind me. He must have nerves of steel! If I were him, I would not want to be trapped in a small room with something like me. Then he walks back over and continues to look at me with increasing intensity. Suddenly, he smiles.

"I'm so sorry, where are my manners? Would either of you like something to eat or drink? I bet you must be hungry," he asks.

"I would love some coffee, and I bet Sam is starving!" Emily says without hesitation as she turns to check in with me. "You said you were asleep for almost a week! I know you said you weren't hungry, but if I were you, I bet I would want to eat my own shirt! I'm sorry, I didn't even think to stop for some food along the way..."

As Emily spoke, I considered that some food would not be a bad idea. She's right, after all, I've been asleep for almost a week, but food was the last thing on my mind. I have been so preoccupied with what the hell is happening to me, that nourishment became an afterthought.

"Well, that settles it. Coffee for us, and 'a meal fit for a king' for Sam. Take a seat at that table, I'll be right back."

"Thank you, but I'll just have some coffee as well. Black, please," I say insistingly. "It is the only thing that sounds good right now..."

"No problem," Dr. Mavro responds with slight hesitation. As though trying to wrap his mind around the idea that I am not starving.

Perhaps he is just hoping I'll voluntarily stuff myself. Just as a precaution. In case human flesh suddenly became a menu option with this new form. After a moment, he walks inside his house, while Emily and I sit down at a table in the third bay of the garage.

"How could he be so calm?" I say, sounding almost demanding. "How could you, Em? This is crazy! You should both be terrified of what I am!"

"Sam," Emily responds with utmost sincerity. "I can't imagine what you're going through. I really thought that you were on drugs or making up some bullshit story to avoid seeing me. I had no clue as to what to expect when I came to meet you. Whatever is happening to you makes no sense, but you've always been there for me and I won't turn my back just because you look different."

"Look different?" I reply in a flustered voice. "You make it sound as though I am a foreigner. At worst, it sounds like I am some old friend who was horribly disfigured and you're just able to overlook that fact. But I am not just 'different' I am a fucking monster! I mean shit, I literally have claws and fangs! I-"

She cuts me off with a simple gesture. "You're still my friend… I can tell that this part of you has not changed. The fact that you care about how Dr. Mavro and I feel or should be feeling, tells me that the part of you that I came to love, over the decades we've known each other, is still there. So yes, you might look like something out of a science fiction movie, but you're still Sam… and don't you forget it."

She smiles warmly and the anger raging inside me subsides.

"I'm sorry Em… You're an amazing friend and I appreciate that you're trying to help. I just don't know that Dr. Mavro will have any answers… I mean, he is a physicist, not a warlock."

Suddenly, Dr. Mavro returns with three university-branded coffee mugs and joins us at the table. The aroma of the coffee is palpable. I press the coffee mug to my lips and sip the hot liquid.

"Thank the gods! I still love coffee… I would be really worried if that was gone," I blurt out from behind the mug. We laugh wholeheartedly.

The feeling seems almost foreign. I had been so stressed about what my life would be from here on out, that laughter definitely seemed like it was off the menu. Yet, being here with people who are not judgmental, somehow I feel safe, and for the first time in what feels like an eternity, I allow myself to chuckle.

"All right, let's start at the beginning," says Dr. Mavro, "and please do not leave out any details."

Despite playing through the events in excruciating detail, yet again, I cannot recall anything new. However, as I speak, I notice that Dr. Mavro is thinking about something, as though this was not the first time he was hearing this story.

Chapter VII

What are the Odds?

As I finish my story, Dr. Mavro seems distant and somehow distracted. He stands up and starts walking back towards the door leading into his house.

"I'll be right back," he says and begins muttering to himself. "Could it be? Is this what she was talking about?"

Emily and I stare at each other in confusion. We can hear him walking to different areas of his house, periodically stopping and rummaging through papers. A few moments later he emerges with a laptop. Already open and loading. His expression could only be described as one of impatience.

"Sorry," he says, as he types in his password and begins clicking on various files. Feverishly searching for something specific. "I just need to find something here... It was a while back... Let me see... Ah, yes, there it is."

Emily and I stare at him blankly, as he skims through multiple documents and dozens of pages of notes. He begins speed reading through a long text document. Suddenly, he slows down and zeroes in on a particular section. Although he is talking, it is obvious to both Em and I, that his conversation is not with us. We wait patiently for him to finish reading through the notes...

"Son of a biscuit eater!" He finally exclaims. "I can't believe it."

"You've heard of my condition?" I ask with a glimmer of hope.

"Sort of," he responds. "When I wrote this down, I did it as a joke, to tell my colleagues. You know one of those 'what is the craziest thing you've ever heard at a conference?' stories. When I heard it, it sounded absolutely insane!"

"Any more insane than a scale-covered, black-eyed vampire, with claws sitting in your garage?" I quip and all of us laugh.

"Fair enough," he responds through the chuckle, then continues. "A few years ago, I was invited to a conference in Europe. It was about space travel, time dilation, wormholes, all that fun stuff. However, one of the speakers was a geneticist. Which, made no sense to me - why the heck would anyone invite a geneticist to a conference about space? So, out of curiosity, I went to listen to her speak. At the time, her presentation sounded like such nonsense that I felt I had to take notes just to come back and have a good laugh with my colleagues."

"But..." Emily interjects.

"But," Dr. Mavro continues, "seeing Sam here... I mean this sounds like exactly what she was talking about. In short, she explained that different species of aliens colonized Earth millions of years ago. Then something happened and the elements of the genome that were responsible for the expression of various traits and abilities became locked within everyone. As a result, all the species defaulted to a humanoid form and eventually evolved into us."

"Well that sounds like a cool plot-line for a science fiction show," I interject, "but did she happen to provide any empirical or otherwise credible evidence for this fantasy?"

"If she had," Dr. Mavro responds, "you would've heard about it on every news channel, instead of from my personal collection of 'Crazy Conference Stories.'"

"Fair point," I concede. "So, her theory would be that I am an alien trapped in a human body? Awesome..." I say sarcastically.

"She touched on many different theories" Dr. Mavro continues, "but concluded that whatever caused the genes to get locked would eventually come undone. Then, humans would once again become whatever species of alien they originated from. Again, I thought she was one of those crazy people looking for recruits in a new cult or something. You know those guys: 'The mothership is coming and you can only get on if you give up all your money and wear a tracksuit.'" We chuckle.

"Do you have a way to get a hold of this geneticist?" Emily asks.

"I am sure I can," responds Dr. Mavro. "However, she is in Europe. Even if she were to hop on a plane tomorrow, it would be a couple of days before she gets here. Though, I would imagine that finding someone to cover classes, booking the trip, plus the fact that I would need to be discrete, as to why I am inviting her... it might be closer to a week."

"Why can't you tell her that you found a living example of what her lecture was about? Don't you think that would motivate her?" I ask.

"Perhaps," he responds. "Provided that she knows which lecture I am referring to. If I give too much detail, it may set off some red flags. I mean, university emails and calls are monitored here. I don't know about Europe, but I imagine it's much the same. So, we definitely want to be cautious. We don't exactly want to announce your presence and condition to some university security guard who may feel that it is his duty to report it to a government agency."

"No, we don't!" I exclaim.

"Right!" Says Emily in her decisive tone. "Then it is settled. Dr. Mavro will reach out to the not-so-crazy geneticist and covertly but urgently get her to come here. Until then, Sam, you can come stay at my family's cabin in the mountains. It's secluded, so no one will bother you there. Go team!"

The mountain 'cabin' owned by Emily's family, is as much a cabin as the Empire State Building is a strip mall. The living room has a panoramic glass wall, with an unrivaled view of the mountain range. Multiple bedrooms, a sunroom, wraparound patio, stone sauna, and an outdoor kitchen that would make professional chefs jealous. However, most importantly, it is so far from civilization, that at night you can see the stars and listen to the silence. It is this serenity that earned the cabin its name: 'The Peaceful Place.'

Outside, only a few hundred yards from the house is a tree line, that marks the start of a forest. As beautiful and luxurious as it is, having been here for days, I begin to feel cooped up. In order to truly stay undetected, I had to leave my cell phone with Emily. There is no internet here, no television, not even a landline. For the first time in my adult life, I feel truly disconnected from the civilized world.

If I am to be honest with myself, the first few days here were unbearable. I would search my pockets for my phone, trying to check my email, text messages, even my social media feeds... which I normally despise. It made me realize just how much the connectivity to information has become less of a convenience and more like a drug. A craving that just won't go away. However, now that I've gone through the disconnect - like a withdrawal, but for technology - I feel like I could be happy here.

I decide to take a stroll in the forest that borders the property. Perhaps the serenity of the trees will ameliorate the angst of waiting for answers. Yet, there is that incessant thought of *'What happens if you get hurt or bitten by a snake? You can't call for help nor get to a hospital.'* It's a valid thought that once upon a time would have stopped me. I would have been terrified to venture out there, into the unknown. However, today for better or worse, I feel no fear.

I walk through the trees, smelling scents that I had no idea existed. Even the air had a sweet aroma, that I never noticed in the past. I hear a waterfall in the distance and walk toward the sound. Following a small stream, I find a clearing that can only be described as serene.

It appears to be an underground spring that comes through a rock formation. The crystal clear water creates a beautiful pool that feeds the stream I followed to find it. I think about the fact that this water should be frozen this time of year. I suppose that there is one benefit to this whole 'global warming' thing... I sit by the stream, close my eyes, and begin to clear my mind. In the silence, the tiny waterfall sounds like thunder. For the first time, I begin to forget what I saw in the of mirror my apartment.

The endless loop of thoughts and images streaming through my mind finally slows. Its volume, muffled and made distant by the sound of the water. I can only describe the feeling as 'being pulled out of time' and 'absorbing the peace and calm' that fill this place.

I am not sure how long I have been sitting here. However, for some reason, I suddenly begin to feel uneasy. A strange smell fills the air. I open my eyes and the world floods back into focus. Like a sixth sense, I realize that I am no longer alone. Still sitting down, I slowly turn my head and come face to face with one that is larger than my entire body.

"Shit..." The word involuntarily escapes my lips. Its nose is so close that I can reach out and touch it. The bear's breath, visibly rolling out of its nostrils and from its throat. Billowing into the air like steam from an old train locomotive. My mind begins racing with all the different bear survival tips:

I should play dead... Wait, wasn't that one debunked? Maybe I need to make myself look as large as possible and roar loudly? No, he might see that as a challenge. Is it even a male bear? I know! Make lots of noise -

As the advice from the nature shows, movies, and documentaries all blurs together in my mind, the bear opens its jaw and a deafening roar shatters the serene silence which had enveloped me. Before I have a chance to react, the bear's giant paw swipes at my head and knocks me to the ground like a rag-doll. Instinctively, my arms cover my head and I feel massive teeth clamp down on my forearm.

I am dragged a short distance and then the vise-like grip around my forearm is released. The bear hits me, rolling me over on my back, and begins to maul my torso. In between bites and claw swipes, I try to curl into a ball while still shielding my face and head, but there isn't enough time. Then, a pause. As though the bear just got bored and walked away. I curl into a ball and quickly come to regret the decision to move...

The vise-like pressure I had felt on my forearm, suddenly clamps down on my ankle. I am once again yanked, dragged, and smashed as the bear thrashes its head back and forth with my foot and ankle trapped helplessly in its jaws. I can only imagine that the bear thought it had won and left me alone. However, I proved it wrong by moving, so it felt compelled to finish the job.

Being flung around like a rag-doll, my arms pull away from my head. I open my eyes and the world is a blur of trees, fur, dirt, and white stuffing from my winter coat. Satisfied that I am no longer in a defensive position, the bear lets go of my leg and goes back to clawing at my chest. I can feel each swipe of the claws, but my adrenaline must be in overdrive, as I feel no pain. Suddenly, I remember that I too have claws. Maybe they are not six inches long, but if I can hit him in the eye... As though I had done this before, I spread my fingers with my nails forward, like the claw of an animal, and swipe at the bear's eye as it comes in for a bite.

Much to my surprise, my strike connects. As I examine my hand, in what feels like slow motion, I notice blood and fur on my fingers tips. At that moment, the bear lets out a deafening roar, turns around, and runs deep into the woods.

I flop backward, panting from exhaustion. The adrenaline must still be coursing through my body as I do not feel the pain from my prospectively fatal wounds. Both relief and fear leave me seemingly unable to move. I lay still for several minutes, not daring to look down at my mangled body.

"I have to get back to the cabin," I say out loud, with the hope of somehow motivating myself to get up. Gathering all my courage, I begin to move my foot in a circle. The anticipation of agonizing pain is probably not helpful. However, after the bear flung me around, using my ankle as the grip, I imagine it's shattered and I'm bleeding profusely.

After ten or fifteen seconds, I still do not feel any pain. I bend my knee slightly, but still nothing.

Deciding 'not to look a gift horse in the mouth,' I lift my head from the ground and pan down to assess the damage to my torso. My clothes are shredded. White stuffing from my jacket mixed with saliva, blood, and dirt covers and surrounds me. What is surprising is how little of my body is covered in that crimson color. I imagined I would be lying in a pool of my own blood.

It should be everywhere, I think to myself.

Moreover, I still feel no pain, not that I am complaining, but I should be in agony.

Is this what it feels when you go into shock? I wonder, still trying to gather my thoughts.

One by one, I carefully peel the shreds of clothing. As I clear away all the loose pieces from my stomach, I expect blood to start gushing at any moment. Nausea starts to come up my throat as I imagine my intestines slipping out of my body and onto the ground. Yet, as the mess of polyester and stuffing dwindles, all I see are more scales. Which now cover every inch of my body.

I sit upright, probably faster than I should, and continue peeling away at the shredded jacket. Searching for wounds and broken bones, I am still confused about my level of pain or rather lack thereof. With each messy clump that I brush away, I gain the confidence to work faster. A few minutes go by and I realize that other than the fact that I am nearly naked, there is not a scratch on my body...

But the blood, I think to myself... *No, it couldn't all have been the bear's, could it?*

Not wanting to push my luck, I stand up with caution. Although my scaly skin is evidently intact, it is possible that I missed a fracture while checking for broken bones. If I put pressure on said fracture by standing up too fast, it could be enough to cause a break.

I rise from the ground, without any pain, and take several cautious steps... Still nothing. I turn in the direction that I originally came from and break into a run. I don't look back until my hand touches the door handle of Emily's cabin.

Feeling that modicum of safety, I allow myself a brief glance back at the tree line. A decision that only adds to my confusion. It must have taken me nearly twenty minutes to get to the spot where I was attacked. Yet, running back, took less than a minute.

"How?" I whisper to myself, as I walk back inside and lock the door behind me.

Chapter VIII

More questions than answers...

I lost track of how much time has passed since the bear attack. Without sleep or contact with the outside world, time seems to lose its otherwise precious value. More importantly, dangerous new questions plague my mind. Is this new version of me truly strong enough to fend off a bear or was it just a fluke? Is it always on or is there a trigger?

Ultimately, I can't seem to stop wondering about just how tough I may have actually become. While I wait indefinitely, without any updates, I decide to conduct an informal experiment. Namely using anything I might find around the cabin to test the impermeability of my scales. Cutting myself with a kitchen knife should be a good start.

I place the blade against my fingertip and draw back, cautiously… I can feel the sharp blade as it slides across my scales. Memories and images of cutting my finger flood my mind. I lift the blade...

"Nothing?" I say in a surprised tone.

I apply substantially more force on the second pass, but it seems to make no difference.

Not even a scratch! I think to myself in bewilderment.

Turning the blade upright, I plunge the tip into the palm of my hand... Same result. Perhaps my stomach may prove to be a softer target.

Again, I begin with controlled stabs to my abdomen, but it doesn't take me long to get bored. Without realizing it, I begin to stab myself faster and apply a fair amount of force. Failing to so much as scratch the scales, I stab myself with such ferocity that the blade bends sideways, permanently.

"Shit," I say out loud. Realizing that I just ruined a knife that probably costs more than I make in a week...

By the time I hear a car approaching in the distance, I find myself in the tool shed. Surrounded by anything that cuts, saws, or drills. Even the axe, that I swung repeatedly against my shin, is laying in a pile of broken tools that failed to so much as scratch me.

When I started, I would've bet anything that a chainsaw would make short work of my scales. I was wrong about that too. For all the sparks and dust that it created, it did nothing more than make me uncomfortable. The teeth on the chain simply sheared off as I gripped the running saw with my hand. Eventually, it just ran out of gas.

Prior to my transformation, any of the things I've done to myself would have caused agonizing pain at best. I would be in the hospital, mutilated by most of them. Hell, I should be dead, from what Grizzly did to me... Yet, I'm unscathed.

I step out of the shed as the car pulls up. Emily, Dr. Mavro, and the woman who I could only assume was the geneticist from Europe, all step out of the car. Each of them inhales a deep breath, as they take a moment to appreciate the clean mountain air and surrounding beauty.

"Sam!" Emily yells in an excited voice. "What the heck are you doing in the toolshed?"

"Oh, you know..." I fumble for words, "I just figured I would hide in here. Just in case it was someone else." I finish saying, as I close the door to the shed behind me. Taking care to ensure that no one sees the chaos inside.

"I'm glad you found a change of clothes," Emily continues.

Me too! I think to myself. I can just imagine what the conversation about the bear would sound like if I hadn't.

"We got food," Emily proclaims. "I would have called to see what you wanted, but I have your phone and there are no landlines out here..."

"No worries," I reply, as I walk toward them. "That's why we picked this place to stash me. Right?"

Much to my surprise the geneticist from Europe watches me with complete calm. Perhaps even a bit of admiration. Almost as if she had seen something like me before.

"...ethros," she says quietly, in what I can only assume is a foreign language.

She walks toward me, with her hand stretched out for a handshake. Despite my new look, my professional demeanor has remained unchanged and I reciprocate. Making sure to shake her hand gently.

"I am Dr. Majken," she says with an evident pep in her voice. "In English, it sounds like 'Mike' with an 'N' at the end. You may call me Majk or 'Mike,' if it's easier."

"Thank you, Dr. Majken... Majk. My name is Sam, pleasure to meet you," I reply.

"It is good to see you here, Dr. Mavro," I continue as I wave to him.

"I wouldn't miss this for the world," he responds.

"Let's go in," Emily calls out from the front door, gesturing for everyone to come inside.

As they walk into the living room, I see Dr. Mavro and our guest taking in the splendor of what Emily and her family refer to as a 'cabin.' The high ceilings and rustic design lead up to a glass wall, with an astonishing mountain view. It truly makes the place feel more like a resort lodge, than a getaway for a family of three.

"What a beautiful view!" Dr. Majken comments. "This is a lovely place,"

"Thank you," Emily responds. "Please sit, make yourselves at home."

As everyone finds a comfortable seat, Dr. Majken quickly becomes the center of attention. The anticipation of what she may be able to tell us is almost palpable.

"I can imagine all of you have many questions," she begins. "I will do my best to answer them. But please understand that my knowledge comes from ancient history along with research that I conducted on my own. So, I may not have all the answers you are looking for."

"When you first saw me," I begin, "I thought I heard you say the word 'ethros' or something along those lines."

"Almost," she replies. "I said Millaethros. It is what your kind used to be called."

"Sorry! My kind?" I ask, in utter confusion. "I may not look like it right now, but I assure you that I am quite human. I only turned into this monstrosity a couple of weeks ago. Are you implying that there are others going through this transformation?"

"I understand your confusion," Dr. Majken responds calmly, "but I assure you, that on a genetic level, you have been a Millaethros your entire life. Have you ever heard the terms 'junk' or 'ghost DNA'?"

"I've seen them in article headlines," I answer while trying to recall if I actually read any of them.

"Although I would love to get into the details of the research behind it," Dr. Majken continues, "suffice it to say that these terms refer to elements of DNA, for which science has little or no explanation."

I knew the hospital would've been a complete waste of time! I think to myself with vindication.

"In other words," Dr. Majken explains, "imagine that your DNA is an instruction manual. The first two or three pages contain all the information your cells need in order to build a human, as opposed to an animal or an insect. However, the manual is one hundred pages long! At present, science sees those remaining ninety-seven or so pages, as blank! Just 'junk,'" she makes air quotes, implying the absurdity of the term.

"Ghost DNA," Dr. Majken continues, "refers to DNA of unknown origins. In other words, we can see that we have shared DNA with ancient human remains. However, there are portions that scientists cannot connect to any species ever found, human or otherwise."

"So, how does this relate to Sam?" Emily asks.

"Well, my guess" Dr. Majken responds, "is that something triggered the 'junk DNA' to reveal what is written on all or at least some of those blank pages. Think about Sam's transformation as building a structure. All humans are like the foundation and a pile of materials. Without the instructions, you have no idea what you're actually building. As the genetic instructions become available, the body starts to change into what it is supposed to be. In Sam's case, it is what I know as the Millaethros."

"Wait!" I interrupt. "You said whatever... ethros was 'my kind.' Are there others like me? More importantly, is there a cure for this? I don't think I can call my old job and say: 'Hey! Sorry, L-O-L! I was transforming into the stuff your nightmares are made of! Can I come in to work tomorrow?'"

"Milla - Ethros," Dr. Majken responds through a chuckle, "is a combination of two species. The first part of the word stems from Millanthea, a distant galaxy from which a long-extinct alien race originated. The second, part of the word is Ethros. The name of a species local to Earth, with which these aliens merged, to form the Millaethros."

The expression on Dr. Mavro's face is a combination of fascination, disbelief, excitement, and confusion. Probably much like my own.

"You are probably familiar with the species," Dr. Majken continues "but not the word 'Ethros.' In legends and fairytales, we now refer to them as dragons..."

I knew it! I knew that there is no way that I walked away from that bear attack unscathed! When it hit me in the head, I must have ended up with severe auditory hallucinations and brain damage, because I just heard her say 'alien' and 'dragon!'

"I'm sorry, Dr. Maj, Mike, Dr. M!" I stumble for her name while interrupting her out of bewilderment. "Did you just say the words 'dragon' and 'alien?' Because if that's the case, you're implying that I am a hybrid species. Presumably the result of an alien that either fucked or got fucked by a mythical creature! Pardon my French..."

I look to Emily and Dr. Mavro for support in questioning the sanity of her statement, but the expressions on their faces appear to resemble those cartoons, where the character's jaw just hit the floor and stayed there.

"Yes," Dr. Majken says affirmingly. "You are indeed half-dragon, half-alien. At least that is the case according to the texts."

"What texts?" I ask, still maintaining my bewildered tone.

"Although I am a geneticist," she responds, "I am also a part of an order. An order, whose mission was to retain the true history of this planet. So that when this day came, the world would not fall into utter chaos."

"I love a good story as much as the next person," I say incredulously, "but 'the true history of this planet...' That sounds like another origin story to me. Perhaps one that never took off as well as the Bible, but we already have dozens of such myths and tales. So, you'll have to forgive me when I say that this sounds like a bunch of horse shit!"

"I know how crazy it sounds..." she retorts. "Perhaps, I should start at the beginning. It may make a little more sense."

Her confidence is undeniable. Either she is an amazing liar, completely off her rocker, or she really believes whatever fairytale she is about to tell. If this is anything like what she talked about in the conference that Dr. Mavro had attended, it is no wonder that he perceived her ideas as the ramblings of a lunatic. Had I heard this under different circumstances, I would have thought they were talking about a video game or a science fiction film.

"I get it," Dr. Majken continues calmly. "It's not easy to accept, but I assure you it is the truth. If nothing else, look at yourself, Sam. Do you resemble anything short of something you would read about in some ancient myth?"

I open my mouth to fire back a response, but I have no words. More importantly, I don't have anyone else standing in line to tell me a story that might make more sense. I suppose, at this point, the least I can do is listen...

Before she begins, Dr. Majken lowers her eyes and gazes into the cup of coffee she had picked up on the way here. Her expression changes from that of a calm, matter-of-fact scientist, to someone who is about to tell a chilling tale. Without lifting her eyes from her coffee, she takes a deep breath and starts speaking:

"The story begins millions of years ago and billions of light-years from Earth... In a distant galaxy, where a war has raged on for over a thousand years."

Although she can't be more than fifty years old, as she speaks her voice becomes melancholy... soft and distant, like a great-grandparent recalling the memory of a time long gone.

"Like many wars, the exact reason for its beginning was lost to time. It has been widely debated by those who kept the records, but no singular cause has been found. Perhaps, like most wars, it began over resources, maybe it was intolerance or cultural differences. What is not disputed, however, is that so many atrocities had been committed by each side, that every new generation had plenty of reason to hate their enemies and continue fighting. In this way, the war was self-perpetuating."

"To give you some perspective," she looks up from her coffee, "it is said that neither side kept count of individual casualties. Their reports only included losses of entire colonies, battle groups, and massive ships. Some of which had populations that numbered in the tens of thousands."

"How could anyone sustain such losses?" I ask, as if it matters.

"When a society stretches across numerous planets and solar systems, its populace numbers in the hundreds of billions," she responds with confidence, "and it's likely made up of many different alien species. Is it really so farfetched to imagine that, given such numbers, a single battle may extinguish a hundred thousand lives, but not end the war? If anything, it would likely spur the other side to retaliate..."

"However," Dr. Majken sighs, "after a thousand years, with casualties that must have exceeded the entire population of Earth several times over, the war came to an exhaustive stalemate. Each side began to focus resources on searching for or developing a more effective means of finishing off the other for good. That 'race' drove them to explore some of the most distant solar systems of Millanthea. During a remote planetary reconnaissance mission, a simple scouting party found an object that they saw as the potential key to victory."

Even if this is pure bullshit, I have to admit, it is not the worst story I've heard, I think to myself.

"You see," Dr. Majken continues, "even with the technology to travel between stars, neither civilization had managed to travel between galaxies. At least not effectively. After a thousand years and countless failed attempts on both sides, each had concluded that it was simply too vast of a distance to cross. More importantly, neither side could afford to waste the resources on the seemingly futile venture."

I can only imagine the disappointment Dr. Mavro must be experiencing. Hearing that intergalactic travel was deemed 'futile,' by advanced, alien civilizations.

"However," Dr. Majken explains, "whether by accident or fate, the scouting party stumbled on a way to do just that... What they found looked like a massive, black crystal. I do not mean the size of a car or bus, I mean the size of Mt. Everest. This crystal turned out to be a sort of bridge or a gateway to what we now know as Earth."

Dr. Majken pauses to take a sip of her coffee and to let the impact of everything she just said sink in.

"Wait!" Dr. Mavro exclaims, almost popping out of his chair. "A crystal with a wormhole in it?"

"I do not know the details of how it worked, Dr. Mavro," she responds with futility. "All I know is that the crystal somehow connected a planet in Millanthea, to the same type of crystal here on Earth."

"I am sorry," Dr. Mavro countered, "and I do not mean to insult your order. However, this portion of their story makes no sense! I am fairly certain that a crystal that size, one that is likely emitting or consuming an astounding amount of energy, would have been discovered by now."

Dr. Majken takes another sip of her coffee, ensuring that Dr. Mavro finished making his point before she responds.

"I am certain," she finally says with confidence, "that you are aware of the evidence suggesting that what is now New York City, was once the top of a mountain taller than Everest. Yet, it now sits at sea level. As far as the energy it would have to emit, I cannot speak to it. It is entirely possible we have yet to develop a way to measure that particular type of energy or radiation... Heck, we may be surrounded by it at all times. So, it is effectively undetectable by our sensors, because the sensors see it as the baseline. I am certain that you can come up with far more scenarios than I can. Especially, when it comes to these sorts of things. What I can say with certainty, is that the bridge is definitely on Earth."

Dr. Mavro eases back into his chair. Obviously considering the plausibility of her statements. While simultaneously trying to wrap his mind around the rest of the story. Emily and I, on the other hand probably look like children, sitting around a campfire, listening to an enthralling ghost story. Silent, in anticipation of what happens next.

CHAPTER IX

THE WHEEL OF TIME

As Dr. Majken continues to explain the story passed down by her order, for what would literally have to be millions of years, I begin to open my mind to the idea that although difficult to believe, it actually makes some sense. Particularly, given what I now look like.

"My order does not explain why or how," she continues, "but apparently time passes differently on Earth than it does in the Millanthea galaxy. Some records imply that mere hours in Millanthea translate to several years on Earth... So, in terms of the war, it was the perfect solution - A colony that could yield an entire battalion, from birth to combat readiness, in less time than it takes to train a single group of soldiers."

"It also sounds like it was located strategically," I chime in. "If Earth is in a different galaxy, the enemy has no way of getting here, other than through the crystal."

"Precisely!" Dr. Majken responds. "As a result, Earth quickly became the first intergalactic colony. The colony itself was named for the team that found the crystal... I am certain you've heard the name... Atlantis."

"Wait! What?" Emily's voice comes out of nowhere. "Are you saying what I think you are?"

"Yes," Dr. Majken replies with a smile. "Atlantis was quite real and simply named after the team of soldiers who found it. Do you really think that all the myths and legends which you have heard were simply a product of someone's imagination?"

"Well, no," Emily answers quietly. "I mean, I've obviously heard the saying that all stories stem from some modicum of truth. Then, as they are passed down through the generations, they are embezzled and exaggerated. Eventually becoming a myth or legend with which we are familiar."

"Exactly," announces Dr. Majken, "and now you know where many of them originated."

"Wait," I interrupt, "you're implying that your order has passed down actual accounts of all the myths and legends that people have come up with over the millennia?"

"Not exactly," she responds. "Obviously, all of the stories we are familiar with today were written by people. However, many of the concepts and foundations of these stories are far more than figments of someone's imagination... You see, Atlantis was intentionally populated with a vast variety of alien species. Some were here because their abilities made them perfect combatants in specific environments. Others were refugees - the last survivors of an alien species, decimated by the war in Millanthea. Hoping to avoid extinction, they would come here... Because of its landmass, Atlantis –"

"Wait," Dr. Mavro interrupts with excitement. "Does your order explain where it was? Do they have the actual location of Atlantis?"

"Of course," Dr. Majken replies nonchalantly. As though she's oblivious to the fact that people have been searching for it, for over a thousand years. "You are sitting in it."

"Huh?" Everyone except her says in perfect unison.

"The stories of Atlantis," I say with uncertainty, trying to make sure that we're talking about the same thing, "say it was an island, that sank beneath the waves,"

"Again, partially true," responds Dr. Majken. "When it was colonized, Atlantis was one giant landmass, surrounded on all sides by water. It was the largest island in the history of Earth, but technically it was still an island... What was once called Atlantis, today is referred to as Pangea - a supercontinent that eventually split into the continents of today. Hence, you are technically sitting on a section of Atlantis. My guess is that when stories of it were first passed down, it was simpler to just refer to it as an island."

"Hold on," says Dr. Mavro sternly. "You are saying that Atlantis existed over two-hundred-million years ago. That simply cannot be. The oldest human fossils do not date back nearly that far. Plus, if the stories of Atlantean technology and architecture are even remotely based in truth, we would have to have found some by now. There are so many issues with this story that can easily be or have already been debunked!"

"Not necessarily," Dr. Majken responds with certainty. "You forget that Pangea or Atlantis broke apart somewhere between one-hundred-and-eighty to two-hundred million years ago. There are civilizations that have existed within the last five thousand years, that we are still discovering today. Many of them were comprised of cities and hundreds of miles of roads. Some even accomplished things we can't explain to this day. What's most significant, is that their buildings, burial sites, and artifacts did not go through a continental split or more than a hundred million years of erosion."

Yet again, no one can really argue, I think to myself. Who knows, maybe this 'order' just tells a really good tale... or maybe there is something to it. If nothing else, I got a pretty cool name out of this fairytale.

"What about dinosaur bones?" Emily jumps in.

"Yes, we have found some very old dinosaur bones," Dr. Majken responds. "However, the vast majority of them are much less than 200 million years old. Of those that are, we don't have a single complete skeleton. There were millions, if not billions of dinosaurs, yet all we have are fragments. I am simply saying, that like most things in nature, given enough time, everything can be reabsorbed and broken down. Thus, what was once Atlantis and its people, is now simply a part of nature... maybe some of it is deep beneath the sands of the ocean floor. The Earth is vast, therefore, we can't rule out the possibility that something was preserved."

"So, how did Atlantis collapse?" I ask.

"Like any society, Atlantis grew and expanded," Dr. Majken states. "Over millions of years, they sent troops to support the war in a distant galaxy. The governing body of Atlantis, the Atlantean Council of Elders, ensured that the colony never forgot its purpose. At least a few of the council members were always from Millanthea."

"I am confused," Emily interjects. "If Atlantis kept sending troops for millions of years, how long had the war lasted at that point?"

"Not as long as you might think," responds Dr. Majken. "Remember that hours translate to years. So, the Millantheans who came here would live out their lives on Earth. Though the texts make mention of some who went back just before they died. I imagine coming to govern Atlantis was akin to a death sentence for a Millanthean..."

"Why?" Emily inquires.

"Think about it," Dr. Majken replies. "Everyone you know, watches you walk into a portal, as a young woman. Then, less than a day later you come back. However, now you are old and effectively on your deathbed."

"That does sound terrible." Emily retorts. "Why would anyone go back?"

Knowing how emotionally intelligent Emily is, and how crippling that can be at times, I'm guessing she's probably imagining the sadness of a parting party. Saying goodbye to a childhood friend, who is walking to what could be perceived as their death sentence.

"Well Emily," Dr. Majken counters, "if we continue to use you as the example, from your perspective, it may have been a very fulfilling life. You may have lived over a hundred years and governed over a diverse colony, made up of hundreds of alien species. Perhaps you even partnered with someone and had children. Coming back would be like a reunion with friends or family whom you have not seen in decades. Except they are as young as you remember them."

"Plus," she continues, "not all species age the same way. Some had immeasurable lifespans and only died when they chose to end their own existence… or were killed. My order cataloged many of the species, but far from all of them. Some were incredibly fascinating."

Dr. Mavro once again shifts forward in his seat.

"Majk, does your order explain the time difference?" He asks with contemplation in his voice.

"Not in great detail," replies Dr. Majken. "They explain it in layman's terms as the 'Wheel of Time.' It's not my specialty. So, I never spent much time trying to unpack that theory. Consequently, my understanding is fairly rudimentary."

"Please," Dr. Mavro requests, "I would love to hear it."

"Well," Dr. Majken begins, "Picture the wheel of a car. Now take a marker and put two dots on the wheel. The first one will be really close to the center. We will call this point M, for Millanthea. The second, we will put on the very edge of the tire and label it point E, for Earth. If you rotate the wheel one full rotation, point E will have traveled a much greater distance than point M. In this case, the difference in the distance traveled is the same as the difference in the amount of time that has passed. Wait… maybe that was the factor of amplification of the time that has passed… Sorry, it's been a while."

I hope Dr. Mavro is getting this, I think to myself. All I got was a car tire with two dots on it…

"Keep in mind," Dr. Majken continues, "this is simply a visual analogy. It does not imply that the universe is like a giant wheel, nor does it explain how gravity or other laws of physics play into the whole thing. There is also a key element that deals with the expansion of the universe. Which actually reduces the time difference as both Millanthea and the Milky Way galaxies get closer and slow down…"

Dr. Mavro slowly shifts back in his chair, without a word. No doubt he is scouring all his knowledge of physics and astronomy. Trying to make some sense of everything he just heard.

"I wish I had more details for you, Dr. Mavro" she states with regret. "Unfortunately, my order focuses more on the history of Earth and Atlantis itself. In other words, we are more interested in what led up to our current civilization. The causes and effects of the events took place. We also seek to ensure that we can provide at least some answers as more people begin to evolve. Hopefully, others will uncover the science in due time. Who knows, perhaps it will be you?"

CHAPTER X

WHY CAN'T THERE BE A HAPPY ENDING?

While I listen to Dr. Majken's story, I begin to wonder: *What went wrong? After millions of years, thousands upon thousands of generations... Maybe, for once, there was a partially happy ending. Maybe the war finally came to an end?*

"So, what happened to Atlantis?" I ask with intrigue.

Her gaze falls back to the now cold, cup of black coffee. A solemn look once again fills her eyes.

Nope, definitely not a happy ending! I think to myself.

"It was destroyed by the last council. In an effort to prevent a civil war within the colony," she says faintly.

"What do you mean they destroyed it?" Emily presses. "Was the council so afraid of losing power that they wiped out everything, rather than fighting to preserve what took millions of years to build?"

"No!" Dr. Majken responds, almost as if Emily had insulted her intelligence. "Part of the Council's duty was to ensure that no individual or group ever tampered with the gate to Millanthea, the Atlantean Crystal, as it was commonly referred to. Since, as I already mentioned, it was the only known way to travel between galaxies, it was invaluable. The texts make clear, that those who wanted to overthrow the council, intended to sever the link to Millanthea and possibly try to use the crystal to travel to other galaxies."

"Wouldn't travel to other galaxies be a good thing?" I ask.

"In theory," she replies. "If that was really their only intent. However, the key dispute was about sending troops to Millanthea. More importantly, the Atlantean Crystal didn't exactly come with an instruction manual. So, any attempts to manipulate it, could have ended in catastrophe."

"Ok, fair point," I respond after a brief silence. "So, where does the Millaet... Dragons, where do dragons, fit into the picture?"

"Well, Atlantis was not only about expanding the ranks," responds Dr. Majken. "It also served as an optimal place to expand what you might call a 'Super Soldier Program.' Some alien species were able to... mingle with others. Which sometimes resulted in offspring with astounding strengths and combat abilities. In Millanthea, most species kept to their home worlds, only meeting on ships or in preparation for battle. Not exactly the ideal place to have a kid. Atlantis provided a safe place where all the alien species could exist side by side, meet, and possibly procreate."

She pauses to take a sip of her coffee, then continues. "However, it was a species native to Earth that proved most interesting for battle, the Ethros. They had an astounding ability to treat water and air as a continuation of one another. As such, they were able to fly and swim at astounding speeds. Their scales made them virtually indestructible. While their immense size, strength, speed, and claws - that could shred steel - would potentially enable them to tear through enemy defenses like butter."

"Wait, no fire breath?" I ask jokingly.

"No, not exactly," she replies. "However, some individual dragons had the ability to channel ambient energy. Then, expel it in the form of searing heat or even lightning. These were incredibly rare though. Unfortunately, capturing a regular Ethros was nearly impossible. So, it would stand to reason that the Alphas who possessed such abilities, would be absolutely impossible to capture."

"Ok, but you said I am part dragon," I reiterate.

"Yes... It is quite amazing to see," she continues. "When the first colonists came up with the idea of trying to use the Ethros in battle, they did not have any way of transporting them to the battlefield. Let alone training them to fight the enemy. Capturing something that flies, swims, and even runs faster than most of your vehicles, is apparently quite difficult," she says with a hint of sarcasm. "Moreover, when they were able to trap or catch one, the Ethros would just shred through the restraints or containment, often killing those who hunted it."

"Hey, Sam," Emily chimes in. "Just so you know, we're not trapping you."

Everyone to bursts into laughter, putting down their drinks to avoid spilling them. Her timing is perfect as always. We definitely needed the reprieve, since this story is getting crazier by the minute.

"So how did I come to be?" I ask as the laughter dies down.

"Right," Dr. Majken responds, picking her coffee back up off the coffee table. "There was a small group of colonists who came to Atlantis with a very unique ability. Their home world, a planet called Valphet, was completely destroyed by the enemy. In an effort to prevent them from joining the opposing side."

"You mean the side that established Atlantis?" I interrupt.

"Yes," she responds. "I am sorry that I keep using the term 'enemy' but not naming them. My order never actually named either side. All the texts are written from the perspective of Atlantis. As I am sure you have heard the saying that 'history is written by the winners.' In this case, all we know is that regardless of species or solar system, the side that opposed Atlantis was the enemy."

"So," Dr. Majken pauses to sip her coffee, "the small group that happened to be away from the planet as an envoy to discuss their neutrality in the war, was all that survived of the species. There were too few to even attempt restoring the population..."

"What was their ability?" Inquires Dr. Mavro.

"Well," Dr. Majken says with a tone of contemplation. "It is difficult to explain the full scope of it. To put it simply, they could construct new bodies. Once an individual reached a certain age, they could extract their... living essence or soul, as some would call it, and generate a new body from surrounding matter."

"That is a pretty cool trick," Emily chimes in. "So, they could live in a body made of rock or water... Kind of like an elemental?"

"I don't think so," Dr. Majken answers. "My understanding is that they would combine elements from organic matter - like plants and animals - to generate a new, young version of themselves. This effectively made them immortal. However, the process took time and concentration. They couldn't simply eject their souls. So, if they were killed, they died like anyone else."

"So, when their planet was destroyed..." I begin.

"Yes, all but about forty or fifty of them, perished instantly," Dr. Majken finishes my sentence poignantly. "It was the Valphetans who found a way to essentially tame the Ethros and bring them to the fight."

"How?" I inquire.

"Valphetans had an alternative ability," Dr. Majken explains. "Rather than generating a new version of themselves, they were able to implant their living essence into a host body. You can call it a consciousness, soul, life force, or some combination thereof."

"You mean they were able to take over a dragon's body?" I ask, trying to imagine what the process looks like.

"Not in the simple sense," she replies. "It was more of a melding than a takeover. The Ethros were not mindless creatures. As such, the process created an entirely new being. The resulting 'Millaethros' retained the shared experiences and memories of both. My order assumes that this is why Valphetans could not perform such a merger with other species that were fully self-aware. It is theorized that the existing consciousness would reject the merger or constantly fight for dominance of the new form."

"Fascinating!" Dr. Mavro interjects.

"Unfortunately," Dr. Majken continues, "this alternative ability was a one-way trip, so to speak. It destroyed the Valphetan's individuality and consequently their innate ability to transfer consciousness. However, the resulting being, a humanoid creature with the speed, power, and near indestructibility of the Ethros, was practically unstoppable. You, Sam, are a distant descendant of one such merger."

"How could that be? According to what you said, there could only have been forty or fifty such combinations. More importantly, why have I been human my entire life, then suddenly this?" I ask.

"There were very few indeed," she replies. "Almost all of them went back to fight in Millanthea. As far as being human your whole life, that has less to do with you personally, and more with the fall of Atlantis -"

"I hear something," I say, as I cut her off abruptly, raising my hand, in a surprisingly tactical manner.

Watching all those action movies finally paid off, I think to myself.

Seemingly perturbed at first, everyone quickly realizes that I obviously hear something they do not. Within a moment, I identify the sound as tires on gravel.

"Someone is coming…"

CHAPTER XI

BULLETPROOF!

I race out a back door and run straight to the tree line. Hopefully, it is dark enough that I can make it without being spotted. If not, Emily will have a bunch of explaining to do.

I press my back against the first tree large enough to hide behind. Peeking out cautiously, I try to identify our surprise guests. It is far, but as I focus on the vehicles, my vision enlarges them somehow. I am able to make out details quite clearly. If I was a few feet closer, I might even be able to read the license plates!

I am going to call this ability 'Dragon Vision.' I think to myself. *Seeing as I am part dragon and all that... Nope, Emily will not stop giving me shit for it. She'll probably say something along the lines of "Oh? You didn't want to call it 'Dork-o-Vision?'*

Much to my surprise, the large SUV with tinted windows drives past Emily's car, without slowing down. It drives around to the back of the cabin and stops. Two more, drive up and park on the sides. Three more pull up and form a wedge fifty or sixty feet away from the front door. The doors open and my heart sinks.

The men exiting the vehicles are heavily armed and wearing some very impressive tactical gear. They work as a unit, getting into position. Each one has a clear line of sight to a specific section of the cabin. The lasers, on their weapons, move back and forth along the walls, stopping at every window and vent. Scanning for movement in their respective section. They are confident but cautious, still taking cover behind the open doors of their vehicles.

"These guys are definitely not here to enjoy the peace and quiet," I whisper to myself.

One of the men puts on a light jacket with those three letters that I really did not want to see right now, 'FBI.' Another man has a word written across his jacket. It is harder to make out...

"Shit," I say quietly, "it's Interpol. What the hell are they doing here?"

"Dr. Majken!" A voice from a loudspeaker breaks the silence. "This is agent Alexei with Interpol. We have the house surrounded. Please come out with your hands up... and bring your accomplices with you."

The front door opens slowly. Dr. Majken, Emily, and Dr. Mavro emerge, complying with the order. As they walk out, multiple lasers shift from various windows and converge on my friends. At least two agents are aiming at each of them. Blatantly adding to the already tense situation, Emily is holding a light in her right hand.

Of course, you are recording everything to your phone, Em. I think to myself.

Agent Alexei, raises his hand, signaling everyone to stand down. The lasers shift away from my friends but remain pointed in their general direction. He walks towards them calmly. I close my eyes and imagine myself standing among them.

Maybe dragons had magical hearing too, I think to myself while focusing on drowning out all other sounds...

I open my eyes and look at my friends. The sound of my breathing and heartbeat become faint, almost distant. At the same time, the radio chatter coming from inside the vehicles seems to get louder. It is almost as if I turned down the volume of anything close to me and increased it for everything in the distance. I close my eyes once again and listen.

"What is the meaning of this?" Emily demands. Her voice filled with frustration. "Unless you have a warrant, you are trespassing on my family's property."

"Are you aware that you are harboring a person of interest in an ongoing Interpol investigation?" Agent Alexei asks calmly, obviously prepared for Emily's demand. "We just have some questions, but if you need us to obtain a warrant. Agent Smith of the FBI here can make a few calls and obtain one. Though, I imagine you would prefer to keep your family out of this, Miss Adams."

This guy obviously did his research, I think to myself as new concerns flood my mind. *He clearly knows quite a bit about Em, and is even implying that he can connect with her dad… This is bad news.*

"Moreover," Alexei continues, "given your father's post in the military, I don't think he would object to us having a friendly chat."

"I'm a geneticist," Dr. Majken exclaims in frustration and utter disbelief. "Why would Interpol have an investigation listing me as a person of interest?"

"Like I said," responds Agent Alexei, "we simply have a few questions. If you voluntarily cooperate, we will likely be on our way. If not, or if you choose to lie, my FBI friends can detain you as threats to national security, for your suspected involvement in numerous conspiracies."

"What the fuck are you talking about?" Dr. Majken demands, her European accent becoming far more pronounced than before, but I still can't place it.

"We've been keeping up with your research, as well as your travel," responds Alexei. "You have mentioned some intriguing theories about mutating people through genetics. Although this all sounded a bit farfetched initially, when you received an invitation to America, concerning a 'potential validation of one of your presentations,' it sent up some red flags for my team and I."

"You're reading my e-mails?" She asks in a bewildered tone. Obviously recognizing something he said as a quote from her correspondence.

"We do not have to," he responds with evident sincerity. "Your university's servers already scan all communications, both in and out for potential threats to safety and security. Additionally, they flag items that could damage the university's reputation. Whether you realize it or not, some of your colleagues are involved in research that… Let's just say that in the wrong hands, it could prove devastating on a global scale. Therefore, if there is ever a concern about any call or email, the communication is automatically flagged and passed on to us for review."

"I am sorry if I got you into this, Dr. Majken," Dr. Mavro says, with evident dismay in his voice.

"Don't worry," says Alexei. "No one is in any trouble, so long as you are not hiding anything. As of now, your 'Alien Genes' theories are of little concern to us. We just need to make sure you're not actively doing anything to make them 'valid' yourself... You know injecting people with various chemicals, developing mutagenic viruses, etc."

"We aren't hiding anything," Emily, cuts in, still frustrated by the intrusion. However, now she also sounds perturbed by the fact that Alexei threatened to involve her father. "You want to search the house? Fine! Go for it! Then I want you off my family's property!"

"Thank you, for your cooperation," replies Alexei.

Wasting no time, the FBI agent, who had been silent throughout the altercation, speaks up.

"Alpha team, green light," is all he says.

"Copy, green light, Alpha moving," another voice responds. Almost immediately followed by the sound of multiple pairs of boots walking along the gravel.

I can hear the agents' tactical gear shifting around as they begin to move from their covered positions. The sound of their footsteps remains concise and coordinated. Aside from their movements, they make no sounds. Suddenly, I feel a cold, round object press firmly against the back of my neck.

"No sudden moves," A male voice says quietly from behind.

"Shit!" I say as I open my eyes. My vision and hearing snap back from the distant interaction.

"Put your hands on your head and turn around really slowly," the voice says calmly, but sternly.

I comply and slowly place my hands on the back of my head. The cold object is slowly removed from my neck. As I turn, I am able to quickly confirm that it was the barrel of a rifle. Aside from the agent who was backing away, there are five others. All, with weapons pointed at me.

"What... the... fuck?" Says the agent whose weapon was against my neck.

Obviously disturbed and terrified by my looks, he takes two more steps back, but they are no longer calculated. He is simply trying to put distance between us. On his last step, his foot slips on a large stone and he squeezes the trigger of his rifle. I hear multiple explosions, followed by searing pain.

For a split second, my mind goes blank. The pain is processed into a gut-wrenching roar. I am not sure what just happened, but I do know that suddenly I am nothing but a passenger in my own body. My vision shifts and I no longer see men all around me. They are silhouettes, pulsing in various colors. My talons extend from my fingertips. As my heart rate skyrockets, my arm swings out at the man closest to me, in a blinding flash.

The man's rifle falls to the ground in multiple pieces. He looks down in what can only be described as astonishment. Then, a thin red line forms at the center of his neck.

"Contact! Con-" another begins to yell.

Before he can get the word out a second time, my claws lunge through his chest. There is no effort nor resistance. His 'bulletproof' vest might as well have been a paper napkin.

A couple of the other agents manage to fire a few rounds. This time, I did not even feel the bullets hit my flesh. Maybe they missed, I am not sure… What I am sure of is that I didn't. The entire encounter lasts less than ten seconds. As I look around, I see six bodies around me. It looks like they were shoved through a giant lawnmower. Some of their arms are separated, still holding on to pieces of their assault rifles, that look like they were cut with a laser. Blood is gushing from their arteries. I think I am going to be sick.

"Saaaam!" I hear Emily's voice cry out in the distance. Then, darkness...

CHAPTER XII

PUPPET

Camera flashes begin to go off incessantly, as the President walks onto the stage and approaches the podium. As the noise subsides and he begins to speak.

"I want to start by saying that foreign interference in our elections is a thing of the past. I will place sanctions on any country that dares to tamper with our systems. This year –"

"Mr. President! Mr. President!" Reporters begin to interrupt. Their volume increasing and disrupting his speech.

"What about the reports all over the internet?" Shouts one reporter.

"As I was saying, the elections this year will -"

"Mr. President!" The reporters continue to yell. "The people deserve answers. Is the White House's official stance to ignore the reports?"

"The elections -" he attempts to ignore the barrage of questions.

"Mr. President," another reporter yells out. "Why are you dodging the question? Is the government not going to do anything about the sightings?"

Suddenly a phone rings and echoes through all the audio channels. The room falls silent, as everyone is caught off guard by the disruption. The President reaches into his pocket and pulls out a red smartphone to ignore the call. Before he is able to put it away, the phone rings again.

"This is apparently urgent government business. I will be right back. He turns and steps away from the podium.

"Do you understand," the President answers the call, obviously perturbed by the disruption, "that I am giving a press -"

"If you ever ignore my call again," the voice on the other end cuts him off ominously, "I will leave you alone with those inmates for a full hour."

The President's face fills with horror, as his hand instinctively moves over his wrists and he recalls the abuse that only lasted five minutes. Though at the time felt like an eternity. Although the bruises have long faded from his body, the helplessness left a permanent mark on his mind.

"When I call, you will answer. I do not care about your bullshit speeches," the caller continues. "The time for politics may be over sooner than you think."

"You told me that you would manage the incidents," the President responds meekly.

"All anyone has at this point are blurry videos and hearsay," the caller responds. "Even I have limits when it comes to being in multiple places across the globe. It seems like things are unraveling much faster than I anticipated. You need to pay a visit to an Air Force base in Colorado. I will text you the details and meet you there when you land. Go now." The voice says with authority.

"What about the press?" The President asks in frustration.

"Tell them that you have resources dedicated to investigating the reports." The voice replies in a perturbed tone. "However, thus far it seems like this is just a coordinated group of alien conspiracy theorists, who are trying to create chaos before elections. Then, have your Press Secretary take over."

The call disconnects abruptly, as the room grows louder as the cameras continue to flash. Once again the President stands at the podium and begins to speak.

"I just got an update from the intelligence team I have assigned to investigate these reports. It looks like it's just a hoax, put on by a resourceful group of alien conspiracy hunters, trying to disrupt our elections. We are taking care of it. You have nothing to worry about. My press secretary will answer any questions."

The President immediately turns away from the podium and quickly leaves the stage, as reporters continue to shout questions.

"Tell them to prepare Air Force One," he instructs his aide.

"S-Sir," the aide stammers, "You have multiple meetings on your agenda for the next two days."

"Cancel them all... We're going to Colorado."

Chapter XIII

Guinea pig...

My eyes open slowly. The sunlight coming through the blinds forces me to squint, straining to adjust to the light. I scan the room without moving my head. Emily is sitting in a chair, in the corner. She must have fallen asleep waiting for me to wake up.

My body feels numb. It doesn't take long to understand that I am in a hospital. For a moment, I am filled with overwhelming hope. Maybe, just maybe I was involved in a horrible car accident and this entire thing was all just a shitty dream while I was in a coma... I lift my hand and bring it closer to my face.

Nope, still living the fucking nightmare, I think to myself as soon as I see the scales.

I begin shifting in the bed, trying to get comfortable. The bed makes a slight creak and Emily opens her eyes.

"Oh, fuck Sam…" she says with evident relief in her voice. "I was really starting to worry."

"Why? How long have you been here?" I inquire wearily.

"Three days," she responds.

"Three days?" I can hear the shock in my own voice. "Well, I suppose that this proves I wasn't ignoring you for all those days. I truly was knocked out for an entire week." I smile.

"I definitely believe you, Sam," she replies. "Though I believed you back then too."

Her tone is disconcerting. Much like when she first saw me, Emily sounds both sad and worried.

"Hey… Em," I say with concern. "What's up?"

"Sam, I've been here three days," she says quietly, "but you've been out for over three weeks."

"What?" I gasp in bewilderment. "How? What happened? Did all that stuff at the cabin really happen? Please tell me that it was all a bad dream!"

Emily's gaze shifts towards the floor. She does not need to say anything for me to understand that she knows full well what I did.

"Why am I not chained up?" I ask quietly. "If what I remember is even remotely accurate, I should be in some underground black site. One of those where they lock you up and throw away the key. Oh shit! Where are Dr. Mavro and Dr. Majken? Are they ok or did they get arrested?"

"Sam, those men had cameras on them," Emily responds sympathetically. "No one doubts that you acted in self-defense."

But I didn't, I think to myself. *That wasn't me at all. I wish I could explain it to you Em... but I have no clue what the fuck happened. I'm just not sure you should be here. Though I imagine if I told you to leave, you would just slap me... Then, I might lose control again...*

"Everyone else is fine..." Emily continues, as she lifts her gaze from the floor to look at me. "Dr. Mavro came up with some theories about what is happening. So, he was invited to explore them with some of the top physicists at an undisclosed location. Although he dropped enough hints to indicate that he could not pass up the opportunity to work in Area 51."

"Dr. Majken is still here," Emily goes on. "She is debriefing a bunch of top government officials and generals from all the branches. Providing them whatever information her order has about you and what they believe is coming..."

She pauses for a moment then smiles and says: "It is kind of ironic that you are the reason she's finally being listened to. That she's no longer dismissed as another looney-bin trying to start a cult... Please, Sam, look at me."

I turn my head towards her. "How can you just sit there, Em? How are you so calm about all this? I still don't get why they haven't turned me into a Guinea Pig… It has something to do with your dad, doesn't it?"

"Look, Sam," she responds with a solemn tone. "A lot has happened in the time you've been knocked out… Yes, my dad stepped in, but it took two weeks for me to find someone who would finally contact him. As far as why you're not a Guinea Pig… To my understanding, it was not for lack of effort on their part." Emily's tone grows shameful, as her gaze shifts back toward the floor.

"What do you mean?" I ask.

"From what my father told me after he arrived… " she responds with difficulty. "For the first 19 days that we were here, they tried everything. They wanted blood samples, tissue samples, skin samples, anything, and everything. They just couldn't get it."

Ah, they ran into the same problem that I did back at the cabin, I chuckle to myself, silently.

"Their needles bent or broke against your scales," Emily says with the tone of someone delivering great news to a terminally ill patient. "Drill bits and saws dulled out within seconds without leaving a mark. I heard that some doctor was so determined to get something, that he dragged a plasma cutter in from the motor pool. But even it shorted out after running at maximum power for too long. What's crazy is that after all that your scales were unscathed and still cool to the touch."

"Hmmm..." I respond with a smirk. "I guess I was right about the hospital thing... I suppose I have your father to thank for not waking up in chains as well?"

"Yes, well..." Emily retorts knowingly. "After watching the footage from the body cams and seeing the damage to that team's weapons and armor... plus a very long chat with Dr. Majken. I think my dad came to the realization that if you woke up in captivity, it could end badly for everyone in this facility."

"I wouldn't hurt anyone," I say with concern in my tone. "Not intentionally... When I got shot, something else came out. I know it sounds crazy, Em, but it wasn't me. Not really. I felt like a passenger in a car that was about to crash. I could see it coming, but there was nothing I could do... That is what terrifies me."

"It must have been the 'Ethros' side of you," Emily responds with more intrigue than concern. "Dr. Majken has told me a bit more about Atlantis and the Millaethros over the last week. You are quite incredible, you know? And you have amazing potential."

Emily's voice suddenly sounds like that of a teacher. Genuinely, trying to encourage a student who is flunking math.

"Thanks, Em..." I respond with sincerity. "I only wish I saw what you see. Unfortunately, when I look in a mirror, all I can see is the monster that I feel I've become... Speaking of... I don't feel restrained, but I'm having a hard time shifting in this bed... What gives?"

"Well…" Emily responds slowly. "That might be due to the fact that you have developed a couple of new appendages."

"What?" I yell out in confusion, as I sit up.

The moment my shoulders lift off the mattress, I hear a loud crack from the hospital bed and feel something connecting me to it.

"Careful!" Emily exclaims.

I look behind me but cannot see what is tethering me down. As I pivot to put my feet on the floor, I catch my reflection in a full-length mirror mounted on the wall. Each of my shoulder blades appears to have a scale-covered rod growing from it. Each one firmly anchored into the bed.

"What… the… fuck?" I mutter in confusion.

"We're not sure," responds Emily. "At first, we thought they were dragon wings or something, but they're more like whips or… tentacles. Dr. Majken said that it might be a result of mixed DNA from another species manifesting itself. Remember she said that everyone became humanoid after Atlantis fell? Well, her new theory is that once that happened, your ancestors could've mixed with any number of spices from various alien worlds. So, it's possible that a whole bunch of other DNA got mixed in."

I stand up and move towards the mirror. Turning my back to it, I look over my shoulder for a better perspective. The long, whip-like appendages protrude through small holes in my hospital gown. Without much thought, I tear off the gown, to get an unobstructed view.

The narrow, spiraled whips appear to extend from the corners of my shoulder blades. Though they likely begin somewhere much deeper underneath the bone. They feel like they are made of cartilage, flexible but not fleshy. The tips, which hang only an inch or two above the floor, somewhat resemble the talons on my fingers.

A thin layer of skin connects to the base of each whip and stretches down to the small of my back. Coming together to form a 'V.' From there they become flush with the rest of my body…

"Fuck, that looks weird," I mumble as I examine my back.

I reach my arm around, trying to feel the protrusions from my shoulder blades. Frustrated that I won't be able to reach, I turn my head forward and notice Emily's gaze dart toward the floor. Like a complete idiot, I didn't think about the fact that tearing off my hospital gown to get a good look at my back, I would be giving Emily more show than she bargained for.

"Shit! I'm sorry Em, I didn't mean to…" I fumble for words as I grab the gown and do my best to cover myself.

I imagine that if I wasn't covered in gun-metal gray scales, I would be countless shades of red from embarrassment.

"Don't worry," Emily chuckles. "Nothing I haven't seen… Okay, maybe the scales are new, but otherwise, nothing I haven't seen… I am sorry though, I didn't mean to make you uncomfortable."

"No Em, it's my fault," I say shamefully. "I didn't even think… I was just trying to get a better -"

"Stop, Sam," she cuts me off obviously not at all bothered to see me in my new birthday suit. "Unfortunately, all they have here are military uniforms. I asked my dad to get a set for you."

I slide the hospital curtain between myself and Emily. The camouflaged pants and blouse are folded neatly on a chair next to my bed. The pants slide on rather easily and from the slits cut into the back of the t-shirt and blouse, it looks like they have already taken my new appendages into account.

"Let me know if you need help," Emily says kindly.

Much to my surprise as I slip on the t-shirt, the appendages slide through rather effortlessly. Then as soon as I slide my arm through one sleeve, the tentacles come up and slide through the openings cut in the back. It looks so strange but feels no different than moving my arms or legs.

"Well that's cool," I say baffled.

"What is?" asks Emily.

I open the curtain as I finish buttoning the uniform blouse. "These things are like tentacles and moving them is not much different from moving my arms or fingers. Like when

117

you go to grab something, you do not have to think about lifting your arm, extending it, etc. Well, these things are just like that. Watch…"

I say as one of the tentacles moves forward and pulls the curtain the rest of the way back.

"Whoa!" Emily says in astonishment. "That's a bit creepy, but also kind of cool."

She looks me over as though I just stepped out of a fitting room. "Hey, the Air Force colors work with your scale tones really well."

"Ha, ha," I say in a snarky tone. "Here I am growing tentacles out of my back, but as I was putting this on, all I could really think about was 'I'm not really sure if this uniform is going to work with my complexion.'"

Emily and I both burst out laughing.

"Yes," Emily responds with an aristocratic tone and a posture to match. "That uniform does suit you nicely, indeed!"

"So, what now?" I ask. "Will they let me out of here, or am I doomed to roam some abandoned wing of a military hospital for the rest of my life?"

"Unfortunately," Emily begins, "you will have to remain here forever… Once a week, they will bring you some stupid teenager who stumbled into a restricted area and saw something he shouldn't have. You will be allowed to hunt him and feed off his body until they send in another one. It'll make for a great horror series," she says mockingly.

"Yes," I respond, "we can call it 'Hospital of Horrors' and you will make lots of money… See, this isn't all bad."

As we both chuckle again, I begin to reminisce about moments like this. When we could make light of the most terrible situation. Knowing that regardless of how much we poked at one another or even in a tragic event, it was never to be mean or spiteful. Instead, it helped to break the tension and make it easier to move forward rather than be stuck in dread and misery.

"Actually, Sam," Emily's tone gets serious, "quite a bit has happened while you were knocked out. I need to catch you up… Oh, and I voluntold you for a newly formed, joint operations unit…"

"Huh," the confusion in my voice is blatantly obvious.

"I'll explain on the way," Emily says. "Just get ready. Now that you're awake, we are going on our first mission. You got fifteen minutes."

"Wait! What?" My words fall on deaf ears as Emily is already out of my room.

Chapter XIV

I didn't sign up for this...

Emily is sitting in the seat in front of me, as the helicopter formation banks right. I stare at her with both frustration and amazement. Turns out that 'voluntold' is just a nice way of saying volunteered by someone else, for something you didn't actually volunteer for. The unit I apparently joined, without knowing it or wanting to, was created exclusively to take on others who changed. Others like me.

Although some part of me is relieved to no longer be the only one going through this metamorphosis, another part of me is extremely concerned. I cannot imagine the chaos that will come as people throughout the world wake up looking like a bunch of fairytale creatures. Apparently, some idiot set up a website that compiles all the videos, reports, and stories from anyone who claims to have seen an Elf, Dwarf, Mermaid, Centaur, or some other creature. Until a few weeks ago people spent weeks designing cosplay outfits to look like those things. Now, they just wake up that way.

According to the site, most of them are like me. Keeping to the shadows and away from society. Trying to figure out what the hell is happening to them? How their lives went from normal to nightmare? However, there are always a few that fuck things up for everyone else. Those who use their newfound abilities to take what they want, when they want it.

After consulting with Dr. Majken and learning about my newfound abilities, Emily's father set up a special team to bring in those who are terrorizing others. He officially made Dr. Majken the intelligence officer of the team. Hoping that her knowledge of the alien species will minimize casualties… All that makes sense, but what the hell was he thinking assigning Emily to it? She's no soldier…

"I know what you're thinking," Emily's voice cracks through the chopper's intercom system.

"Are you developing telepathy or something?" I ask, caught slightly off guard.

"I wish," Emily replies. "No Sam, no telepathy. I am just really familiar with your 'what the fuck is happening?' face."

"Well, I'm glad that you can still kick my ass at poker," I respond dryly. "Maybe this species we're going to take on is just ripping people off at cards. Then you can take it on single-handedly,"

"Look Em," I continue, but now with sincerity. "I know you've gone through some great combat simulation, martial arts training, and all that good stuff… I get that your dad is a

Colonel and he wanted his baby girl to be able to take on anyone. But, how could he be ok with this?"

"I never said he was…" Emily replies. "In fact, he doesn't actually know that I am here."

"What?" I demand in bewilderment.

"Look, Sam," she continues as though there is nothing to be upset about. "I knew my dad would not deploy the team unless you were on it. I also knew that you would not go on this mission because you still have a ton of questions. But we were out of time…

"Time for what?" I ask, still frustrated.

"This guy that we're going after," Emily replies, pulling out her tablet. "In the last week, he's already killed six people, sent 40 to the hospital in critical condition, and injured dozens more… and those are just police and SWAT. Now, all the local gangs are falling in line behind him. I know you would've agreed to go eventually, but I couldn't just sit around while you pick Dr. Majken's brain about the history of Atlantis… I knew you wouldn't hesitate if I were going, so I did what I had to."

"Damn it, Em!" I cry out in frustration, but before I get a chance to say anything else, several small monitors light up in front of us, and the intercom is taken over by someone back at base.

"Ladies and gentlemen," the woman announces. You are going in to take on a Behemoth. We are still working on the classification system, but based on intel, he is incredibly powerful. According to our resident expert, Behemoths once ranged between eight and twelve feet in height and weighed in at over two tons. Reports correspond to our information, confirming that this Behemoth's skin is impermeable to most small and medium caliber weapons."

"Although he is incapable of using firearms himself," the woman continues, "he has developed a large following, made up of local gang members. Many of whom are armed and dangerous. The target has taken over a warehouse complex and has several dozen civilian hostages. Your mission is to provide fire support -"

Suddenly, my intercom clicks, and I can no longer hear the briefing that everyone else is listening to.

"Sam… This is Colonel Adams, Emily's father," his voice solemn and almost full of regret. "I can't imagine what you are going through and I know you didn't choose for this to happen to you. But the men and women on those choppers wouldn't stand a chance without you. I've watched you grow up and I know you have a good heart. But if what Dr. Majken says is remotely true… I am going to have to ask you to make some hard choices and likely do some things that I would not wish upon anyone…"

"Colonel!" I interrupt him. "Emily is on the chopper with me —"

"I am so sorry…" he continues. "Emily and I will see you when you get back. Godspeed."

"Colonel Adams!" I yell, as my intercom switches back over to the briefing. I hang my head realizing that he couldn't hear me.

"… Good luck out there," the woman's voice sounds upbeat, "and happy hunting."

I am not sure about everyone else, but the operator's attempt to motivate everyone didn't do shit for me. The helicopters bank again. This time to the left, and I can feel that we are starting to descend quickly.

"All right boys and girls," the pilot says with pep. "Here we go. Touchdown in 3… 2… 1…"

As we move down the street, we hear gunshots in the distance. The Colorado Springs police department formed a perimeter, cordoning off an entire city block. Some of the vehicles are smashed, some flipped over on their roofs. Police cars from neighboring cities are scattered down the streets leading up to the warehouse. Ambulances race past us as we approach the command vehicle a block away from the front line.

"Sam," Captain Hunter, the team's commander says as he approaches me. "I'm not gonna lie, this feels crazy. Even for me and my team, this whole situation is surreal. But! We understand that you're the only one who can take this thing down effectively. I guess I am just a bit concerned about the local cops… They'll probably have a much harder time with the idea that we have a half-dragon, half-alien on our team."

"Look," I respond dryly, "I don't need them to like me. Hell, I don't like me! I was just like everyone else here a few weeks ago… I am here to do a job and keep the promise I made: To try and keep this thing, this Behemoth, from crushing all of you."

From the side, I imagine that we look like a misfit band of adventurers, in military uniforms. Of those of us with prior military service, Senior Airman Michaels is the youngest and lowest-ranking member of the team. Prior to joining our merry band, he was in the Marines. Short and stocky, Michaels looks like a machine-gun-wielding dwarf. Ready to bust out his battle axe and talk shit while decapitating his enemies.

Senior Master Sergeant Payne, on the other hand, is quite the opposite of Michaels. She is tall, slender, and looks more like a librarian than a combat engineer. If this team was a family, Payne would definitely be the mother.

Senior Master Sergeant Jefferson is standing next to Payne. Jefferson is a tall male, strapped with a bunch of medical bags. Supposedly, he's a decorated veteran, who has saved many lives over multiple tours. However, I imagine that out of uniform, he just looks like a regular guy who spends way too much time preparing to run marathons.

Technical Sergeant Gonzales and Master Sergeant Clark, both served with Captain Hunter prior to becoming part of this team. Both are tactical operations experts and despite looking quite average in stature, their eyes look like they have each seen some things that are too dark to talk about. It would seem odd that Clark, being female, would've been assigned to covert operations, but I suppose it is a sign of the changing times.

Finally, there's Staff Sergeant Collins. During the helicopter ride, all he talked about was what kind of mythical creature he wanted to be and what powers it would grant him. Although his attitude is a bit cocky, like the rest of the team, he carries himself well. I just hope that his experience in combat is as vast as his imagination.

Then, there's Captain Hunter. He is the definition of a battle-hardened soldier. His uniform fits perfectly. Every pouch and piece of gear is positioned with intent. It is clear that combat is his profession and he is prepared for anything.

Emily and I are the only ones with no military background. I am still pissed that she jumped on the helicopter to get me to come along. How could she be so reckless?

I'm not sure, I think to myself, *how a team of eight men and women plus a half-dragon, are supposed to stop an army of gang-bangers, led by a Behemoth. If this isn't some stupid action movie, I don't know what is.*

"All right Sam," Captain Hunter proclaims. "I will brief whoever is in charge here and try to get as much information as I can before we move in. Do me a favor and hang back. The locals will probably freak out a bit if you just come strolling up."

As he walks away, I see Emily chatting and laughing with the other members of the team.

"Is this a private party or can anyone join?" I ask as I walk up.

"Hey Sam," Emily responds still chuckling. "We were just talking about the first time we played paintball together."

"Paintball? You know these guys?" I ask in utter confusion.

"Yeah," Gonzales chimes in. "The Colonel used to make Emily train with us. He never wanted her to join the service, but she has more training in squad operations than most soldiers after twenty years."

"You didn't actually think we'd let some random chick onto a chopper with us, just because her daddy is the commander, did you?" Clark asks rhetorically.

"Plus, she's a hell of a shot," Michaels chimes in.

He must have noticed the look of concern on my face. "Don't worry about your friend, Sam. She can hold her own. I've only been with these guys for a couple of years, but I tip my hat to her when it comes to tactics," he adds in a reassuring tone.

"Well shit, Em," I respond. "You never cease to amaze."

"Let's move," says Payne. "The Captain is calling for us."

The look on the Police Chief's face said it all, as he saw me approaching. I am not sure what Captain Hunter told him, but I am pretty sure that regardless of what it was, he did not have enough time to prepare.

"I sure hope y'all know what you're doing," is all the chief could muster.

"Alright team," Hunter begins. "SWAT has snipers all over the perimeter. So, our entry is clear. Apparently, the Behemoth periodically runs out, smashes a few cars, and retreats. They've hit him with .50 caliber bullets, and a couple of grenade launcher rounds, but nothing seemed to do any lasting damage."

"Sam," he continues, "you do not know our team's tactics, so just hang with me. When I move, you move. We will get you as close to the target as we can. All of us have armor-piercing rounds, but the chief told me that SWAT tried those, and it didn't make much difference. We're going to do our best at keeping you from getting shot. I know your skin is seemingly impenetrable, but from the videos I watched, you still feel pain. So, we will try to minimize that and allow you to focus on taking down that shit show. Are we good?"

"Good-to-go!" The team sounds off in unison.

"Got it," I reply.

Without another word, Captain Hunter raises his hand. Radios click all around and a ceasefire is issued across all police channels. We cross the street and the team spreads out to either side of a metal door, leading to a building that is adjacent to the warehouse.

"Let me get the door," I say. "Bulletproof and all that."

The team gives each other a concerned look and then everyone looks to Hunter for approval.

"Do it, Sam," he says decisively.

I pull the door open. Collins and Michaels move past me, scanning the corridor as they walk. Immediately after they take a knee, Jefferson and Payne proceed inside. Suddenly, I hear multiple shots from their suppressed rifles.

"Clear!" Collins shouts.

The rest of us enter the building. Moving from room to room, ensuring that they are all empty and that no one will pop out behind us. By the time we get to the end of the hall, I've lost count of how many bodies we left behind. A few of them were just kids, they could not have been older than 16.

"Ammo check," announces Hunter.

Everyone takes turns patting down their magazine pouches and checking the ones in their rifles. One by one they all respond with "Good." Hunter looks at me, giving me the go-ahead to open the door to the courtyard. As I push down on the lever, multiple shots ring out on the other side of the door.

I feel a searing pain in my leg and my stomach. As I stumble backward, I let out a horrifying roar and begin to feel myself start to lose control.

CHAPTER XV

THE LION'S DEN...

The team backs up. From the anxiety on their faces, I can tell that they are fighting the urge to point their rifles at me. At this moment, I imagine that they are far more afraid of me than they are of the guys with guns on the other side.

They must have all seen the footage from the body cams at the cabin, I think to myself.

Emily is the only one who doesn't flinch. Seeing everyone's nervous looks, she quickly breaks the tension.

"Sam! Are you good?" She asks in a commanding tone.

Although I am pissed that Emily came along, I am sure glad she's here now. I don't know that I would be able to get through this without her. It's hard to fathom how people can become so accustomed to death. I understand that in the moment it's 'kill or be killed,' 'life or death' and all that.

Maybe it's the fight or flight response and consequent adrenaline rush that allows one to disregard the horrors in the moment. However, at the end of the day, when you're staring at a lifeless corpse, that moments ago was a walking talking person. Someone who had a childhood, learned to speak, had dreams and aspirations... Knowing that you ended all that, even for good reason. That has to leave a mark... Doesn't it?

Emily's voice brings me back. The pain quickly subsides and my talons retract.

"Good," I respond with confidence, as I regain my composure.

"How many do you think are out there?" Gonzales asks.

"Judging by the fact that they just turned a metal door into Swiss cheese," Michaels quips, "I would say at least seven or eight... What's the play, Cap?"

"We need to find another way," Hunter responds. "Even if we pop smoke and their aim is shit, odds are they'll hit somebody, and I am not sure how far the nearest cover might be... It is too risky."

"What if I buy you a window?" I ask, surprising everyone, including myself.

"Sam, have you lost your mind?" Emily asks bewildered.

"No, I am serious," I reply. "If I run straight through the door and charge in a random direction, it will give you an opportunity to take them out with minimal exposure."

"I know you're tough Sam," Hunter acknowledges. "But I can't ask you to do that."

"You're not asking me to do anything," I reply with confidence. "Get ready and stand back from the door."

I take a few steps back, recounting my escape from my apartment building. Then with a deep breath, I charge the door. Neither the gang members in the courtyard nor my team are prepared for what happens in the span of the next two to three seconds.

As my hands hit the metal, the door, hinges, and frame separate from the wall. I charge, still carrying the door and frame, plowing through two gang members before they get a chance to squeeze the triggers.

A third manages to step out of the way. But, as I run past him, one of my tentacles reacts faster than I am able to process the situation. The talon on the end slices his rifle in half as it swings. Then, it turns pointing straight up and punctures through his jaw. Emerging through the top of his skull. Instantly retracting, like a scorpion's tail, so as to not slow me down in any way.

As the other shooters begin firing at me, Captain Hunter and the rest of the team take them out from inside the hallway. Moving like a well-oiled machine, with complete trust that as they move in front of one another, they won't get shot in the back. As I run, I can hear the bullets bouncing off the concrete behind me. By the time I come to a stop, the gunfire subsides.

Bodies litter the scene. One draped over a picnic table that he tried to use as cover. Another is hanging off the railing. His rifle, still swinging in midair because the sling got caught as he fell forward. Most are slumped against the wall behind them, with blood splatter clearly indicating where each one had been hit. Each team member, now in cover continues to scan every doorway and window. Making sure that no one is hiding and waiting for that opportune moment to shoot us, the moment we let our guard down.

I approach a large commercial garage door…

Here it is, I think to myself.

My imagination's images of what is on the other side are quickly cut short. In fact, I do not think any of us had much time to process anything. The vibrations get faster and louder. Then, the garage door rips open! Just like one of those banners that a football team tears through, when they run out onto the field.

Shit! I think to myself. *No wonder all those gangs wanted to join him… This guy puts the 'I' in 'team.'*

By contrast, he makes the bear, that attacked me near the cabin, look like a plush animal that you might win at a fair. In his hand, is a club that is almost as big as I am.

Behemoth seems like a very appropriate name for this species. I think as I try to process what I am looking at.

He glances around the courtyard and lets out a deafening roar. Then, without a second thought, he grabs a dead body with one hand and flings it toward me. The body of the gang member soars through the air as if were a pebble that someone tried to skip across a pond.

Again, my tentacles react faster than I do. Lashing out in front of me, they split the flying corpse in half. The two halves hit the ground only a few feet behind me and bounce repeatedly until they hit a wall on the other side of the courtyard.

Suddenly, I realize that the body was meant merely as a distraction. The behemoth immediately follows up with a swing of his massive bat. Gauging by its shape, that bat once had a light attached to it.

Awesome! I think to myself, as I jump to dodge the sweeping attack. *This guy beats people to death with street lights.*

I duck, to dodge another incoming blow. This time with a counterattack of my own. One of my tentacles swipes at the Behemoth's forearm when it is closest to me. As he completes the swing, he begins to draw his arm back for a backswing. His eyes locked on me, as though I were a tennis ball that he is about to hit out of the court.

But the razor-sharp talon on the end of my tentacle had done its job. Although it was not long enough to slice all the way through the Behemoth's forearm, it definitely cut through some of the bone. The weight of the bat and the momentum of his swing appear to be more than enough to cause it to break completely. As the Behemoth realizes what just happened, he cries out in utter agony.

"What have you done?" He cries out in a mix of shock, anger, and disbelief. "You fucking insect! I'll turn you into a stain!"

Before he finishes his threat, he charges at me. The Behemoth's massive strides close the gap faster than I expected. With his left arm, he swings a powerful backhand. I jump back to avoid the hit, but the split second that it took me to assess how quickly he moved, apparently made a big difference...

The backhand connects and sends me tumbling through the air like a rag doll. My back slams into a brick wall on the far end of the courtyard. I hit it with such force that I literally go through it. Between the Behemoth's blow and the wall, my world goes black. Without missing a beat, my team opens fire.

The Behemoth shields his face with his good arm, turns, and begins charging toward Captain Hunter. However, in the barrage of bullets, one hits his broken arm. The Behemoth staggers backward, reeling from the pain.

"Concentrate fire on his broken arm!" Captain Hunter yells out.

But it is too late... I do not know if it is the pain, the sense of danger, or something else entirely, but as my vision returns so does my rage. Once again, I am in the passenger's seat of my own mind. My fingernails extend and curve slightly. Once again turning into long, black talons.

In the blink of an eye, I realize that I am moving towards the Behemoth at such speed that it feels like flying. Then, from what seems like twenty feet away, I leap toward him. My hand slashes across his face. The talons slice through his bulletproof skin, flesh, and bone like a hot knife through butter.

The friction of my four talons slicing through his skull is just enough to allow me to swing around his head and land behind him. As my feet touch the ground, I plunge my talons into his lower back and slash upward. Although due to his massive height, I am only able to reach the middle of his back, I know that the damage is done. His kidneys, spine, some ribs, and lungs, along with the muscles in his lower back are all shredded.

My arms are covered in his blood. The Behemoth opens his mouth to let out what I imagine should be a deafening cry. However, the damage to his lungs and face stammer the sound. Instead only gurgling and wheezing noises can be heard. The moment he tries to take a breath, the front of his jaw detaches and comes clean off. The Behemoth stumbles forward and falls flat on his disfigured face.

As his heart stops beating, my claws retract, and my vision begins to fade. Unlike the first time that the Ethros took over, I do not pass out. Everything comes back into focus and I regain control of my own body. Then, one after another dozens of voices begin to scream inside the warehouse, all repeating some variant of:

"Shit, they're all dead!"

"Run! Get the fuck out! Run!"

"He's dead! Run!"

Hundreds of footsteps can be heard as the gang members who were holed up in the warehouse begin to flee in every direction. My team and I emerge from the building to the scene of dozens of gang members littering the street. Some are on their knees with their fingers interlaced on top or behind their heads. Most are face down, on the ground, sprawled out to show that they are not a threat.

"I think I need a drink..." I mutter. "Can I even get drunk?"

"First round is on me," responds Hunter.

"Good... Because I got fired a few weeks ago," I quip.

"So long as you drink responsibly," Payne chimes in. "It would be a shame if you blacked out and the Ethros ate all of us."

We laugh, as we push through the wall of police officers who are scrambling to handcuff the countless gang members.

"Hey, Em... You know what?" I ask.

"What, Sam?"

"You're in so much trouble," I say teasingly...

"Yeah?" She asks wryly. "Maybe, but you're officially this team's bullet sponge."

"Son of a bitch!"

CHAPTER XVI

YOU CAN CALL ME JOE

The blades of the helicopter are still spinning, when the steps lower to the ground. The President walks down and then across the courtyard. Automatic doors slide open as he approaches and he is saluted by two soldiers as he enters the building.

"Mr. President," a Captain says in a formal tone, as he drops his salute. "We were not aware that you were coming. Colonel Adams is currently in an after-action review. I will inform him that you are -"

Before he can finish his sentence, a dark slit begins to form in the air next to the President. As it widens, a figure steps through and the dark portal closes as though it was never there. Without a second of hesitation, the Military Police draw their weapons and take aim at the man with white hair and glowing blue eyes. Dark ribbons swirl around his leather duster, then gradually subside and disappear.

"Don't fire!" The President yells out in a panicked voice.

"Mr. President," the Captain says concerned. "Please stand aside. This man is an Evolved."

"It's all right," the President responds, "he is with me. Go get the Colonel."

The soldiers lower their weapons with trepidation. Completely unfazed by the commotion, the mysterious newcomer does not so much as face the soldiers to ensure that they are no longer aiming at him. As the glow recedes from his eyes, he looks completely human. However, his crystal blue pupils still look somewhat too bright. Almost like they should be emitting a faint glow.

He looks at the President. Rather than respect or reverence, his body language is akin to that of a parent inspecting their child's outfit.

"Do not ask any stupid questions," he says with contempt in his voice. "When the Colonel arrives, inform him that I am to be given access to all information about the Evolved regardless of the security clearance required."

The President simply nods in affirmation and looks impatiently at the elevator doors, at the end of the long hallway. As though he is perturbed by the fact that it is taking too long for the Colonel to arrive. Within moments the elevator dings. As the doors open, the Military Police Captain, Colonel Adams, Captain Hunter, and Senior Master Sergeant Jefferson exit and head toward the President. They salute mid-stride, and the Colonel begins speaking before dropping his salute.

"With all due respect Mr. President," he says, clearly perturbed. "This is a military research facility! Bringing anyone who does not have top-secret security clearance onto this base is a clear breach of protocol. Especially, someone who is Evolved and may pose -"

"Colonel," the President cuts him off before he can finish. "This man is with me. He has been working for me… with me, in resolving many of the issues we face and doing so with discretion. I trust him and have granted him the maximum possible security clearance. He is to be given access to any information you have about these 'Evolved.'"

"I'm sorry sir," responds the Colonel, "but I cannot simply share everything we know, without getting his clearance through the proper channels."

"I am the Commander and Chief!" The President exclaims, "I am giving you a direct order! You will provide any information you have to this man! Regardless of what 'secret code' you have classified it under. I have very important things going on! But I flew down here, in person, to make this introduction. If I need to fire or demote you or whatever, and put someone else in command of this facility, then I will."

The Colonel considers the President's threat. He has seen him behave this way in the past…

"Very well, sir," Colonel Adams responds. "I will set up a briefing on the latest developments for yourself and Mr…"

"You may call me Joe," the Evolved responds.

His tone makes it evident that 'Joe' is not his real name. However, there is clearly a certain, underlying urgency. Almost as if he does not have the time to be bothered with something so trivial as a name.

"Please have Dr. Majken, give the briefing," Joe continues. "I have specific questions that I need to ask her."

"Mr. President," the Colonel fires back with concern. "How does he know about Dr. -"

"I have been following her research long before you even knew her name," Joe cuts him off. "Please set the briefing, time is not on your side and neither is my patience."

Clearly caught off guard, the Colonel returns to the room where the rest of the team is guessing as to what could have possibly spurred a presidential visit. As Colonel Adams enters the room, Captain Hunter stands up.

"Room," he announces in a command voice, "attention!"

"At ease," the Colonel says before anyone beside Captain Hunter has time to fully stand up. "Dr. Majken, do you have any records of a species that can travel through portals?"

"No," Dr. Majken responds with some confusion. "There are records of some who can become nearly invisible. So, they have been mistaken as being able to teleport, but nothing about portals. Why do you ask?"

"Because there is one sitting in the briefing room," Colonel Adams responds in frustration. "He just showed up with the President, knows about your research, and asked for you by name... I need you to brief them. But don't volunteer any information about our team or about Sam."

"Sam," he continues as Dr. Majken gathers the papers in front of her. "I need you outside the door. The President says he has been working with this Evolved. But the President has about as much sense as that trash can... I just want you there in case something goes wrong. Hunter, Jefferson, you are with me in the briefing. The rest of you, locked and loaded in the hall. If shit hits the fan, I will cover the President while you take out his new 'friend.'"

The tone of his voice makes it clear that he is a well-practiced strategist. He is not loud or overbearing, but when you hear that decisiveness, you know it is the tone of a real commander.

"Lima, Charlie, sir!" Most of the team responds in unison.

"Oh, and Em," says Colonel Adams as he stops before exiting the room. "You will stay here. We will talk about your actions when this is over."

Hearing the switch in his tone, from command-voice to dad-voice is quite disorienting.

That explains quite a bit about Em, I think to myself.

Everyone but Emily leaves the room, wondering what shit show we are about to see unfold.

"Hey Payne," I say inquisitively. "What the hell is 'Lima Charlie?'"

"It stands for the letters 'L' and 'C,'" she responds. "Military uses words for each letter, like Alpha for 'A,' Bravo for 'B,' Charlie for 'C' and so on."

"So, why did you guys say 'L,C' when the Colonel finished speaking?" I ask.

"Lima, Charlie," she answers, "is another way of saying 'loud and clear.' In other words, we heard what he said and clearly understood the orders."

"Then, why not just say 'loud and clear?'" I press.

"This is why you would be a shitty soldier, Sam." Michaels quips. "When you join, logic, reason, and all that critical thinking nonsense has to go out the window. We're not paid to think. Point, shoot, kill!"

"Don't pay attention to the jarhead," Payne says calmly. "He means that 'he' is not paid to think. It's a sad story, but after the Marines were done with poor Michaels here, he only had two brain cells left. Unfortunately, one is always lost, the other is constantly out looking for it."

Everyone busts out laughing, including Michaels.

It is crazy to watch their interactions, I think as the laughter subsides. These guys will constantly insult each other, their branches of service, and even their families. Yet, they are like a family. Each one, willing to die to save the others... Imagine if all of society was that way...

CHAPTER XVII

YOU'RE A WHAT?

E veryone sits around a large briefing table. Dr. Majken enters the room with several binders and notebooks under her arm. Joe immediately pivots in his leather office chair. Seemingly confused by something.

"I am Dr. Majken," she begins in a scholarly tone. "According to records passed down by my order, Atlantis was a colony -"

"We don't need the entire backstory," Joe cuts her off. "What does your order know about the Council? More specifically, what did they do in order to close the gate to Millanthea? I need every detail of what happened to Atlantis, leading up to the collapse."

"I would like to hear the rest of the story," the President chimes in.

"Go sit in the corner and play on your phone!" Joe fires back in frustration. "Didn't I say no stupid questions?"

"There isn't much, not in terms of data," Dr. Majken responds with some trepidation.

Her focus clearly split between Joe's question and the President obediently rolling his chair away from the table and into the corner of the room. His gaze never leaving his phone.

"I'm sorry," Dr. Majken says inquisitively, "but what species are you? I was told you are able to travel through portals. Yet, my records have no documentation of any alien or hybrid species who were capable of that."

"It's not relevant," Joe answers abruptly. "Tell me what you know of the gate."

"Well, it 'is' relevant to me!" Demands Colonel Adams. "You show up here with the President, talking to him like he's a child, and demanding information. You need to start answering some questions before you are given anything else!"

Joe looks around and reads the room. Then he slowly gets up... Captain Hunter reaches for his sidearm but remembers that he surrendered it before entering the room with the President.

"You won't need your gun, Captain," Joe says calmly. "If I wanted to kill you, you would be dead well before you could pull it from the holster. You must forgive my frustration with your inquiries. Your lives are very short and the information I provide would be of no significance to you. Other than to sate your own curiosity."

"Moreover," he continues, "there is little that you can do to change the course of events taking place. As such, explaining myself feels like a moot point and a waste of time. However, I need the information that the good doctor has gathered. Since, it would likely be faster if you provide it voluntarily, I will answer your questions for the next five minutes… So, ask away, what do you want to know?"

"Let's start with what Dr. Majken just asked," responds the Colonel. "What species are you?"

"I am an Archon," Joe replies.

Instantly, Dr. Majken's face changes from that of a curious researcher to someone who just saw an actual ghost. A look of horror and confusion fills her face, as she slowly lowers herself into the chair behind her, nearly missing it entirely.

"You're a what?" She asks quietly, almost inaudibly.

"I am sincerely surprised that my being an Archon means anything to you at all," Joe says in a pleasant tone. "The Archons didn't join the fight until long after Atlantis had been established. At that point, millions of years would have passed here on Earth. The few of us who did join the fight were never sent to Atlantis. So, I am curious… How did you come to hear about us?"

"What do you know of Archons, Dr. Majken?" The Colonel cuts in with concern, doubling down on Joe's question.

She composes herself, walks over to the water dispenser, and fills a cup. Then sits back down in her chair and takes a deep breath.

"They were myths," Dr. Majken says calmly opening her eyes. "Spooky stories that Millantheans told children about. The most evil of all creatures..."

"To be fair," the Colonel cuts in, "the stories about elves and dragons are proving to be quite real."

"Yes," Dr. Majken retorts, "but those are just different alien species, who were genetically reduced to a base form. Archons were... they were supposed to be something else entirely... According to myths, they were the antithesis of creation. In current culture, they would effectively be considered demons at best. Perhaps even the incarnation of the Devil. Their entire existence was centered on destroying life."

"That was billions of years ago," Joe jumps in defensively. "We lost that war with the Second Suns and have paid for it for many solar evolutions."

"You cannot expect me to believe that this is truly what you are," Dr. Majken continues in disbelief.

"What do I have to gain from lying to you?" Asks Joe in frustration. "More importantly, how would you know any of this, if you were truly human?"

Before anyone can even react. Joe pulls Dr. Majken from her chair and pins her to the wall. His sword a hair's width away from her throat. The blade is black... Not just a shiny finish. It appears to almost absorb light. Dim waves of purple and blue coursing over the blade. The same way that light would travel along a normal sword.

"If the fall of Atlantis locked the DNA of all the species, how were you not affected?" Joe demands. "What aren't you telling me?"

The rest of the team and I burst through the door. A pistol is tossed to Colonel Adams and everyone takes aim at Joe. Again, with little concern about being shot, Joe pulls the sword back. Just enough to allow Dr. Majken to take a breath.

"A Millaethros," Joe says, again sounding pleasantly surprised. "What other tricks are you humans keeping up your sleeve?"

"Let, her, go," I growl through my fangs.

"Not until she agrees to answer my questions... honestly!" Joe fires back. "I know how fast you are... or rather will be. It appears that you have not finished evolving quite yet. So, at this stage, you don't stand a chance against me."

"Let! Her! Go!" I say each word with increasing menace.

"I didn't come here to kill any of you," Joe says calmly. "So, retract your claws, and let's let the good doctor tell us her 'entire story.' After all, based on how this meeting started, it sounds like she has not been completely honest with all of you either."

"Alright…" Dr. Majken says begrudgingly.

Joe slowly moves away from her and sheathes his sword. Dr. Majken straightens her blouse. Then looks around the room, clearly searching for the right words.

"For starters," she says through a sigh, "Joe is right. I am not human…"

CHAPTER XVIII

VALPHET

D r. Majken sits back down in her chair. The rest of us also take a seat around the large table. She folds her hands and closes her eyes. Obviously, thinking back. The look on her face is the same as when she first began telling us about Atlantis in Emily's family cabin.

"I was born on a small planet in the Millanthea galaxy. Our solar system was much like this one, with only one inhabitable planet. By the time the war reached us, it had been going on for over a thousand years."

"What planet are you from doctor," asks Joe.

"I… am from Valphet," she responds somberly.

"Wait!" I jump in. "Isn't that what you said the other half of the Millaethros is?"

"Yes, Sam," she responds quietly. "You are actually a very distant descendant of my own brother…"

"I'm sorry, what?" I ask in shock.

"He and I were the last of my kind in Atlantis," she says in a melancholy voice. "The others had all merged with an Ethros and returned to Millanthea. At the time that Atlantis broke apart, he had been gone for over two years. Searching for an Ethros to merge with…"

"I was astonished," she continues, "when Dr. Mavro and Emily described you on the drive to the cabin. I was certain that my brother had been killed. Either on his journey or during the collapse. Even if he had managed to survive, without his abilities, he would've died of old age."

"The last messenger through the gate," Joe cuts in, "informed us about the situation here. As well as what the Atlantean Council planned to do… What I need to know is how they managed to do it?"

"Wait!" I interject. "That would make you -"

"In total," Dr. Majken responds, "well over 250 million years old. I have been through many, many bodies, and lived many different lives."

"But everyone else's genetic code was locked. How did you avoid that?" I ask.

"That is the first good question you've asked," Joe chimes in.

Dr. Majken reaches under the collar of her blouse and gently pulls out a thin chain. On it, a small, unassuming, clear pendant emerges. At first glance, it appears to be a simple glass sphere. Perhaps one of those fancy, translucent crystals at best. However, as she holds it, I realize that there is something radiating from inside.

"This sphere contains some of the ambient energy from the crystal here on Earth," she explains. "No Valphet has lived nearly as long as I have. I've lived many lifetimes, during which I wanted to be done with my life. But, I made a promise to the other Council members... That I would be here when the crystal was restored. That I would explain to everyone what was happening to them, where they came from, and what our mission is."

"So, no mysterious order?" The Colonel asks. "Just you, by yourself, all this time?"

"Yes," she responds sadly. "And before you ask, Sam, yes, I am the one who started some of the tales about wondrous and mythical creatures. I traveled among thousands of human populations. Some had stories that they passed down from their ancestors who had been in Atlantis. However, new generations, without any abilities, emerged and faced their own challenges. After a few million years and some early wars, their history was simply lost to time."

"So, you started telling people about the past?" I ask.

"Yes," Dr. Majken responds. "I began talking about Atlantis again. Roughly five thousand years ago. It was hard to explain intergalactic wars, aliens, and powers... So, some dismissed me as a traveling lunatic. Others probably cut out anything that they could not understand or remember. The stories also crossed cultures and languages..."

It is obvious to everyone that Joe stopped listening a while ago. His mind is somewhere else, searching for an answer to a problem that the rest of us are apparently unaware of.

"Did all of you lose your fucking minds?" Joe suddenly shouts. "You fucked with something that even the Archons could not fully comprehend! Do you know that each galaxy has only one of these crystals? Not one per solar system. One per entire god-damn galaxy! Yet, you and your council decided to say 'Fuck it! We should bury it!' What gave you the right?"

"We…" Dr. Majken begins. "We sent word -"

"Do you realize," Joe continues, as though she had not said anything, "that you could have destroyed the entire planet? Fuck only knows what would have happened if the crystal shifted from its place in the universe!"

He throws his hands in the air in frustration. Then takes a breath, as though to calm himself.

"Sometimes," Joe mutters to himself, almost inaudibly, "I have to wonder why finite beings were ever created in the first place? Stupid Second Suns… Your fucking creations could've screwed up the entire universe attempting to save a single planet!"

"What did you just say?" Dr. Majken asks suddenly.

"It doesn't fucking matter," Joe fires back in frustration! "Do you realize how long I spent trying to find this solar system? My mission to find Atlantis began less than a day after Earth's link with the Millanthean crystal was severed. I arrived here only two years ago…"

"In case you can't do the math," Joe continues, sounding slightly less perturbed. "That is somewhere between a hundred-twenty and one-hundred-seventy-five million Earth years! If the crystal had not pulsed when it did, I would probably still be out there, checking random fucking solar systems!"

"I don't understand something," Dr. Majken asks. "The stories we were told on Valphet, said that the Archons were confined to a single solar system… Noctsola I believe."

"Yes," Joe responds with dread in his voice. "The solar system with only one giant sun and one giant planet. A planet where life flourishes in the light, but is extinguished when night falls. Trapped in an eternal cycle of Ying and Yang for billions of years…"

"Archons are billions of years old?" I ask, only slightly confused.

"For fuck's sake," Joe says, sounding fired up and infuriated. "Why couldn't we leave? How did I get out? Why do I care to restore the crystal? Your fucking questions have no end!"

He takes a deep breath and composes himself again. Then gets up and walks over to a cart with a water dispenser and glasses. He inspects a glass and pulls a flask from the inside pocket of his leather duster.

Unscrewing the cap in an almost ceremonial fashion, Joe pours an amber liquid into the glass. Then, adds a few drops of water from the dispenser... He wafts the liquid under his nose, as though he were smelling a fine wine. Then sits back down in his chair and takes a small sip.

"Scotch anyone?" He asks in a pleasant tone. "It's a forty-year, single malt... This is one of those little pleasures that I can... simply enjoy."

I am not exactly sure why, but no one seems interested in taking him up on his offer. Perhaps everyone is just caught off guard. It's not every day that some ancient, immortal alien, who found an affinity for expensive Scotch, offers you a glass... Maybe no one trusts him, despite the fact that everything he says sounds pretty candid. I suppose it could be that Dr. Majken effectively referred to him as 'evil incarnate.'

"In order to answer all your questions," Joe continues, "I would ultimately have to go into details about the creation of life and existence. There is also the billion-year struggle between the Archons and the Second Suns. I do not have time for all that right now. Maybe another day, maybe you'll never know. Right now, all that matters is what happened to the crystal here on Earth."

Chapter XIX

Fucking Russians...

D r. Majken composes herself and takes a drink of water, as she once again becomes the center of attention.

"Look, you're right," she begins, clearly addressing Joe. "We did not have all the facts, but we did what we could, with what we had. We sent word to Millanthea the moment we learned that insurgents had infiltrated the highest levels of power. The members of the Atlantean Council were the only ones who we were certain had not been compromised."

"How did they know that you were not a spy?" I ask.

"Because, Sam," she replies with shame in her voice, "I was the head of the council."

"How is that possible?" Joe asks, perturbed. "Why didn't anyone in Millanthea know this?"

"Only the council members knew," Dr. Majken responds. "I have been at the head of the council since Atlantis was established. The first council made this decision unanimously, because of my ability to generate a new body. It made perfect sense… To the masses, it would seem like there is a new council member each time. I would retire or 'die' after a normal lifespan in the public eye. Then, join the council as a new member and gradually rise through the ranks. However, behind closed doors, my word always carried the most weight."

"And no one figured out this ruse?" I ask suspiciously.

"No," Dr. Majken responds calmly. "I would mix up my new identity. I was younger, sometimes switching genders, and even other species. It worked perfectly, just as the original council intended, especially because I would never forget why Atlantis was established in the first place. After all, the war in Millanthea destroyed my planet and all my people. So, they knew that I would never stop supporting the Millanthean cause."

"Yet, you obviously did just that!" Joe exclaims. "I would ask why? However, you've had a hundred-and-fifty million years to come up with your excuse. So, I am sure it is a good one. Why don't you just tell me what you did with the crystal? So that I can try and fix your fuckup."

"We did not have a choice!" Dr. Majken shouts back, popping out of her chair and slamming her hands on the table. "You think the council just decided to destroy Atlantis? Or to obliterate billions of lives? You think I would vote to undo something that I had dedicated millions of years of my life to?"

This is the first time I have seen her lose her temper. As she fumes, the room fills with an energy like I have never felt before. It is like being in a thick fog, except there is no fog to be seen. The pendant around her neck begins to emit a dark blue color, as do her eyes.

Although he is calm, it is evident that even Joe is taken aback. Then, she takes a deep breath, and as suddenly as it began, it is over. The blue glow subsides, both in her eyes and the pendant. Dr. Majken composes herself and sits down again.

"I apologize," she restarts calmly. "I will not make excuses for why we did what we did. However, I will say that I abstained from the vote. The council knew that if we did not act, the consequences would be dire. No matter what the rebels planned, their actions would have likely destroyed billions upon billions of lives, both in the Milky Way and Millanthean galaxies. Possibly even beyond. So, the other members voted unanimously to do anything and everything necessary to keep our issues from impacting the rest of the universe."

"Perhaps someday, I will ask you to tell me that story, Dr.," Joe responds with a hint of respect in his tone.

Holy shit! I think to myself. He sounds like he actually believes her... Maybe even cares a little!

"However," Joe continues, "I truly need to know what happened to the crystal? Because right now, it may be Millanthea's last hope."

"We spent millions of years analyzing and studying the crystal here on Earth," responds Dr. Majken. "Always with little to no meaningful new knowledge. Eventually, a new species emerged. One who had the unique ability to trace energy. According to them, the crystals worked in some type of symbiotic or reciprocal relationship. It was like one of them put out energy that fueled the other. Much like the exchange of oxygen and carbon dioxide between plants and humans."

"Fascinating..." Joe mumbles.

"However, what was truly baffling," Dr. Majken's voice fills with excitement, "is that the crystals were more than just similar to one another. For a time we believed that they were two halves of the same crystal. They are not! They are both literally one crystal! Somehow, existing in two separate galaxies simultaneously!"

"Ooohhh. This is making my head hurt," groans Captain Hunter.

He had been sitting in the corner next to the President. Both men staring at Dr. Majken, Joe, and myself as though we were from another planet... though I suppose, we technically are.

"Moreover," Dr. Majken continues, "this new species was also able to figure out, that this energy exchange is cyclical. And! It is what activates the potential of the genetic code in all species."

"Wait," Joe interjects. "You knew this for millions of years, but decided not to inform anyone in Millanthea?"

"It was useless information," Dr. Majken retorts. "How would it have helped the war, unless there was something actionable about it? It would be akin to sending a report that concludes that the Sun is hot. We archived it, along with tens of thousands of other research projects, that had no military value. Which, is the only thing that anyone in Millanthea gave a shit about."

"So, how is it relevant to today," Joe persists.

"The dissent against sending troops to fight in Millanthea had existed here for quite some time." Dr. Majken explains. "Throughout the generations, we always handled it through education and public information. By the time we realized that this opposition had truly taken root, those who supported it held most of the key positions of power. They became the ones responsible for enforcing and adjudicating almost all of our laws and policies."

"Why was that such an issue?" Captain Hunter asks.

"Because," Joe responds. "If the people who were supposed to prosecute traitors, were instead supporting them, there is nothing a council could have done. Their only option would have been to force everyone out of their positions of power. Which, at that point would make the Atlantean Council appear to be tyrannical. It would only give more credence to the claims of the traitors… In other words, it was a lose-lose situation."

"Precisely," Dr. Majken jumps back in. "We sent word to Millanthea, requesting assistance. However, due to the time difference, years passed with no response."

"So, you decided to weaponize the crystal for yourselves?" Asks Colonel Adams, apparently understanding more than anyone had thought. "Use it to lock everyone's abilities."

"In a manner of speaking," Dr. Majken responds. "Our first priority was to ensure that the insurgents did not take control of the Atlantean Crystal. They had crazy, radical ideas... Such as invading Millanthea and potentially other galaxies. After all, hybrid species were pivotal to social desirability."

"Why?" I ask.

"Why?" Joe responds, in a tone implying that the answer is self-evident. "Would you prefer a team member who is only effective in one specific situation or a wide variety of circumstances? Perhaps someone who can fight but also heal the wounded. The more abilities a single individual possesses, the more versatile they are. Both in and out of combat."

"That makes sense," Colonel Adams chimes in.

"Yes," Dr. Majken adds. "However, in Atlantis, it also became a social status. Elite families sought to add more and more diversity to their bloodlines. Creating a new, sustained hybrid branch in a family's bloodline, put them in the highest echelons of Atlantean society... Today, it would be akin to a family, where every single generation produces top-level athletes."

"And expanding to new galaxies," Joe cuts in, "would yield new abilities, more hybrids, etcetera."

"Exactly," Dr. Majken nods in agreement. "Their propaganda sounded great, on paper. It presented splitting from Millanthea purely as a benefit to Atlantis and its people. Of course, they had no plan on how to actually do any of the things they promised. They just wanted support to get rid of the council."

"So," she continues after a brief pause. "They created a false dichotomy: 'You either support Millanthea or Atlantis!' in other words 'You are with us or against us!' Obviously, it was bullshit, there were countless other solutions. However, if you present a lie enough times and for long enough, to the masses it becomes just as real as the truth."

"So," Joe cuts her off, "you decided to destroy the crystal?"

"As a last resort," she responds. "The plan was to use the combined powers of all the council members. However, we quickly realized that this was impossible. All that power funneled into a single blast of energy literally had no effect at all."

"I know," Joe chimes in. "Even at the peak of our civilization, the Archons did not possess the power necessary to destroy these crystals. That is why I am so confused as to how a few finite beings were able to shut it down, so to speak."

"We didn't," Dr. Majken responds. "Once we realized the crystal can't be destroyed, we realized that there was a better option. Rather than attacking the crystal, we focused our combined energy to disrupt the connection for a brief period of time. It was like interrupting a stream of water from a garden hose, for a split second. We knew that someday it would reestablish itself. The hope was that it would be enough time for a few new generations of Atlanteans to be born and the insurgents to die off."

"I suppose that when time is on your side, it is an effective tool," says the Colonel.

"Yes," responds Dr. Majken. "We devised a plan to preserve some of the crystal's energy, in pendants just like the one I have. They would allow the council to be unaffected by the disruption. We would then restore order, and establish new, better systems of governance. After a few hundred years, the crystal would come back into balance and everyone's abilities would be restored. In Millanthea, the gate would only be down for a few days at most... or so we thought"

"I've always enjoyed the human saying, 'If you want to make god laugh, make a plan,'" Joe says as he chuckles. "So, what went wrong?"

"We spent years attempting to extract enough particles from the crystal." Dr. Majken responds. "Taking turns, working around the clock, and even combining our efforts... It all proved futile. Finally, as time was running out, a council member sacrificed himself. None of us knew exactly what he did, nor how he did it. But in his moment of death, he was

165

able to extract or perhaps exchange just enough energy with the crystal, to fill this one, single pendant."

She pauses, takes another drink of water, and touches her pendant as though reaching out into the past.

"Although we had one pendant, we lost our most powerful council member. Without him, even the combined power of the Council would not be enough to disrupt the crystal's energy… So, they held a vote without my knowledge, Electing me to be the bearer of the necklace and Atlantean history. Then, they barred my access to the crystal and performed the ultimate sacrifice. Jointly giving up their lives, in an effort to protect Millanthea."

"Fuck…" Colonel Adams mutters under his breath.

"I urged them to find a different way," Dr. Majken continues as her eyes fill with tears. "I tried to break into the chamber, as our enemies were breaching the walls. We were out of time... and they knew it. The last council guard had fallen. Betrayed by his own commander. So, I donned the necklace and promised to fulfill my charge as keeper of Atlantean history. As I escaped through the secret tunnels, the crystal's energy faltered, just as we hoped. Unfortunately, this didn't just halt the connection to Millanthea. The entire crystal began to sink deeper into the Earth."

"Shit…" Joe says, visibly pondering her story.

"To put it mildly," responds Dr. Majken. "Over the next few million years, I came to understand that this single event actually fractured the Earth's crust. As the crystal sank deeper, it created the tectonic fault lines, Pangea began to drift apart, and eventually lead to the formation of the continents we have today."

"Alright," Joe says in a decisive tone. "Do you know where the crystal would be today?"

"Based on my calculations," Dr. Majken responds "it is beneath lake Baikal, in what is now Russia."

"Great!" Says the Colonel sarcastically. "You mean the same Russia that we have tons of sanctions against; the one that supposedly messed with our elections; and has been spying on us since the 1950's? The one that wouldn't let our military in, if it meant stopping the end of the world, that Russia?"

"Yes, Colonel, that's the one," she responds to his rhetorical line of questions.

"I suppose I should be glad that it's not North Korea," he retorts in a compromising tone. "So, Joe, now that you got your answers, what are you going to do?"

"Now, I am going to Russia!" He responds decisively.

Chapter XX

Lake Baikal

Several thousand feet above the surface of Lake Baikal, in Russia… Against the backdrop of a star-filled sky. Sparse clouds are illuminated by a full moon. A black slit forms in midair and grows wider, turning into a dark portal.

Joe steps through and begins falling toward the ice-covered lake. His fall can easily be misconstrued for flight, as he gracefully shifts his weight forward. Resembling a hawk, diving after prey. The waves of dark energy that extend from the dark portal, stretch out in a beautiful tail of purple ribbons. Eventually disappearing into the night, as the portal closes and disappears.

As Joe reaches terminal velocity, he grips the sword firmly, with both hands and fully extends his arms. A burst of energy explodes from the sword and Joe's speed increases fivefold. The air friction seemingly charges his sword with energy, as he gets closer to the lake.

Joe impacts the thick frozen surface, creating an explosion of ice and water. Causing massive sheets of ice, several feet thick, to career and shift chaotically away from the point of impact. The absurd speed propels Joe through the water, deep into the abyss that is the deepest lake on Earth.

Only a few feet from the bottom, Joe slows down and turns right side up. He touches down calmly, but the energy coursing through his sword is begging to be discharged. Spinning the blade gracefully, more than five thousand feet below the surface, Joe points the sword down and swiftly thrusts it into the lake's floor.

The pent-up energy instantly releases a monstrous shockwave. Akin to a bomb exploding underwater, the ice on the surface rises several feet, as a massive wave swells from beneath.

The blast of energy clears out all the sediment and leaves a huge crater at the bottom of lake Baikal, with Joe gently floating above its center. There, close to the epicenter of the lake, a small pyramid juts out from the sand.

Finally! Joe thinks to himself.

He floats down and calmly lands next to the black crystal, which is only slightly larger than him. Joe makes a motion with his hand, releasing a small shockwave to clear out the remaining sediment around the pyramid.

Aside from its polished surfaces, the crystal is unimpressive. But, it is merely the very tip of a mountain, that is lodged deep into the Earth's crust. Although he has looked into the Millanthean crystal countless times, never has Joe been on the other side.

As he looks into it, for the first time in what feels like an eternity, he is able to see Millanthea. His face flushed with a look of relief. Joe walks around to each side, as though searching for someone who has been waiting for him for as long as he has been searching for them. Suddenly, horror replaces the relief.

His mouth opens and he lets out a roar that reverberates to the surface.

Three-foot-tall, blue-metallic blades of grass sway gently in the wind, otherwise completely undisturbed. Covering hundreds of miles of open space. From the air, lakes of silver water can be seen scattered across the landscape. The scene is reminiscent of a serine meadow at the foothills of a mountain range that stretches beyond what the eye can see.

The mountains have a majesty to them. Almost resembling guards at their king's back. But unlike the rest, the tallest peak comes to a perfect point. It is polished, smooth like a dark crystal that neither reflects nor refracts the light. It is the peak of the Millanthean Crystal. Providing an unparalleled view of the stars in the Millanthean Galaxy.

Displaying only what is on the other side. It is like a screen showing a picture from a camera that is entombed in stone. The five-thousand-foot crystal extends from the ground like a pyramid. Made from what appears to be one solid piece of glass. The blue grass comes all the way up to its base, but on this side of the mountain range, it is no empty meadow.

The grass grows from underneath and around a tan-colored, armored boot. The boot extends up into a set of armor, that perfectly conforms to the body inside. Unlike anything on Earth, the various pieces of armor are joined by a scaly mesh to protect the joints.

The left arm looks like it is inserted into a massive gauntlet. Instead of a hand and fingers, the entire thing looks like a narrow shield. Rectangular vents run up either side. Instead of coming to a point, the gauntlet ends in an arc, with two long, razor-sharp tips. Giving it the appearance of a futuristic disc launcher.

The helmet contains an array of sensors and cameras, instead of openings for the eyes. Inside, the wearer's nose and mouth are covered with something that resembles a flight helmet, that is connected to the external face shield.

For a brief moment, the top of the crystal emits a bright light. Within seconds, multiple lines begin to display on the inside of the visor. The wearer's eyes open, in response to the glow in front of them. The pupils are faded almost as though the wearer was partially blind.

The set of armor that stood lifeless at the base of the crystal lifts its head. As though examining the situation or waiting to see another flash of light. Behind the first armored creature, row by row, other suits of armor stand in the same position. Each row lifts their heads as though coming to life.

Otherwise motionless, the seemingly endless ocean of armored suits covers the landscape.

They stand in formations. Separated only by the tall, blue grass. It appears as if they had not moved in years. Lifelessly, waiting for the moment when they would be called upon to march into the crystal.

Shaking with rage, Joe turns around and focuses all his attention on the sword. Then, with a single swing, he cuts open that familiar slit in the fabric of reality. Waves of dark energy envelop him as he steps inside.

Chapter XXI

War!

D r. Majken's face looks perplexed, as she ponders Joe's ability to create portals by slicing through the fabric of space.

"Well…" announces Captain Hunter, "if I may be excused, Colonel. I think I am going to go get very drunk and pretend I did not just see a guy cut open thin air and walk into the nightmare zone."

"Excused," the Colonel mutters quietly, without taking his eyes off the spot where Joe was standing a second ago.

"Also," Captain Hunter adds, "Dr. Majken, are you really older than the fucking dinosaurs?"

"Yes…" she responds nonchalantly. Still preoccupied with her own thoughts.

"Yup," Captain Hunter mutters under his breath, "time to break out the good stuff."

"Dr. Majken," Colonel Adams says softly. "I really need you to make sense of this for me. You're an alien, that has been around longer than our continents… And are one of the key reasons that an intergalactic colony has lost its connection to its parent galaxy, Millanthea?"

"That about sums it up," Dr. Majken responds after a long silence, blatantly distracted.

"I need you to focus," Colonel Adams states with urgency. "I must notify the President, and you are responding like Emily does when she is replying to text messages, but acts as if she can talk to me at the same time."

"Yes?" the President asks still in the corner of the room, "what is it that you would like to notify me of?"

Colonel Adams suddenly realizes that he too was distracted. So much so that forgot the President was right there all along.

"My apologies sir." He says as he regains his focus. "I forgot that you are here." He clears his throat. "If I may, sir, how do you know Joe?"

"It is a long story," the President responds. "He has been 'taking care' of some of those sightings that you may have heard about. Obviously, he is also… what did you call them, evolved? I need to get back to Washington. I have some very important things to attend to."

"Of course, Mr. Presi-" Colonel Adams, begins to respond.

"As for you Colonel," the President continues, "I am promoting you to General! You are now in charge of figuring out and resolving this situation. I will make the announcement via Twitter monetarily and my staff will file all the necessary papers."

"Uhhh, do you mean Brigadier General?" The Colonel stammers. "Because just 'General' by itself refers to a four-star, and Brigadier General is a one-sta-"

The President walks out of the room before Colonel Adams can finish his questions.

"Congratulations! General Adams," says Captain hunter, as he snaps to attention and salutes.

"He can't just promote me at his own whim," Colonel Adams says, as he returns the salute. "It requires Congressional Approval. Also, I thought you went to grab a drink."

"Yes sir," Captain Hunter responds. "I just heard you talking to our resident alien over there and wanted to make sure that your summary matched my own. Otherwise, I would wake up tomorrow, thinking it was all a bad dream. Also, this President has Congress in his pocket. His tweet is as good as a promotion."

"Fair point," Colonel Adams says through a chuckle. "You may still go get that drink, Captain. However, before you leave, I have my first order for you as General."

"Sir," Captain Hunter responds smiling.

"On your way out," Colonel Adams says with a smile, "please notify my daughter that she can stop hiding by the door and join us. Then go into my office. In the bottom drawer of my desk, you will find a wooden box. Grab that, along with a few glasses, and bring them here. I think all of us need a drink."

"Sir, yes sir," Captain Hunter responds, obviously suppressing a child-like giddiness.

"Congratulations, General," Emily says as she walks in, obviously having heard him 'give the order.' "How do you always know?"

"I am your dad first and foremost," he responds. "It is my special power. Sam here, is part dragon, Joe makes portals, Dr. Majken lives for millions of years, and I always know what my daughter is doing. Just like I knew that you were on that helicopter."

"Wait! What?" I jump in, utterly flustered.

"Yes, Sam," Colonel Adams responds calmly. "I knew well before you took off… I also knew that you and the rest of the team would keep her safe."

"I suppose that with all the times I've screwed up, you wouldn't have faith in my plan," Emily replies with the utmost sincerity. "That, and I imagined you would just yell at me and then send me away…"

"Look sweetheart," the Colonel says softly, "you've made your share of mistakes. However, at the end of the day, you have learned to take responsibility... I know I haven't always been the most emotionally supportive father. I imagine that at times I can even be scary to talk to, but if there is one thing that will always be true, it is that I love you."

"I will do everything I can to keep you safe," he continues. "It is why I had you train with the incredible men and women under my command. It wasn't just about toughening you up, but about showing you that you have a whole other family. Who will look out for you and protect you? They might not always be sweet or kind... sometimes they're probably emotionally stunted... but they'll always have your back."

"I get that, dad," Emily responds. "I just wish you could communicate that better."

"Look, you've become a remarkable young woman, Emily." Colonel Adams says with an air of pride in his voice. "However, with all the unknowns out there, now more than ever I need you to trust me. So, no more going behind my back. Deal?"

"Deal..." Emily says with a smile. "Thanks, for trusting in me."

Suddenly, the door opens and Captain Hunter walks in backwards, pulling a bar cart in with him.

"Well ladies and gentlemen," he says joyously, "I would've bet against it, but I just saw the President's tweet. Looks like he really did put you in for that promotion. However, it also looks like our General has been keeping a big secret! Should I tell them, General, or will you come clean?"

Everyone gives the unofficially promoted General Adams a puzzled look.

"Yes," he responds. "It is time you all knew... I have been keeping a 40-year-old, single malt scotch hidden away in my desk."

"How could you, sir?" Demands Jefferson, as everyone bursts into a relieved laugh.

"All right, everyone grab a glass. That's an order," says General Adams. "Captain, you may do the honors."

Captain Hunter carefully removes the priceless bottle from a wooden box, takes out the cap, and pours the amber-colored scotch into 11 crystal glasses.

"It was given to me by my predecessor," says the General. "I was really hoping to save it for a celebration, but with the insanity that our world has become, I would really hate to die not having tried it..."

General Adams looks down, admiring the deep amber liquid as he gently swirls it in his glass. Then, brings it up to his nose and takes in the smooth, smoky aroma of the scotch.

"To Sam and Dr. Majken," General Adams toasts, raising his glass in the air. "The newest members of our crazy family."

"And to your promotion, General," I chime in.

"Here, here," everyone responds in unison, as they raise their glasses and take a sip.

As we stand there, enjoying the calm before the storm, a young Lieutenant bursts through the door.

"Sir," he says, clearly winded, "We just received a call about some major Evolved activity in Great Britain! They're requesting guidance."

"We'll give them one better," General Adams responds. "Tell them a team is on the way."

Chapter XXII

The New Normal

G eneral Adams clearly has some grand plan that he has yet to share. What is more perplexing, is that he doesn't seem surprised that the British are reaching out to us.

How did they learn about our team? I wonder as everyone stares at the General with anticipation. Do they have a spy here?

"General," Captain Hunter finally breaks the silence, "how would the Brits know to call this base to request help? Plus, don't they have their own units who can deal with this?"

"Unfortunately," the General responds, "your dance with the Behemoth drew international attention. Between the media coverage and videos uploaded to social media, it was every covert operation's nightmare. We covered it up as much as possible for civilians, but foreign intelligence had wind of it before we could get the online streams removed."

"Oh good," I sigh with relief. "I was just beginning to wonder if perhaps you had set up a hotline and forgot to mention it. You know 'Thanks for calling one-eight-hundred-evolved! What type of creature are you dealing with today?'"

Thankfully, everyone got the joke as they burst into laughter. Presumably, imagining a little old lady answering calls. With people screaming in terror as they run for their lives from a monstrous octopus... All right, perhaps that was just what I was visualizing.

"No," General Adams says, still chuckling. "However, it would not be a bad idea, to go along with what I had in mind."

"Why do I get the feeling that I am about to be 'voluntold' for something?" Asks Captain Hunter.

"Not you Captain," the General responds. "I am volunteering Emily for this role."

"Thanks, dad!" Emily quips.

"Well," General Adams retorts, "You wanted to be part of the team, sweetheart. So, you don't get to cherry-pick your assignments."

"Damn..." Emily concedes, realizing she put herself in this predicament.

"I have come to realize," General Adams continues, "that we won't be able to keep everything under wraps for long. So, by the time that all of you return from your 'vacation' to England, we will have a task force and facilities set up for newly Evolved individuals. As General, I will ensure that none of them are harmed or experimented on. You and Sam, however, will need to craft the messaging to put them at ease. No one will come here if they're worried about being made into Guinea Pigs."

"You mean like I was?" I ask with sarcasm.

"I just realized that I never apologized for that, Sam," the General responds with shame in his voice. "I had no idea that either you or your friends were here. Interpol and the FBI didn't even notify me about Emily until two weeks after you were here. I am well aware that they use this base for some of their 'less publicly known projects.' However, in the past, it has always been a pissing contest about who has the 'more' top secret clearance. So, until I found out that they were holding Emily, I didn't act… I sincerely apologize for how you were treated…"

"It's all right General," I say, much to my own surprise. "I suppose I didn't really expect anything else. Plus, since I still have all of my appendages, I can't be too mad."

"Speaking of experiments, General," Dr. Majken cuts in, "may I take blood samples from the team? At the end of this, all of you will have some new elements of your DNA activated. Due to the countless generations of interbreeding between the species, I may not be able to identify everyone. However, it may be good to know what species we have to start with."

The unease in the room is palpable. Everyone begins looking at one another, then to the General, then at their own hands.

"You may start with me," says General Adams.

"I will also volunteer," Emily pitches in.

"Thank you," replies Dr. Majken. "As I said, I cannot promise that I will be able to identify every prospective Evolved. But, at least the ones I can identify will be able to prepare for what they're going to experience."

"Fine," replies Captain Hunter in a disgruntled tone. "I suppose I might as well know what to expect."

"Look," Dr. Majken continues, "just because the re-emergence of the crystal will unlock your DNA, it does not mean that you will necessarily transform into anything different than what you look like now. Many of the species in Atlantis looked exactly the way we do now. What made them unique were their abilities, not their appearance. I know all of you look at Sam and imagine that this is what's coming for you, but don't forget that Sam is part dragon. Dragons were the only species actually from Earth. The rest of us came here from Millanthea."

She pauses to take her last sip of scotch. Then continues. "Remember that my DNA was never locked, yet, I have lived among humans for countless generations, and no one could tell me apart. Therefore, it is likely that the vast majority of people will remain exactly as they are in terms of appearance."

Senior Master Sergeant Payne suddenly perks up. "Wait, so I might have the power to fly and shoot lasers from my eyes, or throw fireballs?" She asks.

"Not unless you grow wings," Dr. Majken chuckles, "and no lasers. Though there were several species that could manipulate ambient energy into fire. So technically you might be able to do that -"

"Sweet!" Payne cuts her off with a child-like excitement in her voice. "Test me first. I want to know what powers I have!"

"This will take time," Dr. Majken says calmly. "I've only had the ability to study DNA for the last 70 years. The technology we had on Atlantis was completely different. Identifying a species with the tools we have today is incredibly challenging. Plus, as I mentioned, I am concerned about all the new DNA combinations. Although for some, this would mean incredible complimentary abilities, it could just as easily neutralize others."

"What do you mean," Emily asks.

"It depends on how the DNA of two species merged inside an offspring. For instance, if your father could manipulate fire, while your mother wielded water, you might be able to manipulate both, neither, or you may be able to create a new element. At least that's how it used to work. Now, you have to take into account these combinations have stacked for thousands of generations. So, if it started with only fire and water, but then you mix in force, or a mental ability like telekinesis, it gets really messy."

"You've been researching this for some time though," General Adams says. "Have you found any patterns?"

"Some," Dr. Majken replies. "Abilities are not unlike eye and hair color. Let's say your mother was able to charge items with energy. While your father could manipulate certain metals. Based on the genetic dominance, you would most likely retain the charging ability. Metal manipulation is incredibly rare. Because in and of itself, it is a hybrid ability. So, just like dominant traits, the dominant abilities have likely persevered through the countless combinations..."

"So, it is possible to have multiple powers or abilities?" Asks Staff Sergeant Collins.

"Yes," Dr. Majken responds, "however, it is most likely that billions of people will have no abilities whatsoever. Simply because their DNA has become so diluted. Like everything else in this world, abilities require balance. Too much interbreeding and they are neutralized. On the flip side, too much inbreeding and... well, we've all heard the stories of those royal families. That is why I want to run some tests. With a large enough sample, we would theoretically be able to identify whether someone will evolve or not."

"Alright," General Adams says decisively. "Sounds like all of us have a mission. Captain Hunter, you and your team will head to Great Britain and figure out what they're dealing with. Doctor Majken will figure out how to test for various ability lineages and compile them into a database. I will establish accommodations for newly Evolved individuals. Perhaps if they have a place to go as their new abilities come through, it will reduce the number of incidents that we need to respond to."

"Yes," I chime in, "and when Emily and I get back, we will figure out how to get the word out. So, that it comes across as a safe haven rather than an internment camp."

"Go team!" Emily exclaims, we head for the door.

CHAPTER XXIII

NOT WHAT YOU THINK...

A s I make it to the airstrip, the team is already onboard of the massive C-17-X military transport plane. The 'X' designated that it was some special model, outfitted for extra-long flights.

"Hey Em!" I shout over the sound of idling engines, as I enter the back of the plane. "Perhaps you can show me some cool sites, if there's time after the mission!"

"I'd love to Sam," she responds in an equally loud voice. "But I'm not sure if the Brits have any more tolerance for half-dragons than we do here!"

"Quite all right!" I shout in my best imitation of 'proper English.' "I'll just wear one of those fancy hats! No one will be the wiser!"

We chuckle at the idea as everyone gets situated.

"Hey," I ask as I put on my helmet with a built-in comm system. "Can anyone tell me why the hell we call it the 'pond' whenever we talk about flying across the damn ocean?"

"The world has become much smaller over the last couple of hundred years," replies Captain Hunter.

"It's a small world after all, it's a small world after all," Emily begins singing. Causing everyone to cringe at the idea of the song getting stuck in our heads.

"Nooo!" I yell out of desperation. "Please stop! You know I can bring this plane down, right?"

We all laugh at the idea that we would rather die a fiery death than spend the next ten hours with 'It's a small world after all' playing on a relentless loop in our heads. I strap in, and the ramp shuts behind me. The overhead lights turn green, and the plane begins to taxi toward takeoff.

"Ladies and gentlemen," the pilot announces, doing his best impression of a commercial airline. "Welcome to Air Force Airlines! We appreciate you flying with us, even though we know you didn't have a choice! We are on our way to England. Home of tea, crumpets, shitty weather, and apparently some monsters that have been terrorizing a local village. So, strap in, and keep your parachute handy!"

"Alright team," Captain Hunter says through the plane's communication system, as we accelerate down the runway. "This mission sounds like massive a clusterfuck! The only details that we got from the Brits is that this is a group of flying Evolved. They took over a castle in Ireland, and are terrorizing the surrounding villagers. Something about dismembered bodies and heads on spikes, on top of the castle walls!"

"Wait," Emily interjects. "If the castle is in Ireland, why did they tell us England?"

"Like most international affairs," Captain Hunter responds, "it was a shit show. The Evolved came from all over Great Britain. However, they settled in an Irish castle. Since the situation involved citizens of multiple sovereign countries they picked England to reach out to us."

"Ah," I chime in, "got to love international bullshit. Though I think the whole 'head on a pike' idea speaks clearly in every language."

"Can't argue with you there, Sam," Captain Hunter responds. "I thin -"

Although I can see his lips moving, I can no longer hear Captain Hunter over the plane's communication system. A few moments later General Adams' voice comes through.

"I hope none of you were planning on taking a nap," General Adams says. "Unfortunately, Joe got back shortly after you left and all of you need to hear what he has to say. We've set up a speaker in the conference room. You should be able to hear us and vice versa. Can I get a quick mic check from everyone?"

"Hunter here," Captain Hunter says to ensure that everyone can hear him.

"Lima Charlie, Captain," General Adams responds.

"Emily here," Emily announces.

"Lima Charlie" General Adams responds again.

One by one, Payne, Jefferson, Collins, Gonzales, Clark, and I check-in.

"All right," General Adams says, "Joe, have a seat, have a drink, and bring us up to speed."

"You are wasting time going on this mission," Joe begins bluntly. "You need to focus on mobilizing all the major military forces on Earth and prepare for war."

"Look Joe," General Adams responds, "I appreciate that you obviously know quite a bit more than the rest of us, being an Archon and all. However, you cannot expect that we just drop everything and gear up for war, without any details."

A small monitor lowers from the ceiling of the plane as a pixelated video feed is established with the base. We see Joe sit down in one of the chairs. Placing his sheathed sword on the table in front of him. As he swishes what I can only imagine as more scotch in his glass, it becomes evident that he is trying to figure out where to start.

"I found the Atlantean crystal," Joe says calmly. "It is at the center of lake Baikal, just like doctor Majken said. Thankfully, it is still buried in the rock below. So, my guess is that you have about a year before it fully emerges. More importantly, is that I was able to see the other side. Your enemy is already gathered there. However, this enemy is unlike anything you have ever faced."

"Well, based on our encounter with the Behemoth," Captain Hunter jumps in, "I doubt anyone is expecting anything 'familiar.' Especially, if this enemy is coming from another galaxy!"

"You don't understand," Joe continues. "Regardless of who or which species you have fought, all of them have a survival instinct. This enemy has no such thing. I'm not even sure you can consider them to be alive."

"What are you talking about, Joe?" Dr. Majken demands. "The gate in Millanthea is controlled by –"

"- Was," Joe cuts her off, "controlled by our side. You are familiar with the two Millanthean empires, each fighting for control. Each would take a few solar systems, then lose a few, and so it went for over a thousand years. Until our side found the crystal and established Atlantis."

"Right…" she responds waiting for the 'but.'

"After Atlantis was established," Joe continues, "the influx of battalions and hybrid abilities of the species from Earth, gave us a massive advantage. We were able to capture and hold more solar systems than anyone thought possible. Including my own. Howev -"

"Wait," Dr. Majken, cuts him off. "Our side found Noctsola? Is it really how the myths describe it?"

I am not sure if it is excitement or surprise that I hear in her voice. For a split second, this alien, who has lived over a million lifetimes, sounds like a kid who found out that she was getting a pony for her birthday.

"Yes," Joe responds. "Please focus!"

"Wait, what exactly is an Archon?" I ask via the speaker.

"Fine," Joe sighs, clearly understanding that our curiosity outweighs our concerns. "Archons were the second set of conscious beings to exist in the universe. The Second Suns, were the first, before you ask. Those original Archons, are what we now refer to as Grand Archons. They came about sometime toward the end of the third Solar Evolution. Their sole purpose was to wipe out all life, throughout the universe."

"Sounds lovely!" I quip.

"After the War of Life," Joe continues, unamused, "the Grand Archons were reduced to their lowest and weakest form, by the Second Suns. In this weakened form, they were neither able to withstand light nor draw on dark matter for power. As a result, they were all placed and consequently trapped on a single planet. A prison that needs no walls. Damned to run from daylight for the rest of eternity."

"What is a 'Second Sun?'" I inquire.

"Simply put," Joe says nonchalantly, "by human measures, they were gods. They are responsible for the creation of life throughout the universe. However, they did not create consciousness. They simply planted the seeds which, billions of years later and under the right circumstances, flourished into the multitudes of species throughout the universe."

"How did you manage to escape Noctsola?" Dr. Majken asks.

"The Kailet," Joe responds, "a rare hybrid species that originated in Atlantis. They have the unique ability to bond with Archons. Allowing us to exist in the light and leave our damned solar system."

The silence and static that permeate my headset, make it evident that everyone is suddenly contemplating the implications of Archons roaming the universe. Is this the enemy that Joe is trying to warn us about?

"I am familiar with the Kailet species," Dr. Majken finally breaks the silence. "Did you kill the Kailet that you were bound to?"

"No!" Joe replies, seemingly shocked at the accusation. "First of all, that would be suicide. The bond is mutual, so if the Kailet dies, the Archon perishes as well. For the few of us who had the opportunity to leave Noctsola, that would be the last thing we would want."

"So, how were you able to travel the universe?" General Adams inquires. "More importantly, why risk being lost in the vastness of space?"

"Think about it General," Joe responds. "If you are fighting a war and your greatest ally stops sending the support that has turned the tide, would you not send someone to investigate?"

"Of course!" The General replies.

"I came to Earth, with a singular goal," Joe says with sincerity. "To restore support from Atlantis. As far as how I was able to, that is a bit more complicated..."

Joe lifts his glass, takes a sip of his scotch, and pauses for a moment to appreciate the smooth, rich flavor of the antique beverage.

"Everyone understood," Joe continues, "that without support from Atlantis, our Empire would collapse relatively quickly. Since there was no technological way to reach Earth, there was only one potentially dangerous and experimental solution - dark matter travel. All Archons know it is possible, but in our base form, it was inaccessible."

"Wait," I say inquisitively. "Is dark matter travel something that Archons are capable of innately or would it utilize technology?"

"It is an ability," Joe responds, "but one that we cannot use in our base form... Having fought alongside living species for decades, Archons learned about a previously foreign concept – self-sacrifice. In order to exist in light without a Kailet and to travel using dark matter, six individual Archons would need to willingly sacrifice themselves. In doing so, they would merge into a single tier two Archon."

"So, six other Archons had to die," Dr. Majken presses, "in order to create you?"

"For mortal beings," Joe responds, "it is impossible to truly grasp the idea of infinity. Even if you live for an exceedingly long period of time, such as yourself doctor, in your experience everything is finite – it has a beginning and will eventually end. Archons, do not see existence in this way. We are truly infinite. When an Archon's physical manifestation is destroyed, it becomes part of what you refer to as dark matter. Our individuality is extinguished, but this is not death. Merely an existence we would prefer to avoid."

"Mind… blown…" Captain Hunter chimes in quietly.

"Since you are standing here on Earth," Dr. Majken cuts in, "I assume that this is what you are… A tier two or Grand Archon, as you mentioned. That is why you weren't scared of Sam… You are just as powerful, if not more so."

"Oh no," Joe chuckles, "nothing like me has ever existed. I am indeed a tier two Archon, but I imagine it would take thousands of me to recreate a single Grand Archon. Having said that, I am also well aware of what the Millaethros are capable of. The tier one Archons who merged to form me, have fought alongside them many times… It is also how I knew that Sam here, is far from the maximum potential of the species."

"I am still evolving?" I ask with trepidation.

"Absolutely!" Joe says confidently. "Once you reach your full potential, you and I would be quite evenly matched. Not that I would want to challenge you. However, by the time the Atlantean crystal fully emerges, you will be the Earth's single greatest asset, or warrior if you prefer."

"You make it sound as if you won't be joining us," General Adams says.

"Look," Joe responds solemnly. "You may have a little over a year to prepare for the onslaught that is coming, but I must leave immediately and return to Millanthea. I only came back from Lake Baikal to warn you about what is coming... Perhaps with time to prepare, knowledge of your enemy, and lots of luck, you might stand a chance."

Chapter XXIV

The other side...

There is something peaceful about flying high above the clouds. Many times throughout my life, I would look up at a plane flying overhead and wonder about the individuals aboard. Where are they going? Are they traveling for leisure or business? Perhaps a family tragedy or celebration?

As we traverse our respective lives, it is easy to forget that every single person out there has one of their own. Everyone is someone's child. Some are parents, brothers, sisters, friends, etc. Each one has problems and challenges which they find overwhelming. Yet, when we see them on a plane, in a store, or if one of them cuts us off on the highway, how often do we think about their individuality?

"Let me get this straight..." Captain Hunter says in a perturbed tone. "You are a distant cousin of immortal beings, who wanted to wipe out all life throughout the universe. After billions of years, with the help of some new species, you escaped from a solar system that 'gods' created specifically to hold your ancestors! And now you want to save Earth so that we can once again start sending troops to support a war in a distant galaxy. Is that right or am I just insane?"

"It is far more complex than that," Joe retorts. "There is no time to get into the detail -"

"No!" Captain Hunter fires back sternly. "I'm not buying that bullshit answer! We have a long flight ahead of us. If you expect my team and I, to gather the Earth's militaries and tell them that they should go die, fighting some Millanthean army of undead! There's plenty of fucking time for you to explain everything!"

The change in Captain Hunter's demeanor catches everyone off guard. Even General Adams - who appears preoccupied with formulating a strategy - suddenly shifts all his attention to the conversation.

"The Captain is right," General Adams says calmly. "Joe, you are asking more of us, than any other group in the history of human civilization. It is only fair, that you take the time."

Joe takes the last swig of his scotch. Quietly walks over to the bar cart, refills his glass, and adds a few drops of water. Then, he walks back to his seat and takes a long sip.

"When the Archons were imprisoned," he begins. "It was the first time in our existence that we developed individuality. Prior to that, we simply existed as a driven consciousness, an idea... A force with only one goal - to destroy life. Individual needs, including survival, were irrelevant."

Everyone in the room shifts to the edge of their seat. Almost like children listening to a ghost story.

"It may not make much sense," Joe continues. "But in order to be imprisoned, Grand Archons had to be reduced to their weakest form. In this new form, we developed personalities and individual needs. We became independent of one another, and eventually developed the desire to perpetuate our individualized existence. After billions of years of being trapped on our home world, a few of us opted to help the Millanthean empire. In exchange for a kind of freedom from our cursed existence."

"Suffice it to say," Joe continues, "that in my individuality, I have grown fond of the finite species. Also, I am not a 'distant cousin' of Grand Archons. I am a fragment of one... Well, a combination of fragments, to be precise. And as I already mentioned, I would need to merge with countless other Archons to regain the level of power that a single Grand Archon held."

"What exactly stops you from doing just that?" Captain Hunter asks cautiously.

"About a third of the Archons in the Noctsola system," Joe replies. "Imagine trying to convince a third, maybe two-thirds, of Earth's population to give up their lives, so that you can become really powerful."

"Fair enough," Captain Hunter concedes.

The plane banks hard and everyone aboard grabs hold of their respective seat.

"Are you able to use the crystal to get back?" Dr. Majken inquires.

"I can't," Joe responds. "Archons, have never been able to use the crystals... It took me over one-hundred-and-seventy million Earth years to get here. I promise it was not because I took too many bathroom breaks along the way."

Much to everyone's surprise, all of us burst out laughing... For as much of an asshole, as Joe seems to be, it is nice to see that he actually has a sense of humor.

"I was literally searching every galaxy and solar system between Millanthea and the Milky Way," Joe continues. "Now that I know where I am going, I should get back to Millanthea within less than a year of Earth time. Once there, I will try to figure out what went wrong. Perhaps, even flank the enemy or gather Millanthean reinforcements to improve your chances."

"I need to understand something else," General Adams cuts in. "Why help our government fight the Evolved here on Earth? Why coerce our President?"

"When I finally made it to Earth," Joe responds candidly, "I went after those who commanded the largest military forces. My initial goal was simply to reduce the opposition against the Millanthean leadership. Ideally, they would have been welcomed, rather than met with hostility."

"Makes sense," Dr. Majken chimes in.

"However," Joe continues, "since I couldn't find the crystal, I hedged my bets. Focusing on your President as well as leaders in Russia, China, and a few European nations. I figured one of them would know where it was. The hostile Evolved were simply a mutual issue. One which I resolved in order to gain their trust."

"If your relationship with our President is any indicator," Captain Hunter cuts in, "are the other world leaders in your pocket as well?"

"No," Joe laughs lightheartedly. "I mainly have relationships with generals who lead armies. Politicians are puppets. I just figured the one here would be able to open doors for me with the other nations... Plus, your politicians are mostly pampered, self-serving brats. They spend most of their time pandering to the most ignorant, yet loudest fringes of your population."

"This," Joe continues, "made your 'leaders' much easier to influence. Heck, they have no combat or field experience. Despite this, they are the ones who make policies about war and whether or not to deploy troops and combat assets."

"I can't argue..." General Adams admits. "That's pretty ass-backwards."

"Right!" Joe says with a knowing smirk. "If you have no experience with something, just sit back and let those dealing with the situation find a solution."

"I'm sorry," General Adams says calmly. "I didn't mean to take us on a tangent. Please, finish your story."

"You're right," Joe's tone clearly shifting the conversation back to the issue at hand. "I have come to enjoy the political banter here on Earth. It's easy to get carried away... Long story longer, I found the crystal and was able to see the Millanthean side. Unfortunately, it appears that our side lost control of the planet. So, when the crystal that's here fully emerges, you will not have a delegation waiting for you, but a slaughter."

"But what are we facing exactly?" Asks General Adams.

Joe slowly swirls the scotch in his glass. Evidently searching for a way to explain something that doesn't simply boil down to 'guys with guns.'

"Since I was the first Archon not tethered to a Kailet," Joe responds, "I decided to do one last recon mission, before leaving Millanthea. Although we had driven back our enemies, I wanted to be sure that they were not preparing some grand counterattack, or developing some secret weapon."

"That was noble of you," General Adams says.

"General," Joe retorts. "Despite your rank, you're a soldier first. Are you not?"

"Of course," General Adams responds proudly.

"Then," Joe continues, "you should be able to appreciate, the fraternal bond that forms between those who fight alongside one another."

"More than you know..." the General says solemnly.

His response makes it evident that he has lost someone close to him. Probably more than once.

"As I mentioned," Joe goes on, "I hold memories and emotions tied to those alongside whom the Archons have fought. Therefore, I have grown to value the lives of individuals... Especially those who fight for something worthwhile. Having lived on Earth, I can say that the Millanthean Empire for which I fight is akin to the European Union or the United States. It is more of a conglomerate of solar systems and cultures with similar ideals and values."

"So, a republic," Emily corrects him, "more than an empire."

"Sure," Joe concedes, "let's call it the Millanthean Republic... The opposing side of the Empire is more like a kingdom. Where all cultures serve a singular purpose and group, above even themselves."

"Is that who took control of the planet?" I ask. "Did this 'Millanthean kingdom' push back your Republic? Is that what you saw through the crystal at the bottom of lake Baikal?"

"I wish," Joe replies solemnly. "Unfortunately, what I saw at the bottom of the lake is far worse..."

He takes a long sip of his scotch and continues.

"As I jumped from solar system to solar system," Joe recalls, "before leaving the Millanthea galaxy, I did not find anything that I would classify as a great threat, to the Republic. A few colonies, and some small battle groups, but nothing our forces couldn't handle with relative ease. However, I did discover something incredibly disturbing, in one of the more distant solar systems."

"It was a planet" Joe continues, "that did not belong to either the Millanthean kingdom or the Republic. Despite this, they already had some rather advanced technology… This is rare, without the intervention of an advanced civilization. A standalone population seldom achieves the level of technology it had. Some of it was so advanced or unique, that I had never seen it."

"Was it weapons or just benign technology?" I ask.

"Both," Joe responds, "but, nothing interplanetary. However, their ground weapons were advanced enough to rival our own. More importantly, I wanted to explore the source of this advancement and make sure they weren't going to side with the kingdom. It was then that I learned a terrible truth. The species there had developed an incredible artificial general intelligence - AGI."

"Great," Captain Hunter chimes in, "A planet of terminators."

"Worse!" Joe replies. "What I learned was that they initially developed the AGI to solve their sustainability issues. Just like here on Earth, there were concerns about it going rogue and wiping everyone out as 'the solution.' However, they managed to prevent that…"

Joe takes another sip of his scotch. The silence of everyone in the room, and on the plane, speaks for itself.

Likely recalling everything they have read about artificial intelligence and the debates on the pros and cons of using it here, on Earth.

"They used various programming parameters," Joe continues, "that made wiping out sentient life an invalid calculation. Forcing the artificial intelligence to simply disregard any solution where that was a factor. Other parameters centered around the AGI not being able to utilize various weapons systems. Everything centered on directing its efforts towards optimizing resource use and reducing reliance on finite resources – like fossil fuels would be here on Earth."

"Sounds perfect," says the General, "we could use a computer like that."

"Yes," Joe responds with satire in his tone. "Except that since it was not simply an artificial intelligence, but an artificial 'general' intelligence, it found two major problems that had to be fixed, in order to minimize waste and optimize consumption... As depicted in all your science fiction movies, this never ends well."

CHAPTER XXV

INCONSISTENCY...

I begin to imagine a true artificial general intelligence, here on Earth. There are so many different ways in which it can destroy its creators. Ultimately deciding that 'we' are the problem that it must solve.

"Look," I interject, "I get where you are going with this, but you just said that the creators figured out how to keep it from killing them."

"Yes, but it wasn't trying to kill them," Joe responds. "The first issue that the AGI identified, was that the species who built it was in and of itself an inconsistent variable. There were massive disparities in how individuals utilized various resources. For example, some individuals ate more than they needed, while others were not getting enough food; some used more fuel by flying to their destinations instead of using ground transportation; or they would take scenic routes, which were less than optimal; and so on."

"Yeah…" I say quietly. "Earth definitely has some similar disparities."

"Right," Joe says, confidently. "So, in order to optimize resource use, the AGI had to first eliminate the inconsistencies in consumption. There were no protocols preventing this."

"So," Senior Airman Michaels cuts in. "For those of us who don't have PhDs and aren't science dorks. What is the difference between artificial intelligence and artificial 'general' intelligence?"

"Basic AI," Dr. Majken responds, "is still a computer. It can learn, but only within certain guidelines. An AGI is more like a person. It can evolve its understanding and learn anything, much like a person can."

"Yes," Joe agrees, "unfortunately, that also means that it is aware of itself. My guess is they tried using AI, but it didn't achieve the desired results."

"So…" Captain Hunter chimes back in. "Self-actualized terminators?"

"Initially," Joe continues, disregarding the Captain's comment, "in order to identify what caused these inconsistencies among individuals, the AGI needed a baseline. In other words, access to a sample of thought processes from the species. To accomplish this, it created a device that could be attached to the neck of an individual. This device allowed the AGI to gather neurological data of both the bodily functions and psychological motivations of an individual."

"Oh," Emily chimes in. "I can already see how this goes wrong,"

"Yes," Joe continues. "At first, prisoners were used to conduct the research. In order to pacify their desire to escape, the AGI 'neutralized' certain aggressive tendencies. The device triggered neural stimulation that made the wearer feel content and even happy at times. So, the research project in and of itself resulted in an amazing solution to a major problem -"

"Pacifying the prisoners," the General interjects, finishing Joe's point. "They would no longer need prison guards or prisons for that matter. The economic impact alone would be monumental!"

"Even better," Joe corrects him. "The test subjects began eating optimal amounts of food for their body mass; sleeping for the minimum amount of time necessary; and performing their assigned duties with exceptional results. Moreover, with their violent tendencies suppressed, prisoners became the model workforce. Best of all, instead of millions of prisoners rotting in cells and using up precious resources, they could serve time to the AGI. Thereby, contributing back to society, building and maintaining infrastructure, doing dangerous jobs, etcetera."

"That is actually quite brilliant," Dr. Majken says, obviously reflecting on the prisons here, on Earth.

"This unintentional consequence," Joe continues, "prompted the planet's leadership to subject anyone convicted of a crime, warranting incarceration, to serve under the AGI instead."

"Sounds great, so far..." Captain Hunter chimes in.

"It was a remarkable solution," Joe agrees, after taking another sip of his scotch. "Especially because after serving their time, the convicts would have earned a place to live; already had a job in which they were skilled; and had been cured of any addictions, they may have had. Moreover, they were so accustomed to their productive lives, that even after their sentence, they were actually happy as functioning members of society. It truly was the perfect system. Except for one flaw..."

"Ah, here comes the 'but,'" I say hesitantly.

"The issue," Joe goes on, "was the gradual return to inconsistency. As time went on, those individuals would sleep more, eat more, become more wasteful in their commutes, and spend too much time on entertainment and leisure. You know, all the things that living species enjoy, but computers perceive as a waste of the most precious resource - time."

"Oh, shit..." Dr. Majken says, realizing the implication. "The AGI decided that they would be better off under its control, permanently."

"Yes," Joe responds. "As it cycled through prisoners, the AGI figured out how to convert electricity into bioenergy. It was able to effectively 'feed' the bodies of living beings with minimal food and water. This technology was built into armored suits that the AGI upgraded over time. Eventually, the armor became so efficient that it was able to absorb ambient energy from the surrounding air, feeding the body, and even healing the wearer. This efficiency also extended the life of those wearing such an armor by decades and eventually eliminated the need for traditional nourishment altogether."

"So, how did it enslave the populace?" Asks the General.

"It hid a more advanced version of the control units that it used for prisoners into the armor… In less than a generation, over sixty percent of the planet voluntarily wore the armor. That is when the AGI activated the control units. Except that the advanced control units didn't just induce neural impulses. They locked out the consciousness of the wearer. Giving the AGI total control."

"Wow," I whisper, as I imagine the fall of an entire planet, without a single shot being fired. "Why build robots, to fight the living when you can just take control of them?"

"Precisely," Joe, agrees. "From there, the AGI began to optimize every element of life. It bred only perfectly paired individuals, allowing those with various issues or genetic mutations to die out. Those who refused, to wear the armor, were simply rounded up and forced into it or killed."

"How?" Asks Captain Hunter. "I thought the AGI could not use weapons?"

"I'm not sure," Joe responds. "The group of survivors or rebels, I found, had several theories. Some believed that since the wearer of the armor was still an individual, the AGI wasn't technically controlling the weapons. Rather, it would simply issue requests, that wearers had no choice but to comply with... Perhaps firing at a target yielded pleasure, while choosing not to yielded immense pain."

'Moreover," Joe continues, "most of the weapons were designed simply to incapacitate living targets and get them into an armor. Lethal weapons were only used to destroy vehicles, strongholds, or equipment."

"So," General Adams cuts in, "if people 'happened' to get killed because they were inside a building or vehicle, or wearing equipment that was targeted, the AGI technically did not violate any of its protocols."

"That was another theory," Joe continues. "Since the intent was merely to destroy an inanimate object, the AGI's 'no kill' protocols wouldn't have been triggered. Intent thereby became the key factor. Remember, the original goal was optimization. The most effective way of achieving it without killing everyone was to eliminate variance."

"You mean individuality?" I ask.

"Yes," Joe agrees. "Although twisted, the logic made sense - individuals who survived were put into armor and go on to lead optimized lives, prolonged even. If they died, optimization was achieved through waste reduction. No matter how you look at it, it was –"

"The perfect, twisted solution." Dr. Majken finishes Joe's sentence.

"Sadly, that's right," Joe concurs.

"And now, you believe that this AI is coming here?" General Adams asks, "to attack Earth?"

"I wish it were merely a belief," Joe responds with certainty. "I assume that the Millanthean Empire, the 'kingdom' as we are calling it, somehow found this planet after I did. My guess is that, in their arrogance or perhaps desperation, they perceived the AGI and its armor as a response to the Republic's use of Atlantis for reinforcements. From there, the AGI probably used their ships to spread throughout Millanthea."

"And," General Adams cuts in, "since the crystal went dark, your side would have reallocated the resources protecting the planet."

"Most likely," Joe responds. "What I know definitively, is that there is an army - millions of armored suits, just standing there at the base of the crystal. These looked slightly more advanced than the armor I saw when I was on the planet, and their colors matched the Millanthean Kingdom. So, it stands to reason that the AGI controls them as well."

"I'm a bit confused," says captain Hunter, "are they still alive? If we were to remove the armor, would they return to normal?"

"I suppose," responds Joe, "that is the most disturbing part of some of the theories that I heard. When the AGI takes control of a mind, the individual continues to exist. However, he or she has no control over their own body. Unable to speak, move, or do anything but observe."

"The conscious mind would eventually go insane..." Dr. Majken says in a disturbed tone.

"That's worse than death!" I exclaim.

"That," Joe responds solemnly, "is what all of you are about to face. The crystal will fully emerge in roughly one year. By then, everyone here, who has the genetics to evolve, will have completed their evolution. Once the crystal fully connects with its counterpart in Millanthea, the AGI's army will spill out like a flood. I know that your nations have their differences, but this is a threat that you must face as a planet. One year... that, is how long you have to prepare."

CHAPTER XXVI

IRELAND...

Our plane hits a patch of rough air. Despite its size, the turbulence rattles everyone on board. Master Sergeant Clark, spills some of her coffee during one of the bigger drops. Thankfully, we lost connection to the meeting half an hour ago. So, no one back at base had to listen to her profanity-infused rant.

Did Joe already leave for Millanthea? I wonder. *There are so many questions he didn't answer... I should probably get some sleep before we get to Ireland. Though, I'm not sure that is possible, given what we just learned.*

"Hey... wake up..." Emily nudges me awake. "We're almost there."

I guess it is possible. I think as I chuckle silently.

The rest of the team already has their parachutes on. Their gear bags and weapons strapped onto their harnesses, in order to withstand the descent. Every one of them ready to jump into the hornet's nest. I attach my gear and my mind travels into some void of space and time, as I try to steel myself against the panic that is setting in. The overhead light switches from green to red. Like clockwork, we stand up to head toward the back of the plane.

As the ramp begins to open, I try desperately to recall all the instructions about how to steer the parachute and where we're supposed to land. The chutes are supposed to automatically deploy at a specific altitude. The castle is surrounded by lots of open fields. So, even if I miss the landing zone, the team will wait at the rendezvous point.

All right, I remind myself, *all you have to do is 'enjoy the drop' as Payne put it. She might as well have told me to enjoy a fucking heart-attack!*

I've never been a big fan of air travel. Despite knowing the statistics - that it's safer than driving - sitting in a tin can that is hurtling through the sky at 700 miles per hour, has never appealed to me. Nor have I ever found the idea of jumping out of a perfectly good airplane exciting in any way. Yet, here I am doing both. The initial few seconds are terrifying. I accelerate toward the ground at a blinding speed.

Perhaps, I shouldn't have tried to impress everyone by lying about having done this before, I think to myself, panicking.

Then, something incredible happens. It feels as if I am no longer falling, but rather floating. The feeling is difficult to describe. It is amazing! But just as I begin to enjoy the exhilaration, my chute opens and I am reminded just how fast I was plummeting to my death!

"Owww!" I yell out, as the harness yanks me upright.

The ground comes up surprisingly fast. I see my team below me gathering up their chutes. It is only then I realize that I am coming in too fast and at too much of an angle. I overshoot the landing zone and miss the wall of the castle by mere inches. There is no way that I will make it over the other wall.

I extend my talons and cut away the parachute. Plummeting the remaining twenty to thirty-feet, to the stone-covered courtyard. As I hit the ground, small rocks and debris are sent flying in all directions.

Damn! I think to myself as the terror of the fall subsides. *That must've looked awesome!*

I feel like one of those superheroes, making a dramatic entrance before a battle. The parachute continues on without me and gets hung up on the other castle wall. I immediately begin scanning the walls and windows, searching for where my enemy will emerge.

"Dragon, this is Eagle!" My radio clicks on and Captain Hunter's voice rings out in my earpiece. "Why are you in the courtyard? We were supposed to land outside the castle... Over."

Becoming a part of Hunter's team meant that Emily and I had to come up with call signs. I figured 'Dragon' would be appropriate. Hunter's callsign had always been Eagle; Collins is Wolf; Michaels is Specter; Jefferson is Tomcat; Payne is Fox; Gonzales is Panther; and Clark is Owl. Emily decided to go with Hawk, probably because Eagle was taken.

"Eagle... this is Dragon," I stammer while still scanning the courtyard. "I figured it would be easier open the gates from the inside... Definitely not because I overshot the landing. Over and out."

Satisfied that no one is shooting at me, I make my way to the main gate. It is barricaded by a massive wood beam. Probably the same one knights used when they defended the castle against invading armies. I walk over and attempt to lift up the thousand-pound block of wood.

Just before the beam clears the metal bracket, I feel a blunt object impact my spine and another the back of my knee. My body slams against the massive beam and I collapse to the ground. The beam falls back into place with a thud. Before I am able to gain my bearings, a strong hand clasps my ankle and drags me several feet. Then, I am lifted off the ground. I see massive wings flapping above me, as I am carried higher into the air and quickly ascend past the castle walls.

"Dragon!" My radio cracks and I hear Emily's terrified voice. "What the hell is going on?"

As I am flown higher, I can see twenty or thirty other evolved spread their wings and fly over the castle wall, towards my team. Massive hammers, maces, and swords raised over their heads. Looking down, I realize that I am now over a hundred feet in the air. One of my tentacles lashes up and slices the hand grasping my ankle. A shrieking cry pierces my ears and the grip is released.

I can only imagine what this looks like from Emily's perspective - watching me plummet from that height.

"Saaaam!" Emily screams out in horror.

My body hits the ground with an astounding thud. I feel the impact throughout my body. However, as I regain my bearings, clench my fists, and move my legs, I realize that I am not injured at all. Fractures in the stone, extend in every direction, away from the point of impact. I jump up with surprising agility, baffled by the realization that I am somehow still alive.

The suppressed popping of my team's weapons echoes through the air. Immediately followed by the plinking sound that bullets make when they hit metal. I look up, but my attacker is nowhere to be seen.

In battle, a single second can mean the difference between life and death. Getting to my team is all that matters right now. As I charge back toward the massive gate I notice a normal door, that is locked with a chain. Extending my talons, I slice through the chain and padlock in a single swipe. Then burst through the door scanning the field to locate my team.

"I'm coming, Em!" I yell, nearly crushing my radio as I press the talk button while running to catch up to the flying Evolved.

Somehow, these Evolved manage to evade the barrage of bullets being fired at them. Their armor must be deflecting any that do hit. It is evident as every once in a while one of them drops a few feet, but then continues toward the team.

I can't make it, I think as the panic begins to set in.

Looking around, I see one of the Evolved laying on the ground with a blood-soaked wing. Out of sheer desperation, I decide to do something I never thought I could. I retract all my talons, except the one on my index finger, and stab it through the shoulder. My claw penetrates the heavy armor and pins the Evolved to the ground.

The shriek that escapes through the full-face helmet makes it evident that this is a woman. As she cries out in agonizing pain, the others immediately stop and turn to look toward us.

"I will take off her head!" I yell to the other Evolved. "I don't want to kill her, but I will! We only want to talk! No one needs to die!"

Much to my surprise, the Evolved lower their weapons.

Holy shit! I think in disbelief. *It actually worked!*

They fly towards us and land gracefully all around. I can see the tension in their body language. One wrong move and they'll attack without a second thought.

"I will retract my talon and put pressure on your wound," I say calmly, as I turn to her. "It's going to hurt, but you need to stay still."

She nods and I can feel her muscles tightening as she braces for the pain. I withdraw my talon and use it to carefully cut through the straps of her shoulder guard. Then remove it gently and apply pressure to reduce the blood loss. She lets out a muffled groan but does not flinch.

Emily and the rest of the team run up behind us panting, their weapons still at the ready. However, the Evolved do not attack. Instead, one by one, they remove their helmets and move aside to make way for my team. As I scan the group, I realize that there is not a single male among them.

"Payne," I say forgetting to use her callsign. "Can you help her?"

"Of course," Senior Master Sergeant Payne replies, reaching into a cargo pocket for her first aid kit. "Specter, grab my medic bag. I will need to dress this properly."

The other evolved, all wearing various types of heavy armor, form a large circle around myself and the team. Their massive wings stretch down behind them like capes. They examine us, still unsure of what to make of us and whether or not we can be trusted.

"What are you?" Asks, the injured woman, obviously directing her question at me.

"I am a Millaethros," I respond calmly, "a half-dragon, half-alien."

I must sound like a crazy person, I think to myself.

"And you must all be Valkyries," I continue, as though I magically became an expert overnight.

"We do not know what we are," she responds with a surprisingly calm demeanor. "Many of us are from small towns, all around the UK. But our stories are quite similar."

"What do you mean?" Captain Hunter asks.

"We began to grow stronger and faster than all of the men," she responds. "So, naturally they began suspecting us of witchcraft... I know it sounds stupid saying that in the 21st century, but 'simple minds' and all that."

"Yeah," Senior Master Sergeant Payne quips, carefully tying off the dressing. "I'm not surprised."

"Three of us are from the same place," the Evolved continues. "Once our wings grew in, we knew it would only be a matter of time before we became the government's science experiment. So, we decided to leave before that happened. We took this castle and made it into our little safe haven."

"There," Payne says. "Now, let me take a look at your wing."

"Good aim," the Evolved responds. "I'm Julia, by the way."

"Sorry," Payne counters. "I'm Senior Master Sergeant Payne. That's Captain Hunter, Collins, Michaels, Jefferson, Clark, and Emily. You've had the unfortunate pleasure of meeting Sam, our resident Evolved."

"I'm sorry about your shoulder," I cut in.

"Apology accepted," Julia responds. "I'm just glad no one else was hurt. We've already had a few close calls."

"Yeah," Michaels interjects. "Except you guys are decorating the walls with people's heads on spikes."

Simultaneously, the Valkyries all burst into laughter.

"Would one of you girls please show them one of our victims?" Julia asks, in between laughs.

One of the Valkyries walks up to the wall and spreads her wings. With a powerful jump and just a few wing flaps, she reaches the top and removes one of the heads off its spike. Then she jumps off the wall and glides down gracefully towards Captain Hunter, presenting him with the severed head.

"Mannequin?" Captain Hunter asks in a confused tone, as he inspects the blood-encrusted wig.

"Just props," Julia says nonchalantly. "We figured as long as we were out of sight, people wouldn't harass us. But the locals just kept coming. Some even showed up with torches and pitchforks, while others brought shotguns and rifles. It was just like those old movies where the villagers go to fight some monster."

"We just wanted to be left alone," another Valkyrie chimes in candidly.

"We tried talking," Julia continues, "but quickly realized that stupidity cannot be overcome with reason. A few of us had experience with film props. So, we decided to manufacture our victims. We weren't out to actually hurt anyone. Some dummies to scare the dummies, if you will."

"Well," Emily chimes in, still wiping Julia's blood off her hands. "Despite appearances to the contrary, we didn't come here to hurt anyone either. We were actually hoping to enlist your help."

"You have a funny way of asking for help," another Valkyrie chimes in. "Showing up with guns and dropping in from the sky."

"That's fair," says Captain Hunter. "But our reports said that you were dismembering people and putting their heads on pikes. So, we had to take precautions. Plus we didn't open fire until you dropped Sam here from a hundred feet up and charged at us with medieval weapons."

"I'm sorry about your friend," Julia responds. "Sophie was abused pretty badly before she found us. I told her to scare you a bit and fly you out of the castle. I'm not sure why she dropped you, Sam."

"I cut her hand," I respond, carefully displaying the talon on the end of the tentacle. "It was more of a reflex. A pretty stupid move considering how high I was. I had no idea that I could take that kind of fall."

"Yeah!" Emily says angrily as she punches me in the shoulder. "You nearly gave me a fucking heart attack, Sam!"

"Sorry Em," I respond, feeling guilty.

"Well, perhaps we can start over," Captain Hunter, chimes in. "We are starting a sanctuary for Evolved, back in the States. We also have an expert who can explain why you evolved. Since you haven't killed anyone, I am sure your government would be happy to have you leave with us."

"I'm sorry Captain," Julia retorts. "These girls and I are not looking to become anyone's science project. British or American. We -"

"No one will harm any of you," Emily cuts her off calmly.

And that's why her dad wants her to create the messaging for the sanctuary, I think to myself.

Sometimes, Emily's tone can be so calming and reassuring that you can't help but believe anything she says.

"I know," Emily continues, "that you have no reason to trust me. But more and more people will evolve over the coming months. We won't force any of you to go if you don't want to. However, if you join us, you can find out why this is happening to you."

She pauses briefly, allowing the Valkyries to consider the idea. Some of them turn to one another whispering questions and doubts, but also some support.

"Julia," Emily says after a moment. "You seem to really care about keeping these girls safe. Come with us and help build a place where they can be."

In every sale, there is a decision-maker. Emily quickly realized that Julia is the key to the Valkyries here. Julia looks at the other Valkyries, scanning their faces, trying to figure out what they're feeling. There is doubt, concern, even fear can be seen in their eyes. However, there is also hope. Hope that what Emily is saying might be true.

"Give us a day," Julia responds, breaking the silence.

"Fair enough," Emily says confidently. "Captain, let's book some rooms at the nearest inn. I could use a shower and a stiff drink. We'll come back tomorrow."

She gives Julia a candid smile and extends her hand to help the Valkyrie off the ground.

"Thanks," Julia says, as she takes Emily's hand and gets to her feet. "Oh, and perhaps just knock when you come back."

Chapter XXVII

Nine months...

*A*fter the Valkyries, the Elves began to arrive in droves from all over the country. I still can't believe how many people answered Emily's social media campaign. The first week back from Ireland, only a handful showed up. No doubt skeptical about potentially becoming lab rats. However, with Dr. Majken's help, they quickly learned to control their abilities. As they shared their successes, more and more began to arrive.

Last week, we saw our first Centaur. She was amazing. The horse portion of her body was as black as midnight. The human portion was a beautiful mocha color. Her jet-black tail matched the color of her hair, neatly braided and hanging over her shoulder. As it turns out, she is incredibly strong, able to lift a two-hundred-pound weight with one arm, without much effort.

As the numbers swelled, we began briefing them on what is to come. Surprisingly, only a few of those who considered themselves 'preppers' decided to leave and try to make it on their own. Most, volunteered to stay and use their newfound abilities to help us in the upcoming fight.

Master Sergeant Clark was the first one on the team to begin exhibiting any signs of evolution. She is now able to draw energy from the surrounding air to make small flames in her hands. Dr. Majken insists that when the crystal's energy once again fully permeates the planet, she will be able to create fireballs! Other than this ability Clark looks completely human.

"Hey, Sam!" I hear Emily shout down the hallway. "Wheels up in 10."

Over the last three months, after our success with the Valkyries, we have been traveling almost non-stop. Dr. Majken has been busy compiling a database of all the species from the time of Atlantis. Their abilities, strengths, weaknesses, etc. This list has been invaluable in our fight to stop those who are using their abilities to hurt people. Moreover, it has helped us recruit those who are willing to join the fight.

On a grand scale, most of the Evolved who we come across are just like I used to be - trying to avoid becoming a spectacle or a guinea pig. However, there are enough selfish assholes to keep us busy as well. Akin to the Behemoth we faced when I first arrived here.

Last month, we ran into our first Dark Elf. Turns out they can make all the cells in their body nearly transparent. However, thanks to Dr. Majken's database, we knew exactly what to expect. Still, the son of a bitch eluded us until it got *dark. Then, he snuck up behind Captain Hunter and almost stabbed him with some sort of polymer blade. It was completely translucent. Somehow, I saw him at the last moment and impaled him with one of my tentacles. It came so close to Hunter's head, that he spent the entire flight back studying the nick it made on his Kevlar helmet.*

I have become faster and stronger over the last three months. With Dr. Majken's help, I've learned how to better control the reflex that used to take over my body. While in the past, it has resulted in the slaughter of whatever was attacking me. Last time I retained enough control to spare the guy who triggered the Ethros to take over. He was an Elf, who could conjure massive icicles out of thin air and launch them like missiles. As it turned out, he wasn't trying to kill me, just didn't know what he was doing.

"Five minutes, Sam!" Emily yells out from across the hall.

I put down the pen, close my journal, and grab my supply bag for our next operation. I cannot believe that this journal is almost full. Although it is most likely that no one will ever read it, writing down our missions and the stories about various Evolved species, appears to be helping with the otherwise overwhelming thoughts and emotions.

Ever since Senior Master Sergeant Jefferson nearly got an Elven arrow through his eye upon touching down, I always jump first. I figured that being bulletproof and all that, made me the only logical choice to be the team's bullet-sponge. So, I am always the last to board the plane.

"I appreciate your optimism, Dr. Majken," says Captain Hunter over the phone, while pacing inside the plane. "If the AGI's forces had to fight on two fronts it would definitely improve our chances. However, if I understand the time difference between Earth and Millanthea correctly, even if Joe is already there and convincing them to fight, it may be decades here on Earth before they are able to help us. All I am saying is that I do not think we should count on them."

I stow my bags, sit down, and focus my hearing, to try to make out what Dr. Majken is saying.

"You make a valid point, Captain," Dr. Majken responds, "but even if they attack a different front or possibly the AGI's home world, our chances improve. Regardless of what happens there, we need to focus on gathering as many Evolved as we can over the next nine months. We should also reach out to the other military powers. If dropping Joe's name with the Russians proved effective, we need to enlist other governments!"

"Yes," Captain Hunter responds. "But I can't be everywhere at once! All our teams have been running with virtually no time off. Trying to deal with more and more Evolved incidents. So, between my own missions and training new teams... You can't expect me to play diplomat on top of everything else, doc."

The pilot spins up the engines and I can't hear the remainder of their conversation. Captain Hunter hangs up the phone, plumps down in his seat, and throws his head back against his headrest. Then, quickly straightens up, puts on his headset, and opens his computer. As the plane's loading ramp closes.

"Hey Cap," Payne's voice comes through our intercom, "you ok?"

"I'm…" Captain Hunter pauses, obviously realizing that Payne will call bullshit if he says he's fine. "It's just a lot… The military doesn't exactly have a standard operating procedure for 'Train Your Team to Deal with an Alien Invasion,' you know?"

"They don't?" Jefferson cuts in with blatant satirical disappointment in his voice. "Do they have one for 'Train Your Team to Deal with a Psychotic Artificial Intelligence' or perhaps 'Humans with Super Powers?'"

"Fair point," Captain Hunter responds with a chuckle. "I sometimes forget that we're probably going to be voluntold to write those manuals."

"Fuck that noise!" Michaels cuts in. "If they try to force me to write an SOP, they'll get five-hundred pages of dick and balls drawings!"

"Of course," Gonzales chimes in. "I'm not sure what else they would expect from you. On the bright side, by the time you're done, at least you'll have finally mastered something in your life."

"Alright, settle down," Captain Hunter cuts in.

I've seen this before. One of them leaves themselves open and someone inevitably jumps at the opportunity. Then, the back and forth escalates into a day-long bashing of one another's skills, intelligence, stereotypes, etc. Nothing is off-limits.

I'm just glad that Em and I have been spared from these sessions. I think to myself. *I can't wrap my head around the fact that they can be so fucking mean to one another, then turn around and risk their lives to protect each other. I wonder if it's some kind of twisted version of sibling rivalry?*

"I want to give everyone an update," Captain Hunter continues. "

"You getting married, Cap?" Michaels snarks.

"Yeah, Michaels he is!" Payne retorts on Hunter's behalf, in an equally snarky tone. "To your mom!"

The team chuckles. In part at the joke, and in part at the fact that Payne was the one to deliver it. She always holds a certain demeanor - exemplifying senior leadership. Yet, she is still capable of knocking someone like Michaels 'down a few pegs' to keep him humble. She almost comes across as the mother of our crazy little band.

"I have an announcement too!" Master Sergeant Clark chimes in, excitedly. "I'm changing my callsign! Now that I'm Evolved, you can all call me 'Blaze!'"

"Nice!" Collins responds.

"Hell yeah!" Gonzales chimes in.

"I like it," Payne says with affirmation, "however, the Captain had something to tell us. So, let's give him a second."

All of us mute our microphones and turn our attention to Captain Hunter. Michaels and Clark, clearly feeling guilty for interrupting him.

"Thanks, Payne," Captain Hunter begins again. "Doctor Majken just finished assessing the Evolved who have volunteered to help us fight the AGI. She's working with the General and the leader of the Valkyries, to develop a training program. It sounds like we will have some powerful species on our side, by the time the crystal fully emerges."

"Having said that," Hunter continues, "I know that all of you have been going virtually non-stop since this began. You're all aware of the dangers we face. So, if anyone needs a break, I need to know right away."

"I'm good Cap," Jefferson responds after a brief moment.

"Me too," Emily chimes in.

One by one each member of the team unmutes their microphone to acknowledge that they're not about to leave the team hanging. I stay quiet to build anticipation, and inevitably all eyes land on me.

"Sorry guys," I say, trying my best not to smile. "I'm beat! All this flying around, constantly getting punched, stabbed, shot at, blown up. It's taking its toll, you know?"

The look on every one of their faces is priceless! It is as though someone managed to combine disappointment, shock, confusion, and frustration into a singular expression. None of them expected that I would be the one to back out of a fight.

"Shut the fuck up, Sam!" Emily finally brakes the awkward silence.

A knowing grin stretches across my face, just barely revealing my fangs. The entire team simultaneously bursts out with a mixture of laughter and relief.

"Damn you," Michaels says, "You fucking had me going there for a moment! I mean, I don't give a damn about you, Sam... I just didn't want to become the team's new bullet sponge."

"But Michaels," Clark joins in. "If you become the bullet sponge, we'll feed you extra crayons!"

"Shit!" Michaels fires back, without hesitation. "Why didn't you say so sooner? Sign me up!"

All of us chuckle lightheartedly. I have always found it fascinating that despite being some of the best in their respective branches of the military, each team member still proudly carries their branch's humorous stereotypes. Emily used to have to explain all of them to me - the Air Force is spoiled, so other branches refer to them as the 'Chair Force'; Marines, are referred to as dumb brutes, who love eating crayons; the Army is full of people who wish they could be Marines, but aren't good enough; and so on.

Initially, I was quite apprehensive about laughing at these people who have taken Emily and I under their wing. More importantly, each one of them has sacrificed their personal life to try to make the world a slightly better place, so that others don't have to. However, I have come to understand that this is just their way of keeping themselves both humble as well as sane.

They face atrocities that most people cannot imagine. So, rather than be offended, this is their way of staying grounded. Making fun of each other and being able to laugh at themselves. It makes all the misery just a little more palatable.

"Thank you," Captain Hunter jumps back in. "I am glad you're all in this with me. I have to admit that between training the other team leaders and having to assess their after-action reports, going out into the field with all of you feels like a break."

"I bet," I chime in. "Nothing like charging into uncharted waters to clear your head of bureaucratic minutia!"

"Yes," Hunter responds. "I wouldn't have believed that when we first started. But right now, I can't argue with you, Sam."

A crowd of onlookers watches as we descend into the center of a small German city. Although the residents were told that we are coming, I can imagine that to a civilian, our arrival may resemble an invasion. This feels different from our standard operation. Where we would simply parachute directly into an area where the Evolved are holed up.

According to the briefing, this group has taken up refuge in a dense forest just outside of Baden-Baden, Germany. The reports mentioned guided arrows, that are accurate enough to hit a small drone, mid-flight. So, in an effort to avoid any of us getting skewered, as we dangle helplessly from our parachutes, Captain Hunter made the executive decision of going in on foot.

As I descend, I notice that the morning air actually smells sweet. The city is surrounded by forests and a ruined castle overlooks the landscape. According to history, half of it is built on top of ancient Roman ruins. However, what is most fascinating, are the clouds of mist that cover the trees. I imagine that walking through the forest will be akin to stepping into a haunted fairytale. It is places like this that must give rise to the imaginations of storytellers when they write about mystic forests and magic beasts.

We suspect a group of hybrid Elves, who use a telekinetic ability to guide their arrows. However, by now I have learned that when we are facing a large group, their species, abilities, or country of origin do not matter. They all just want some place to belong. The hard part is starting the conversation and building trust, before catching an arrow to the eye.

CHAPTER XXVIII

SIX MONTHS...

I think if we survive this war, I am going to write a book comprised of my journal entries.

War, it seems to plague everything we are... Like the universe has had some kind of conflict for as long as it has existed. Joe mentioned a war that lasted a billion years. The Millanthean galaxy has been ravaged by war for over a millennium. Atlantis was literally torn apart by civil war. Today, and as far back as we can go within human history, war has plagued humanity...

It does not seem to matter whether the war is fought for territory, resources, or beliefs. It permeates all manner of existence. World War I, was said to be the 'war to end all wars.' Yet here we are, preparing for another.

I pause to wonder about what this means, and where it stems from?

Is conflict simply programmed into our DNA or is there some hidden force that drives us to destroy one another? The irony of it all is that each side always claims that they are fighting in order to end the fighting... This reminds me of something written on the ceiling of a barracks that I once stayed in: "Fighting for peace, is like fucking for virginity."

I close my journal and head to the briefing. Gradually, other attendees begin to trickle in through the doors. At one time briefings like this would be predominantly filled with old, white guys, wearing a ton of ribbons and medals on their fancy dress uniforms. Today's briefing is full of Orcs, Elves, Centaurs, Valkyries, and humans from around the world.

Among the first waves of Evolved, we found much more than just warm bodies for the front lines. Engineers, programmers, social media and marketing experts, and many other professionals, have all come together. Each one bringing some contribution to our efforts against the impending threat.

Many of them come from cultural backgrounds that have been in a perpetual state of conflict for generations. Yet, when they enter this base, these individuals are somehow able to leave their prejudices at the gate. There is no room here for debate over whose religious text is right or what is the proper way to worship.

Ethnic discrimination is nonexistent because your species trumps your skin color and any other feature that may have once set you apart. It is astounding that throughout history, some have used the now insignificant differences to justify hatred, ostracisation, or worse. Where would we be as a species, had we simply afforded others the chance to prove themselves as individuals, rather than deciding their worth based on the box they check on a form or in our minds?

In between training and honing their abilities, everyone pitches in to help with various efforts. From recruitment campaigns to designing armor and weapons. It is quite fascinating to watch groups and individuals who are not just of different ethnicities but entirely new species. All collaborating, in an effort to ensure the other's survival.

Why is it, I wonder, *that people only seem to rally when there is a common threat? The rest of the time, we seem to be at each other's throats. As parents, regardless of culture, people try to teach their children to share. Whether it is toys, snacks, video games, etcetera.*

Parents teach children that greed is wrong. That depriving others, regardless of whom the toy belongs to, is mean-spirited and ultimately leads to conflict. Yet, when these same parents are asked to share their resources, they choose to hoard them. At least until they face a threat that they cannot overcome alone.

It just seems fucked, that those who turn a blind eye to the suffering of others, are put into positions of power, and are then shielded from demise, by the very people they ignored.

"Good morning everyone," General Adams announces. "First and foremost, welcome to everyone who has joined us over the last week. As you may have learned, we have a wide range of task forces that you are welcome to join. Based on your profession and evolutionary skills, you may be eligible to join more than one. I encourage you to meet with the leaders of each task force, and identify which would benefit you most as well as make optimal use of your skill set."

"Before I turn the meeting over to Dr. Majken," he continues, "I want to thank all of you for your discretion about what we are preparing for. I realize that all of you have friends and families whom you would like to protect. I promise you, that we will authorize you to inform them well in advance. We will also do our best to provide them with the resources necessary to weather the coming war. However, for now, it is imperative that information about the AGI threat does not get out. A worldwide panic would make it impossible for us to prepare..."

"Now," the General closes, "I present Dr. Majken. Our resident expert on Evolved genetics."

It was Emily's idea to offer resources and an early warning as a recruitment tool. For every Evolved who joined us, it was a way of assuring that their family would have a better chance, both during and after the coming war.

Dr. Majken sits to the left of General Adams. Julia, the head of the Valkyries, sits on his right. It is good to see that she has healed completely, after the castle incident. Yet, I still feel terrible for having impaled her shoulder.

Although each group of Evolved only sends one representative, these weekly briefings are cast over a secured intranet to anyone on base who wants to watch. Moreover, our sanctuary has become the template for several other countries. They too tune into our secure broadcast. Most importantly, they have all committed to providing support, when the AGI's forces arrive.

Due to the sizes of some Evolved, the briefings are held in an old airplane hangar, that has been converted into a meeting hall. Tables and seats are arranged in a large circle, with cameras placed strategically in the center, in order to focus on whoever is speaking.

"Thank you General," Dr. Majken begins. "Starting tomorrow, all of you will have access to our ETD – the Evolutionary Trait Database. Keep in mind that this database was compiled from information about each of your base species. It is meant to teach you about your respective origins, known abilities, as well as weaknesses. However, most of you are hybrids - two or more species. So, we are constantly updating it, as we learn more about the interplay of your respective abilities. The idea behind the ETD is to help you understand what to expect, what to avoid, and how to optimize your training and abilities."

Funny, I think to myself, *I had early access and the section about the Millaethros is less than a page. While some of the others have a damn encyclopedia written about them...*

"As you use the database," she continues, "please send us updates on your specific abilities or combinations thereof.

It will allow us to improve the ETD. Which will be paramount to our fight against the AGI and to helping those who come later. The ETD will also help our Mission Teams better prepare for what they might run into before the invasion. So, a few minutes of your time now may save the life of someone in the field."

I doubt this applies to me, I think to myself. *Since I'm the only damn Millaethros around.*

"Next," she continues, "there seems to be a very high concentration of Valkyries, Elves, and Orcs in Europe. Although many of them have made contact with us or joined our remote sanctuaries, there are likely many more who have yet to join. So, to our European groups, please make an effort to reach out and bring them on board. With that, I will turn the meeting over to Julia."

"Thank you, Dr. Majken," the Valkyrie says as she turns on her microphone. "We will be sure to use and update the ETD. As some of you already know, we have created thirteen new mission teams, over the last three months. Their goal is to take some of the load off Captain Hunter's original team. Although his team still handles the more dangerous and unknown situations, our new teams play a key role in outreach and recruitment. Having said that, we need linguistic experts as we bring in Evolved from China, Africa, and the Middle East. So, please reach out to your respective leadership, if you are willing to help form a new Mission Team."

Is this a disaster waiting to happen, I wonder. *Some of the Evolved on these teams have a tremendous distaste for one another's culture, religious beliefs, and even ethnic backgrounds... This might turn into a powder keg...*

"We have also received word that the Russians will allow our military to pass through to the Atlantean Crystal, four months from now. They will initially only allow up to 5,000 human infantry units, in addition to all Evolved. If you are among the group that will be staged there, it is imperative that you don't do anything to create unnecessary tension with their military. If we don't stop the AGI's forces as they pass through the crystal, the war is lost!"

"Those who arrive in advance will help clear out all the areas around what is now lake Baikal. We want to create a standoff distance, from the crystal. Our aircraft - drones, bombers, and additional personnel transports, will only be granted access after the crystal fully emerges. So, those of you who are not there beforehand will likely be parachuting into a war zone."

"We don't have much information about the invading force," Julia continues. "Only that they are ruthless, and greatly outnumber our forces. Although it is unlikely that they will have any vehicles, we cannot be sure. Ideally, we will bomb their infantry into oblivion before they get a chance to get close to any of you. Additional, details will be available based on a need-to-know basis. Thank you."

"Alright everyone," Emily begins, as she switches on her microphone. "I will keep this short and sweet. Our social media engagement has been phenomenal. Your support in dispelling false claims about government experiments being conducted on those who come to our sanctuaries has been a huge asset. The flames of fear stoked by the ignorant are always our biggest challenge. Keep posting the truth about your experiences here, as well as how our programs are helping to develop your abilities. As General Adams said, please do not share anything about the invasion. We haven't had issues with that and I would like to keep it that way. You guys are awesome and I appreciate all your help!"

"Are there any immediate issues or concerns?" General Adams asks.

After a brief moment of silence, a Minotaur's head appears on the monitors.

"How, do we know that the enemy will not have vehicles?" He asks in a thick Greek accent.

"As I've mentioned," Julia responds, "we can't be certain. Based on the information we have, only a living creature may pass through the crystal. Aside from armor and anything worn on the body, nothing is able to pass through."

"How reliable is this information?" A man's voice, with a heavy French accent cuts in.

"The ETD," Dr. Majken responds, "contains all the information about the historical texts, predictions, and anything else that may be pertinent to your missions."

We chose not to disclose the details of what Dr. Majken really is, along with her role in Atlantean history, to anyone who didn't already know. General Adams, felt that it may create animosity among the Evolved and present a danger to Dr. Majken if everyone found out. More importantly, it would shift the focus away from the fight. As some Evolved might become distracted by the benign details of their history, rather than preparing for war.

I skim through the newly added sections of the ETD, while Emily, Julia, and General Adams address issues about dietary needs, minor training injuries, and expanding training facilities.

'History of Atlantis,' the first section reads. Atlantis existed well before most dinosaurs... A massive city housing well over a hundred million individuals... Hundreds of species from the Millanthea galaxy... Built without the use of any technology. The collaborative and coordinated use of the unique abilities of various species, built and expanded Atlantis over the course of a million years...

This is interesting, I think to myself.

'The Fall of Atlantis' I click on the heading to expand the section. Even with the advanced knowledge possessed by the people of Atlantis, they were not able to comprehend or control the crystal... When it plunged into the Earth's crust, it fractured Pangea into the continents of today... Killing most of the population within a matter of minutes...

Interesting, I think. Nothing about the civil war or the Atlantean Council. It makes sense that they would choose to leave those things out. Less for anyone to question.

'Abilities FAQ,' The next section reads. 'What are species-based abilities?' Your specie's abilities are akin to your senses. Much like if you were to try to explain what a flower smells like, to someone without a sense of smell. It would be next to impossible. It is not something they could see or touch. Yet, you would be able to identify a rose, for example, simply by its scent. Without ever having to see the actual flower. To them, this may seem like magic! Much the same way, your unique abilities allow you to sense and interact with certain elements. A connection or a bond that others simply cannot experience, because they lack the senses.

'Why didn't I have abilities before this?' The next question asks. Your abilities became dormant as a result of the Atlantean Crystal becoming submerged. It is unclear how or why the crystal impacts individuals in this way.

Suddenly, a group message pops up on my tablet.

"Emergency deployment. Briefing en route to destination. Beast is wheels up in 30."

Chapter XXIX

Final Transformation...

We named our C-17-X cargo plane 'The Beast.' Due to its ability to travel extensive distances while carrying an insane amount of weight. As we gather near the loading ramp, Captain Hunter explains the mission.

"We are headed to Japan. There are reports of ghosts raiding the homes of wealthy families between Nagoya and Tokyo..."

"Sorry did you say ghosts?" Michaels interrupts in a worrisome tone.

"Yes," Hunter responds. "Don't worry, according to our lovely ETD, they are likely Dark Elves."

"Oh good," Michaels quickly fires back with sarcasm. "That's not much better. You think I haven't read the stories?"

"Seriously Michaels," Senior Master Sergeant Payne cuts him off. "You are literally fighting side by side with a half-dragon. But you are going to be worried about some bullshit you read on some fucking Wiki site?"

"Fuck-off Payne," Michaels retorts. "Doctor Majken herself said that those myths are based on stories she told over the years."

"Yes, Airman dumbass," Payne quips. "She also told us that they were exaggerated over hundreds and thousands of years –"

"Enough you two," Captain Hunter breaks them up. "Dark Elves won't haunt your dreams or eat your flesh, or whatever other thing you read, Michaels. According to doctor Majken, aside from being very strong and fast, they have always had stealth. At night they are almost invisible and can appear translucent in the light. Something about their DNA allows light to pass through every cell in their body. So, to someone who has never seen an Evolved, they probably look like ghosts. Ideally, they will simply join us like most of the other species."

"So, who speaks Japanese?" Jefferson asks.

"Don't look at me," Payne responds as though the question was directed at her. "I was born and raised here."

"An interpreter should be meeting us there," Captain Hunter responds, as he walks up the ramp. "Don't worry English is a common language in Japan. After all Michaels, the Dark Elves need to be able to interrogate you."

"That's not funny, sir!" Michaels shouts back, as the plane's engines drown out his voice.

The flight to Japan is quite long. Although it allows Emily and I to read through the seemingly countless pages of the ETD, the rest of the team seems quite content sleeping, playing card games, and desperately trying to beat the next level of whatever game is on their phone. It is quite fascinating to watch men and women who have dozens of confirmed kills, seen some of the weirdest, most horrible shit imaginable, freak out over losing a game of blowing up rows of candy.

As we land, our translator greets us at the ramp. She greets each member of the team with a smile and kind words about how honored she is to be our guide. Her smile quickly fades and her eyes grow extra wide as she catches a glimpse of me walking down the ramp.

"Don't worry," I say smugly, as I notice her unease. "I don't bite."

"I'm so sorry," She apologizes with sincerity after quickly regaining her composure. "I have never seen anythi - I mean anyone quite like you before... I think I need to stop talking before I put my foot further into my mouth."

"Don't worry," I respond with a smile, unintentionally revealing my fangs. "You aren't the first and probably won't be the last. You should've seen my reaction when I saw this mug in the mirror for the first time."

She gives me an embarrassing smile and turns to Captain Hunter.

"Please, follow me," she says in a professional tone, pointing to a tour bus parked nearby. "Japan would like to take part in establishing a safe location for all Evolved. Our government has set up a well-protected facility where you and your team may stay. We hope it is to your liking."

"Thank you," responds Captain Hunter, as everyone walks to the bus. "I am certain that it is wonderful..."

As we leave the city, mountains and forests begin to paint a serene image. The beautiful scenery made the nearly three-hour drive seem far too short. Our bus stops at a military checkpoint, and a young officer boards the bus.

"My name is Commander Tetsuro," he says walking down the aisle, introducing himself to each of us. Pausing briefly as he gets to me.

"I apologize for my fascination." He says with sincerity as he shakes my hand. "I do not mean to stare."

"No worries Commander," I respond. "I am just happy that neither you nor our guide ran screaming."

"Nonsense," he fires back. "Your unique appearance has little to do with my hesitation. I have had the privilege of reading about some of your missions. Your accomplishments are incredible! As is the praise from both your Captain and General. It is my honor to meet an accomplished warrior such as yourself."

I look over at Emily, then at Captain hunter. I guess my transformation has not impacted my facial expressions - since both of them laugh at the look of confusion on my face.

"Hey Sam," Emily says through a chuckle. "I told you that you should read those after-action reports."

"You never told me there was anything in them about me specifically!" I respond. "I thought it was all just summaries to explain what we did in the field, to a bunch of pencil pushers."

"Well," Captain Hunter replies, "that's mostly what they are. However, they also contain the commanding officer's comments about the performance of each soldier... I'll spare you the details, Sam. Suffice it to say that both General Adams and I feel you are an integral part of the team."

Commander Tetsuro goes back to the front of the shuttle and takes over for the driver. The compound that our guide so humbly hoped we would like, turns out to be an expansive resort, near Nagano.

"This is where you will be staying," Tetsuro explains as he drives. "Our government has unanimously voted to turn this entire area into a preparation site for the Evolved and mixed units. Although there are no restrictions on leaving, you will need special badges to get back into the facility, as we wish to avoid tourists from entering. Once you have had a chance to inspect the facilities and provide your approval, we will open this sanctuary to others, throughout Japan."

"This place is amazing!" Payne exclaims.

"I am curious," says Captain Hunter, "why do you need our approval?"

"This facility in particular," responds Tetsuro, "contains the command center for all Evolved. We have smaller compounds open to any Evolved who wish to live away from the general populace. From here, though, you would be able to have secure communications and it will be restricted to those who will be fighting in the coming invasion. It is also meant to symbolize Japan's commitment to supporting the coming battle."

We park in front of what could only be described as a five-star resort. The soldier at the front desk issues each of us an ID card and explains. He explains that the complex security algorithm will grant us access to anywhere in the facility, except areas that require a PIN code in addition to the card.

As we are escorted to our respective rooms, I cannot help but feel uneasy. Despite this feeling, jet lag has taken its toll. Paired with the tranquility of the area, sleep all but beckons to me.

We choose our rooms one by one. Captain Hunter and I, opting for the two closest to the elevator. The door to my room shuts softly behind me and I drop my gear on the floor. Then, I close the curtains and flop down onto a bed that feels like a cloud...

Just as I predicted, I awake incredibly well-rested. Much to my surprise, there was no knock on my door, no one running down the hallway yelling for us to wake up. Just a peaceful night's rest.

A quick shower and then downstairs for breakfast, I think to myself as I step over to the curtains and slide them open.

The sunlight enters my room and I am faced with an astounding mountain view... The silence paired with nature feels tranquil.

These guys must have really invested in some breakthrough soundproofing for this resort, I think, as I realize that I cannot hear anything or anyone else, despite my enhanced hearing.

For a brief moment, I completely forget about why we are here. A part of me feels like I am on a nice getaway with Emily and some friends.

"Oh... shit..." I mumble as I turn and see my reflection in a large, wall-mounted mirror.

The tentacles on my back are no longer thin strands, hanging down to the floor. Instead, they resemble massive, swollen horns. Almost triple their thickness and pointing diagonally up and outward from behind my shoulders. The talons that used to be on the ends of each tentacle are now fused onto the ends of each horn.

"What the fuck?" I ask out loud as though expecting a response. "How the hell am I supposed to walk through doors and hallways with this shit?"

I knew I felt way too well rested, I start to think, recalling my past transformations. *How long was I out this time?*

I turn sideways and try to get through the hotel doorway, in such a way as to not scrape the frame with the talons on the end of each of the horns.

"Nope! Not happening," I say as one of the talons puts a deep gash into the door frame and the other into the adjacent wall.

This is why you can't have nice stuff, Sam, I think to myself.

I close my eyes and begin to focus. Visualizing the flexibility of my tentacles and thinking about moving them around. The feeling oddly resembles how my arm feels after I have slept on it for several hours – I know it's there, I know I should be able to move it effortlessly, but instead of doing what I want, it just feels numb and tingly.

Then, a strange sensation flows through my back and into the horns. My shirt tightens and I hear the distinct sound of tearing fabric. I move back towards the mirror and watch in both horror and anticipation, as the massive horns unravel slowly. A layered membrane drapes from each horn, both of which are now much narrower than they were a moment ago. The membrane looks the same as the one that stretched from my tentacles, down my back.

Finally, the seemingly solid horns, each split into two parts. The thinner portions, unfold outward from where the talons are, on the end of each horn. Almost like a forearm, bending away from the bicep. The membrane continues to stretch, until…

"Holy fuck!" The words involuntarily escape my lips. "I have wings!"

CHAPTER XXX

GHOSTS

Still, in awe of what just happened, I stare at the massive wingspan.

That has to be at least ten feet, I think. *Well, now I have to figure out how these work... Emily is going to lose her shit! Definitely better than tentacles!*

Without much thought, my wings just fold up behind me. Although very cool looking, I realize that although narrow enough, the added height will still keep me from fitting through most doors. Thankfully, this place has 10' ceilings. Otherwise, I would be asking them to patch up holes and replace a broken ceiling fan.

As I wonder how I will walk around, I decide to sit down on the bed. My wings reflexively extend backward and to the sides, allowing me to relax. Then, the tension in them subsides, and they fold over my shoulders and across my chest. I look up at the mirror and realize that I look like I am just wearing a cape.

That actually looks awesome! I think to myself. Sadly realizing that this is the first time that I have truly enjoyed the way I look.

I run out of the room and down the hall. Stopping at what I recall being Emily's door, I begin knocking profusely.

"Em!" I yell out loud, not thinking about the fact that the rest of the team may still be asleep. "Em! You need to check this out!"

They're all probably downstairs, I think after a few minutes without an answer. *They must be out, if Emily has not responded, and no one is yelling for me to shut the hell up.*

I scan my ID to activate the elevator. It takes a few minutes to arrive, and I enjoy the tranquil elevator music as the floors count down to the lobby. The elevator reaches the ground floor and the doors slowly part. The pleasant, tranquil feeling instantly disappears as my entire body is covered with little red dots. Instantly, I recognize the lasers from weapon-mounted sights.

As the doors finish opening, I see over a dozen soldiers aiming at me.

"Tomete!" A familiar voice yells out in Japanese.

Although I could not discern the next couple of commands, the lasers turn off, and Commander Tetsuro runs toward me.

"I am so sorry, Sam!" He says in a tone that is both apologetic and happy at the same time. "I am so sorry, please forgive me and my men."

"Uh..." I stumble for words. "Sure, I am happy to forgive you, but what the hell is going on?"

"We thought you were gone," Tetsuro responds. "It has been thirty-two hours since you arrived."

"Shit," I say. "My body is still evolving. When that happens, I sleep for way longer than normal. Where are Emily and the rest of the team, and what's with the firing squad?"

"We do not know where they went," he responds in a concerned tone. "They disappeared only hours after you arrived."

"Wait!" I interject "Did you just say disappeared? They're well-trained soldiers, not a group of middle-school kids or a set of fucking car keys! They don't just disappear! Where would they go?"

"They were taken, Sam..." He continues in a defeated tone. "The ghosts infiltrated our facility and took them."

"How the fuck is that possible?" I demand.

"There was a brief power outage," Tetsuro responds. "After that, they were just gone. We believed that you were taken as well... So, when my men saw that the elevator was activated, they thought maybe it may be one of the ghosts."

"I thought that this place was secure," I say still frustrated.

"It is," he responds confidently, "but there are miles of mountains. Plus, these ghosts have never attacked a government facility or taken anyone. In all the reports they only take money jewels, art, and electronics, then disappear."

"Well," I exclaim, "it looks like they've expanded their M.O. to include kidnapping! Have you received any demands? How were they able to take the entire team?"

"No... no demands," Commander Tetsuro answers. "We believe that they had someone on the inside. They disabled the power, cameras, and thermal surveillance. The reason we know it was the Ghosts, is that our secret cameras spotted a few of them carrying your team out of the building. Those cameras are tied to a separate server. So, even people who have access to the normal surveillance system, would not be able to turn them off."

"So," I say sarcastically, "let me get this straight... A group of Ghosts who magically knew that we arrived; disabled the security cameras; shut off the power; snuck past the security gate; through the property and into a secured building; got passed everyone and into our rooms; took each team member; and then carried everyone out without being noticed?"

"Sam," Tetsuro responds in shame, "these are not your common criminals. They are akin to the ninjas of ancient Japan. They are well organized and specialize in stealth.

The cameras that spotted them were only functional because they're on an entirely different system."

"We're working on upgrading security," he continues. "But we wanted to limit the personnel allowed inside. So, it takes far longer to cover this size of a complex. More importantly, based on the direction they left, they came over the mountains. We did not expect a coordinated infiltration to come through impassible terrain."

"Yeah, well it did," I state firmly. "Did you send out helicopters, drones, etcetera? Are you looking for them at least?"

"Yes, we are doing all we can." Tetsuro's tone sounds defeated, suggesting that they have absolutely no leads. "We even used dogs to track them, but the scent scatters at the stream and waterfall."

"Take me to where the dogs lost track of them," I say in a decisive tone. "I'm going to find them."

As I approach the waterfall, I begin to understand why they are referred to as 'ghosts.' The dogs surround a small pool, formed by a waterfall, coming from the side of a mountain. There is not a single trace of the Ghosts or my team. I doubt they were airlifted from here. The vegetation is far too dense. There are no vehicle tracks and I cannot pick up any scent, other than those of the Japanese soldiers and their dogs.

"I think they went underwater," I say as I pat myself down to make sure that I do not have any electronics on me. "There may be a cave behind the waterfall."

"We can get divers out here within a few hours," Commander Tetsuro responds.

"We are already behind," I reply. "I will take a look."

I check to ensure that my pockets are secure and jump into the frigid water.

Bingo, I think, as the bubbles around me clear. *That's where these bastards went.*

"Hey, commander!" I yell out to Tetsuro as I emerge from the water. "There is definitely a cave here. I will follow it and see where it goes."

"Don't you want to wait for a dive team?" He asks with concern in his tone.

"Send your men," I respond confidently, "and make sure they're armed. I might be bulletproof and all that, but we don't know what waiting on the other side."

I go back down and enter the cave. My vision quickly adjusts to the dark environment. The cave splits only a few feet beyond the entrance. As I focus, I notice a metal loop screwed into the wall of one passage. They probably tied their gear to it, so that they wouldn't leave traces on the surface.

I tie a small string to the loop, to ensure that the divers notice it. As I swim further in, I realize that my wings are acting like fins. Propelling me along much faster than I've ever been able to swim. A couple of hundred feet into the cave, I find a small pocket of air.

There is no way someone could make this swim without equipment, I think as I stop to take a few much-needed breaths.

My wings propel me through the tight tunnels. After another minute, I emerge from a small pool, inside a massive cave.

"Stop!" A voice behind me announces with authority. "Turn around slowly or you die."

I turn cautiously to find two men aiming at me with compound bows. Each one has a pistol, holstered on his leg. I guess their thought process makes sense - If the arrows don't work, the bullets will.

"Get out of the water..." One of them continues. "Slowly, with your hands where we can see them."

I opt to comply. Figuring that they will take me to the same place they take all prisoners. Hopefully, the same place where they took Emily and the rest of the team. As I emerge slowly, one of the men says something in Japanese over his radio. Likely to alert someone of my intrusion.

I wrap my wings around me like a cape. Doing my best to appear less threatening. Then fully extend my hands in front of me, completing the illusion of my surrender. Despite the fact that I am able to see quite well, I can tell that the cave is pitch black.

These Evolved must also be able to see in the dark. I think to myself.

"Stop," the voice commands after I take a few steps out of the water. "Keep your hands in front of you."

Some sort of bag is placed over my head and my hands are bound tightly. They bend my arms at the elbows and use the remainder of the rope to make a noose around my neck. Once they finish, I feel a tug at my wrists and a thin object is inserted between my wrists and throat. I quickly realize that this is a very clever way of binding someone.

The hands are bound only inches from one's face, but a short stick prevents the captive from reaching the knots with their teeth. The noose tightens if the captive tries to pull their hands away. Then a sort of lead rope is held by the captor. Therefore, if the captor tugs on the rope, it pulls the hands and simultaneously chokes the captive. Providing a great incentive to keep walking.

I hate this feeling of being bound and treated like a dog on a leash. I know I can use the talons on my wings to slice through the rope and rip these men to shreds. It takes every shred of willpower to keep up this charade.

If this helps me find the team, it'll all be worth it. I keep telling myself as we walk silently for what feels like forever.

Suddenly, I begin to hear what sounds like hundreds of voices, all speaking Japanese. We walk another four or five hundred feet. Then my captors stop and remove my hood. I am standing inside a pit, located at the center of a massive cave. Surrounding the pit are hundreds of people, all wearing a wide range of ninja outfits.

"Ghosts, stealth, dark elves, now it all makes sense," I whisper to myself. "Tetsuro was right in likening them to ninjas…"

On the ledge in front of me. A ninja in a white outfit lifts his head and pulls back his hood. He is older, probably in his sixties. He looks over me carefully and then begins to speak.

"Why have you come?" He asks in a thick Japanese accent.

"We are looking for Evolved to join our fight, against an impending invasion," I respond. "Why have you taken my friends?"

"You do not get to ask questions," he says sternly, as my captor tugs the rope causing me to choke. "Your friends have told me a similar story. About an endless army which will come here from another galaxy… Yet, my daughter tells me that you come here on a military plane, bringing with you weapons and technology to find and hunt us. Why should I believe that your intentions are noble?"

The guide! I think to myself. *She is one of them. Sneaky… but smart. I wonder how many others throughout that facility actually work for them. Hell, they probably have eyes and ears within the government and the military. That's why they were targeting the prominent homes. The thefts were just to throw off authorities – random home invasions. They probably coerced all sorts of people to help them through blackmail and threats.*

"We were asked to come here, by your police and military as a response to people's homes being broken into," I respond. "We are a military unit and we had no idea what to expect. So yes, we came prepared for conflict, but we are always searching for allies. Your own government established facilities to help Evolved like yourselves."

"You call them facilities," he fires back with a snarky tone. "We see them as prisons. My family has been in this area for countless generations. If the story your friends tell about Atlantis is to be believed, then it seems our people have been in this part of the world for millions of years. This is our land and you are invading."

"Look," I respond, "I know how crazy it must all sound. A year ago, if you told me that this is what my life would be, I would not have believed it either. But I give you my word, we are seeking allies against a common enemy. Please release me and my friends. We are not your enemy."

"I have lived long enough," he responds, "to have learned that words are cheap. If you wish for the ninja to support you, then you must prove to us that you are worthy."

"How?" I ask.

"We have traditions here," the old man responds. "I was told that you are very powerful. Thus, you will fight my three best ninjas. Should you win, we will release your friends. Loose and our council will decide whether to let them live or die."

"I do not want to hurt any of you," I retort. "Why – "

Before I can finish my question, a sword slices through the stick between my hands and face. I pull my hands apart and remove the rope fragments from my wrists and neck. Three ninjas jump into the pit, without hesitation. Their swords drawn and ready to attack... I can see that the conversation is definitely over.

One of the ninjas charges at me and swings his sword. Although I dodge the attack, it is evident that these guys are much faster than humans. They may be almost as fast as I am. I dodge a backswing from the same attacker by ducking under it and respond with a powerful punch to his sternum. He lets out a groan and staggers backward several feet. The speed and impact obviously caught him off guard. However, he recovers quickly and charges again.

As he swings his sword repeatedly, I dodge multiple attacks in quick succession. I block a kick to the body and deflect several more strikes with my hands.

"Enough!" I yell out.

My wing unwraps from around my shoulders and hits him so hard that he is flung against the wall of the pit like a rag-doll. Both my wings come up as I get into a defensive stance, in anticipation of attacks from the other two ninjas.

Before they charge, I can tell that they cloaked themselves. However, it appears that another benefit of being a half-dragon is that I can still see them rather clearly. I dodge a sword strike and simultaneously grab the ankle of the ninja who tries to sweep my leg. I swing his body like a bat against the other one but miss. As I release his ankle, he goes flying against the wall of the pit. Barely missing the first ninja who is just getting back to his feet.

I turn to the third ninja and I quickly realize that it is a woman. Without hesitation, she swings her sword in a downward chop. I block the overhead strike, grabbing her wrist. Utilizing the momentum, I put my hand on her abdomen and throw her over my head. She lets out a groan as her body hits the floor and the wind is knocked out of her. Fully recovered, the first ninja charges at me again.

As he swings his katana, I step backward, and my wing projects out in front of me. The talon that is in the middle extends out and connects with his blade, which splits into two pieces. He stops for a moment and examines the broken blade in disbelief, before discarding it to the side.

At that moment, I notice the young woman who was our guide standing on the edge of the pit. In her hand is a long staff. She turns it parallel to the ground and spreads her arms, as though wiping the staff. Immediately, I notice that the staff begins to glow blue.

The ninja in front of me runs up the wall, jumps just high enough to grab it from her hands, and then kicks off the wall with his other leg. As he flies towards me with the staff overhead, the blue energy gives off a beautiful trail. I jump back to doge the staff and it slams into the ground giving off a small shockwave of electricity.

She's an enchantress! I think to myself, as the ninja begins to twirl the staff, pressing his attack.

At this point, the others have recovered as well. Each one tosses their sword to the woman the guide. Much like the staff, she quickly enchants each one and throws them back to the ninjas. Except each sword glows in a different color. The female ninja's sword is bright orange, while the other is almost white.

As the first ninja twirls his enchanted staff, the trail it gives off is almost memorizing. I dodge another swing but miss the secondary attack. As it connects with my chest, I feel as though someone shot me with a taser. I take a step back, though more from surprise than the voltage. He begins spinning the staff again, creating a figure eight, and advances towards me.

Immediately, the other two ninjas jump over him on either side, delivering heavy overhead blows with their now-enchanted swords. My wings immediately form a canopy over my head. The talon in the middle of each wing blocks each sword respectively. However, this time the enchantment keeps the swords from breaking. A flash emanates from the white sword and ice covers a portion of my left wing. While a small ball of fire explodes over my right.

At the same moment, I notice the tip of the staff lunging towards my torso. I stop it, just before it connects, by grabbing it with both hands. The electricity courses through my entire body, but I hold on. The ninjas give each other a bewildered glance. The look in their eyes makes it evident that they expected me to cry out and double over in pain.

I yank the staff with incredible force. The ninja wielding it loses his footing and comes toward me. Though he holds on desperately, the speed and power of my pull catch him completely off guard. As he stumbles, I deliver a devastating punch to his chest. I can hear the sound of bones breaking in his rib cage, as he is launched backward from the impact. He flies across the entire pit and slams into the wall. The pain of the staff's shock dissipates and I realize that now I wield the energy of the staff.

I simultaneously push up against the swords with my wings. This creates an opening, as both ninjas are still off balance from their jump. Using the staff, I quickly hit each one in the ribs. Although the strikes are fast rather than powerful, the staff's enchantment is obviously far more powerful than I thought. Both ninjas scream out in pain, drop their swords, and fall to the floor, twitching from the shock.

Not wasting any time, I leap into the air. My wings extend and with a single flap, I end up nearly at the ceiling of the massive cave. Without thinking, I flap my wings again, this time to propel myself forward. Landing in front of the white ninja with a heavy thud. The impact causes him and others around him to lose their footing and take half a step back. Before he can draw his sword, I lunge the staff at his head. Stopping mere millimeters away from his face.

"Are you ready to talk?" I ask menacingly, albeit surprised at how calm he seems to be, given the situation.

"You are a worthy warrior," he responds, with an air of pride in his tone. "I speak for all the ninja when I say we would be honored to fight at your side. There are more than twenty thousand of us throughout Japan... On my honor, we will be there when you call."

CHAPTER XXXI

A SECOND SUN...

The plane finally levels out. I cannot help but think about the worst-case scenario. The command center near the crystal had been issuing updates every hour. The last update we received was that the fighting had not stopped since it started, over 24 hours ago.

We were told that the enemy had sacrificed nearly two million troops, just to get out of the kill zone - an open area between the base of the Atlantean Crystal and the front lines, where there is no place to hide from the bullets and bombs. Two million... and they are still coming.

I am not sure what I should be feeling. Regardless of how powerful our enemies were; no matter how much they loved or hated their evolution; or whether they despised us or wanted to join our cause; all our previous encounters have always had one thing in common - they all wanted to live.

Just as Joe had warned us, over a year ago, this new enemy is different.

Perhaps Joe was right, I think to myself. Maybe these guys are not actually alive?

"That is a fair question." A voice I had never heard before startles me and I immediately begin to look around in search of its owner.

"You can't see me," the voice continues. "At least not yet."

All of a sudden, I realize that I am no longer sitting on the plane. Emily and everyone else for that matter are gone. Instead, I find myself sitting on a camping chair, overlooking a beautiful lake. In the chair next to me is an older gentleman. In his hands is a loaf of bread. Which he is using to calmly feed the ducks, that are running around and swimming in the lake.

"What? How? Where the hell am I?" I demand.

"Well," he responds without looking at me, "that depends on your perspective... If you are asking about your physical body, then you are still on the plane. If you are more interested about where your mind is, we are sitting on the shore of a lovely lake in Scotland."

"Are you shitting me?" I ask flustered. "How am I here and there at the same time? Who the fuck are you and why did you bring me to Scotland?"

"You have nothing to worry about," he continues unfazed, either by my frustration or profanity. "Soon enough, you will be back next to your lovely Emily; headed into the fight that will not only define this planet, but also this galaxy. I brought you here because there is something you need first."

"What would you know about what I need?" I ask. "Also, how do you know me, Emily, or anything about what is to come?"

"You have asked several questions," he responds calmly. "Unfortunately, our time together is limited. So, like most things in life, you will have to choose which ones you truly want answers to…"

"Look," I say in a calmer tone, "if what you're saying is true, and my body is still on a plane, thousands of miles away. Yet, I am able to see, hear, and smell everything here. You're obviously a very powerful Evolved, with telepathic abilities."

"I am not an Evolved," he corrects me. "As far as knowing what you are; what you're about to face; or knowing the future… As I said, that is far more complicated than I have time to explain right now."

Not Evolved, I think to myself. Maybe this guy doesn't use technology. So, he hasn't seen all our social media campaigns. Shit, he'd have to be living under a rock for the past six months, if he isn't familiar with the term 'Evolved.'

"Alright," I say, still collecting my thoughts. "Then how and more importantly why bring me here?"

"The 'how' is of little importance," he says as he stops feeding the ducks. "As far as the 'why,' it is because I know that your true power has yet to fully emerge. However, without it, you have no chance of surviving the battle ahead... So, I brought you here to unlock that power. Your full potential, if you will."

"Ok, now I'm really confused," I say out of frustration. "How could you know anything about the battle or about my abilities? Despite not knowing that you are obviously Evolved."

"It has always fascinated me," he responds lifting his gaze toward the horizon. "That even when they're faced with evidence to the contrary, mortals tend to assume that what they believe, must be absolute."

"Mortals?" I ask, "You sound like Joe. So, if you're not Evolved, who or what are you, exactly?"

"I've been called many things and have had countless names," he responds, finally turning towards me. "When you've been around as long as I have, what people call you becomes rather irrelevant... The most recent cultures gave me names such as Odin, Zeus, Anu, and Raven, among others. Just depends on which mythology you subscribe to."

"Sorry," I respond in bewilderment. "You actually expect me to believe that you are a mythological god?"

"I don't expect you to believe anything," he responds with a soft smile. "You asked who I am... I'm simply giving you a choice. But, if you don't like the ones I've listed, you're welcome to call me Bob."

"All right Bob, the great god of duck feeding," I say in a snarky tone, "let's say, given everything that has happened over the last year, I were to believe you. Is this really what a god does? Just chills by a lake... and feeds ducks, while the world turns to shit."

"Ah," he responds, as though I should be having a moment of epiphany. "This is where your mortality impairs your perspective. From your point of view, I should step in and wipe out your enemies."

"Sure!" I respond as though it is obvious. "You are a god, the enemy is a crazy computer. You know - if rock beats scissors, wouldn't god beat computer? You created the universe, how hard would it be to smite an army?"

"Let's clarify something," he says, implying that I am completely wrong. "First, I did not create the universe. I was simply one of the first conscious beings to appear within it. Moreover, my ability to bestow life onto a lifeless planet does not create consciousness. I only infuse planets with basic living organisms. Sometimes, those organisms evolve and eventually become conscious."

"Second," he continues. "I do not control the lives of mortals nor choose the winners or losers. I merely strive to create a balanced opportunity, with the goal of perpetuating life... Tell me, Sam, what do you think is the difference between a hero and a villain?"

"Huh?" I mutter, obviously caught off guard by his question.

"Heroes and Villains," he restates. "Both usually possess some kind of above-average strength, power, knowledge, opportunity, or combination thereof. It sets them apart from everyone else. But what makes one a hero rather than a villain?"

"Heroes," I respond confidently, "help others. They build people up and protect the weak. Villains use their advantages for personal gain and to empower themselves. I suppose…"

"Alright," he says with a smile. "Then it is simply a question of motivation - one is motivated by altruism, the other by greed?"

"Yes!" I say, appreciating the simplicity.

"But," he interjects, "then, by your definition, the enemy you're about to face would be a hero."

"What?" I demand in confusion.

"This computer," he reiterates, "it seeks to save the environment, reduce waste, increase lifespans, eliminate war, and inequality. Most importantly, it is not seeking to empower itself. If greed is what makes a villain, then this computer is quite the opposite."

"Sure," I respond, "but it's taking away people's ability to choose. It is enslaving them!"

"Ah," he says as though he just proved a point. "So, it is not quite as simple as one's goals or motivations. Now you see my dilemma - If I choose to control how mortals live and what they can and cannot do..."

"You become the villain," I say, proving him right.

"You see Sam," he continues. "Conscious life is about choices. It is about experiencing growth and consequence; balancing personal freedom and social stability; ultimately figuring out who you are. If I dictate how mortals must live, then I remove their ability to determine their own purpose for existence."

"That seems like an excuse," I respond. "The amount of suffering on Earth is incalculable! Starving children, people with horrible diseases, murder, rape... I think you get the picture! You have the power to fix it, but, because in your opinion determinism is worse, you do nothing!"

"That's shit and you know it!" I continue to lay into him. "Maybe Michaels is right when he says 'Opinions are like assholes. Everyone has one and they all stink!'"

Much to my surprise, he doesn't appear to be getting angry. Instead, he tears off a small piece of bread and throws it to the ducks.

"I understand your frustration, Sam," he finally says after he is confident that I am done ranting. "So, why fight?"

"What?" I ask, still trying to calm down.

"Why fight?" He repeats himself. "Why risk your life, Emily's life, and the lives of everyone you care about? The AGI you're about to face offers the solution to all the things you enumerated and more. All you need to do is put on its armor."

"It's not the same," I retort, "and you know it."

"Would everyone in the world agree with you?" he asks calmly.

"I'm sure there would be some who disagree," I concede.

"Right," he says pointedly. "So, it is merely your opinion that my determinism would be preferable over the AGI's control or the world as it stands now. What was that thing you said about opinions?"

He raises one eyebrow and gives me that look, that a professor would give a student, who obviously had not considered all the points of an argument.

"You are half-right," he says. "If I were to exert some control or define a singular path for mortals, it would indeed reduce suffering. However, it would simultaneously eliminate the most valuable aspect of being mortal - Trying out various paths, to figure out the meaning of one's life."

"Over billions of years," he continues, "I've watched countless individuals. The ones who had the most incredible and joyous lives were not those who had the most power or influence; and definitely not the ones who followed some doctrine to perfection. Instead, the greatest lives belonged to those who made mistakes and overcame seemingly impossible challenges."

"Yeah," I cut in, "but how many failed? How many simply gave up and killed themselves?"

"Mortal life is a choice, Sam," he responds solemnly. "Every single day, you get to choose whether to overcome pain, struggle, sadness, the consequences of your previous choices, or the circumstances of society. In the end, each time you triumph, you become more resilient. Even if that triumph is as small as getting out of bed."

"Each little victory," he continues, "is a step towards self-discovery. For most individuals, overcoming adversity helps them to find joy in the little things; results in personal growth; drives them to figure out who and what they love. At times, it even helps others to grow as well. This, in and of itself, is one of the greatest facets of mortal life!"

"Thus," he says conclusively, "in taking away pain, I would also be taking away people's ability to expand their own consciousness and live their short lives to the fullest."

"But," I interject, "you're a god! Can't you provide guidance? Teach people to be decent, to live better lives."

"I never used the term 'god,'" he responds confidently, "nor have I ever desired it. It is a term that mortals attributed onto me... In fact, I never even told you that I'm a god. You yourself began using that word."

"Touché!" I admit. "But to be fair, you rattled off names like Odin and Zeus."

"Look, Sam," he sighs, "when Atlantis fell, the survivors were scattered all around Pangea, which was shattered and drifting further and further apart. Without their abilities, they were defenseless and would all perish. I gave them tools and guidance to succeed in their new lives."

"While you may see me as a god," he continues. "I see myself more like a gardener. Once I was satisfied that Earth was taken care of, I went to check on the other planets, which I had seeded with life. Affording the humans here the freedom to use these tools as they saw fit."

"So," I interrupt, "you have stepped in before!"

"Yes," he says with disappointment. "However, over the generations and millions of years that followed, the mortals here devolved into the most basic and primitive of beings."

"Well," I retort defensively, "their genetic codes were locked. They lost everything that they were."

"I'm not talking about abilities, Sam" he continues. "They used the tools that I had given them for protection, to slaughter each other! Instead of rebuilding society and culture, they became no different than beasts. It wasn't just their abilities that were lost. It was their humanity... When, I returned to Earth, only small, scattered pockets of survivors remained."

"I tried to bring order to the chaos," his tone fills with futility. "However, regardless of how I manifested myself, as divine or inspirational; leader or advisor; male or female... none of it mattered. The peace would only last for a few generations after I withdrew. Then, it was always back to dictators, authoritarianism, and destruction."

"All right," I say, "I understand that you want to allow people to determine their own path. However, why does it need to be so black or white? It seems to me, like a false dichotomy. Why can't you explain how the universe works along with some of what you told me, but stay out of daily life? So to speak."

"Perhaps..." He says with sarcasm, as he pretends to ponder the idea. "Maybe, I could stay hidden, so as not to influence people directly; but leave a set of instructions for a moral and peaceful coexistence? Something people could reference, knowing it came from a higher power?"

"Oh, now you want to make jokes?" I jest.

"Sorry Sam," he chuckles. "However, when you have lived through as much of human history as I have, you truly begin to understand the phrase: 'history is written by the winners.'"

The more I think about it, the more I come to understand his frustration with mortals. Even his guiding principles had been twisted by those in power, at any given time.

"Do you think," he continues, "that Odin was really a conqueror god? Or that Zeus was so petty that he punished mortals anytime he had a bad day? Or that a deity powerful enough to create all life, would damn someone for all eternity, simply because they were born in the wrong place or 'use His name in vain?'"

"Well," I say quietly, "when you put it that way…"

His point is undeniable, I think to myself. *Unless he literally spends all his time enforcing his teachings, there will always be some power-hungry individual or group, who will corrupt and cherry-pick his words. Just enough to where the story will fit their narrative. Providing rationale for waging wars or enriching themselves.*

"You see Sam," he says calmly, "there are some things that simply cannot be conveyed without a point of reference. Just as you would never be able to explain what the color blue looks like, to someone who was born blind; I will never be able to explain the value of a balanced life to someone who is insatiably greedy."

"Trust me," he continues, "I've spent countless millennia pondering this… It seems like every act of war, genocide, and criminal activity you can think of, can be boiled down to fear of loss; desire for more; or wanting something that is being denied. Be it money, power, resources, pleasure, whatever it is, there is always someone who is willing to burn others for their own gain."

"And stopping them," I complete his thought, "requires direct intervention. Which, would make you a tyrant rather than a guide."

"Exactly," he concurs. "When you pair that with my perspective, it should all make sense."

"What do you mean" I inquire, "when you say 'my perspective?'"

"Imagine a cup of water," he responds.

"All right," I say, as I picture a clear plastic cup filled to the brim.

"Now," he says as he bends down to pick up a small rock. "What would happen, if you threw this stone into that cup?"

"Most of the water would splash out," I respond as though the answer is obvious.

"Yes," he agrees. "Now, imagine throwing this same stone into the lake in front of you."

"It would make a tiny splash," I say confidently. "Maybe create a few ripples -"

"But ultimately," he cuts in, "it would not affect the lake whatsoever."

"That is your perspective of the world," I say, as everything he has been telling me finally converges into an epiphany. "Humans see the world as the cup, you see it as this lake…"

"No Sam," he responds in a somber tone, "I see it as an ocean."

With those words, he leans over and presses his index finger in between my eyebrows. Suddenly, I can feel everything around me in a way that I have never felt before. As though in a dream, I can see myself floating above the center of the lake.

My eyes beam with energy! Emitting a radiant blue glow. Electricity crackles between my fingers and along my wings. I draw energy from the surrounding air. It courses through my body like rage. Then, I look at the sky and let out a deafening roar!

At that moment, all the energy is released in a translucent, blue sphere of destruction. It empties the lake of water and eradicates everything it touches. As the blast disburses, the peaceful lake and surrounding shoreline become little more than a desolate crater.

Shit! I think to myself in horror, as I assess the magnitude of destruction.

Then, I am suddenly back in my chair, sitting next to the old man. The lake, the ducks, the trees, everything is back to the way it was.

"Before you go," the old man says with a kind smile, "I have one more experience to share with you."

"All right," I respond, still feeling the after-effects of the power I just unleashed.

"Now that you have felt the rage," he says softly, "and experienced the destruction it can cause, you need to feel its counterbalance."

With those words, he waves his hand and the world around us becomes completely still. The feeling is like sitting inside a painting. There is no noise, no ducks quacking, no insects buzzing. In all my years I have never experienced such tranquility.

Then, the sun begins to turn red. Its warm glow, replaced with cool circulated air. Distant voices disrupt the perfect silence and grow louder... As suddenly as I came to be at the lake, I am back. Strapped into my uncomfortable seat on the plane.

The ramp at the back begins to open. The silence and serenity are completely dissolved by the noise of the engines. Emily reaches over and takes my hand, as though reassuring me that it's all going to be ok.

CHAPTER XXXII

24 HOURS EARLIER...

A s the earth around the crystal stops moving, what was once the deepest lake on Earth is now completely filled in. In its place, a mountain stretches towards the clouds. Its faces are smooth mirrors, but instead of reflecting what is in front of them, they provide a glimpse into a different world...

A purple sky stretches toward the horizon. The ground is a sea of blue grass, dotted randomly by lakes, that look like they're filled with liquid silver.

The crystal releases a pulse, that passes through Earth's forces as a gentle breeze. It expands away from the crystal, in a limitless sphere, that encompasses the planet, almost instantly. Then, it continues through our solar system and beyond the Milky Way, into the far reaches of space.

Earth's forces surround the crystal. Pilots sitting in various types of jets and helicopters, stare in awe at the towering mountain in front of them. From their vantage point, they can see an ocean of enemy troops, who stand perfectly still as if awaiting their marching orders.

Several of Earth's tank battalions cover the hills overlooking the two-mile perimeter of empty space at the base of the crystal. The engineer units from the U.S., Russia, and several other nations, did their job well. Over the preceding months, they worked tirelessly to flatten out the terrain. Removing or destroying large rocks, and cutting down any trees or bushes. All collaborating to ensure that there would not be so much as a blade of grass for the enemy to hide behind.

Thousands of Earth's troops sit within their respective fighting positions. Many of them, nervously move their fingers along their weapon's safeties and triggers. Various species of Elves, Orcs, Behemoths, and countless other mythical creatures, stand alongside the human troops. As they wait for the first wave of onslaught.

Several hundred centaurs, anxiously lift and lower their hooves. In their hands, they hold mini-guns, each with at least five barrels. Belts of bullets, stemming from massive drums of ammo that are mounted onto either side of their horse-like torsos. As a last resort, customized sledgehammers are strapped onto their backs. Each with a long spike protruding from one side.

Snipers and spotters peer through their scopes, trying to identify the single target that is closest to the crystal. Meanwhile, several dozen high-ranking officers sit inside a distant bunker. One of them, nervously gripping a red nuclear launch control key, hidden in his pocket.

Finally, a single enemy soldier begins to move toward them. As though stepping out of a mirror, the enemy scout looks around, examining the situation. It takes less than ten seconds. Then, the scout kneels down and places a small object on the ground; turns around, and walks back into the crystal.

"Well that was uneventful," a sniper says to his spotter.

"Yeah," the spotter replies sarcastically, "maybe the guy saw us, shit his pants, and is now going back to tell them that walking into a killing field is not such a good idea."

"Anyone have eyes on what he left behind?" A staticky voice inquires over the open communication channel.

"This is Delta Leader," another voice responds. "It's just a box."

"I got it," another voice cuts in.

Then a centaur breaks into a gallop downhill, toward the crystal. As he bends down and touches it, the plain metallic box opens. Extending a series of small crystals, into an intricate carousel. A bright beam of blue light blasts out of the box, refracting through the crystals. Instantly creating a massive hologram. The blue, two-hundred-foot image is of a beautiful, almost-human, female.

"Please, do not be alarmed," she begins in a soft tone, though it is loud enough for everyone to hear. "The army in front of you will not attack without my order. Thus, there is no reason for any of you to die here today."

"Well," a soldier says turning to his platoon. "I was definitely not expecting that. If this is how hot all the aliens are, sign me up!"

"Your bravery," the hologram continues, "is undeniable. But it is misplaced. If your lives are anything like those of the people on my planet, then most of you must work, struggle, and make sacrifices throughout your entire lives. All in the hopes of a peaceful existence during your final years. Your life does not need to be so futile."

"Yeah!" Another soldier says, in a mocking tone, to the squad in front of her. "Just be a drone in my army and you got nothing to worry about. No stress, no fear, no thoughts of your own… It's bliss!"

"All of you," the hologram continues, "may enjoy a much longer and more rewarding life. Why die here? Even if you had a chance at victory, the reprieve would only be temporary. All of you would just return to your lives of struggle and sacrifice."

"I will permit you some time to consider my offer." The hologram says, after a brief pause. "Should you accept, simply lay down your weapons and approach the crystal. You may have my armor and no compensation is required of you... I hope all of you will make the intelligent choice."

With that, the message ends, and the hologram disappears. An hour passes... Then two... Then five... Finally, the hologram reappears. Only this time, the woman is a blood-red color.

"Your time has elapsed," the hologram announces. "Now you will all die."

As the hologram disappears, the ocean of soldiers on the other side begins to move.

"Movement!" Various voices announce on all open radio channels.

A wave of two hundred troops charges through the crystal. Clustered together as though they are centurions from Ancient Rome.

"Hey, look at these idiots," a chopper pilot says to his gunner. "Maybe they think we'll send the centaurs in as cavalry. Did this chick think that we're going to use swords against her army?"

"They forgot their shields and pikes," the gunner laughs in response.

"Tango 6," their conversation is interrupted by their commanding officer, "fire a rocket at the center of the group. Let's hope this was all a big waste of time."

The gunner locks onto the group that has suddenly expanded to over 400 soldiers.

"Fox 1," the gunner announces, as he pushes a red button on his control stick.

A flame erupts from the back of one of the helicopter's rocket silos. The rocket emerges in a streak across the vast open space. A single AGI soldier aims his gauntlet toward the incoming rocket and fires a small ball of energy. It connects with the rocket, which explodes harmlessly in mid-air.

"Shit..." A spotter says quietly as he watches pieces of the rocket fall from the sky, through his scope.

"Switch to the thirty-mike-mike," the commander says calmly to Tango 6.

The gunner flips a switch on his console and the reticle on his screen changes to a crosshair. He squeezes the trigger on his control stick and a burst of bullets streak across the night sky.

The front line of enemy soldiers all raise their gauntlets as though they were shields. Small perforations on the sides begin to emit blue light. As the rounds from the helicopter hit the group of AGI's troops, the rounds explode. But the flames and shrapnel harmlessly pass over or bounce away from the enemy.

"They have fucking force fields?" The gunner says in a panicked tone.

More and more enemy troops pour through the crystal, and their numbers quickly exceed several thousand. Edging closer to the Earth's forces as they continue to fill in the kill zone.

"Fire at will," A voice comes through the intercom to all helicopter units.

Almost immediately, the night sky lights up with rockets and tracer rounds streaking across it. Thousands of explosive rounds blow up inside AGI's troop formations. While most of the rockets are intercepted, exploding harmlessly in the air, a few make it through.

As the dust from the first volley settles, several hundred of the AGI's soldier's bodies lay scattered and dismembered throughout the battlefield. Leaving large patches of dead in the once-perfect formation.

"Yeah!" A helicopter gunner screams across the open radio channel. "Bring the rain!"

The helicopters fire several more volleys. All with devastating effects to the enemy troops. One at a time, each chopper breaks off from the formation, as it runs out of munitions.

As the first half of the helicopters fly back to rearm, another command is issued via the comms. From behind them, the soldiers of Earth's forces feel a dozen shockwaves. Massive fireballs light up a row of perfectly aligned artillery units, each one sending a 155-millimeter round into the sky. Within 30 seconds the rounds begin to impact the enemy formations. Massive explosions send bodies flying hundreds of feet in all directions.

The dust settles, and the ten-thousand-strong AGI force is reduced to a few hundred, scattered troops. Cheers and shouts begin to rise from all around. Some of Earth's soldiers begin to remove their helmets and wipe their foreheads in relief.

"Fuck…" one of the snipers says with a sigh, as he rolls over on his back. "For a minute there, I thought they were indestructible."

"Here they come again!" His spotter responds, and the sniper immediately flips back over to look through his scope.

Within seconds a new wave of AGI forces enters through the crystal. This time they do not set up a defensive perimeter. Instead, they charge away from the crystal towards the front line. Another volley of artillery rounds soars into the sky.

The rounds splash down in massive explosions, killing and dismembering thousands. Despite this, numerous AGI troops make it safely around the blasts and advance toward the front line with astonishing speed. As thousands more continuously pour through the crystal in a seemingly endless stream of enemies.

Chapter XXXIII

2 HOURS OF FIGHTING...

The hill surrounding the two-mile kill zone in front of the crystal suddenly lights up with flashes the size of small cars. Dozens of tanks begin firing into groups of AGI soldiers who make it past the artillery barrage.

The tanks fire flechette rounds. Each one, filled with a dozen spikes that shred enemy troops like pellets from a shotgun. The command room, in a reinforced bunker, is filled with computer monitors. All clearly displaying the carnage around the crystal. The video feed streams from a set of drones, circling thousands of feet above the fight.

The forward command center, only a few miles behind the front line, then beams the footage to a set of low-orbit satellites, above what was once Lake Baikal. Ensuring optimal communication and providing live feeds to other command centers, across the globe.

Only two hours after the first round was fired and it is already impossible to calculate the death toll. The artillery batteries now fire in rapid succession, rather than in volleys. Leaving mere seconds between the impacts of their rounds.

The fighter jets armed with bombs and air-to-ground missiles have yet to use any of their armaments. Those AGI troops who make it past the artillery, helicopters, and the barrage of flechette rounds, are then mowed down by the tanks' machine-gun fire.

The few who make it within 500 yards of the troops, entrenched at the edge of the kill zone, are taken out by snipers. Not a single AGI soldier has been able to make it close enough to effectively engage the Earth's infantry, and not a single human or Evolved has fallen.

"I might be speaking out of turn," a German Colonel standing in the front-line command center announces, in a thick German accent, "but it seems that this Artificial Intelligence has underestimated our forces."

"For all our sakes," responds General Adams, "I sincerely hope you are correct. Our assessments showed that the AGI's army was close to 10 million units. Even at the current rate of loss, the attack may last several more days."

"Do not worry General," says a Russian Colonel, with Zhukov written on his name tag. "My boys will keep our forces in the fight. Our system of logistics was set up to be able to sustain continuous fire into the kill zone. Even if the enemy draws this out, we have fresh troops and fueled vehicles, ready to relieve those who need to a break. We have learned quite a bit about holding ground from the two World Wars."

"I am not doubting the military prowess of the Russian forces, Colonel," responds General Adams. "I too have several thousand men and women out there. All of whom have spent months preparing for this. I am more concerned that our enemy is not just hoping that we'll run out of ammo. We are fighting a supercomputer that was able to conquer an empire. Which, at one point, stretched across multiple solar systems."

"With all due respect, General," Colonel Zhukov retorts smugly. "My people, have a history of beating computers at strategy."

"With all due respect," General Adams fires back, clearly both irritated and concerned, "we are not playing chess here! However, since you have made the analogy, if this AGI was doing just that, it is presently sacrificing pawns. In chess, when you sacrifice pieces, you are typically moving into position to either take the queen or checkmate the king..."

"Are you implying that this AGI, will target the command center?" The German Colonel asks hesitantly.

"It doesn't seem possible," replies General Adams, "but neither does a checkmate in five moves..."

The continuous bombardment from artillery has made it impossible to identify the number of casualties or troops pouring through the crystal. Most die within a few seconds of stepping foot on Earth. Arial surveillance clearly shows several million troops, still remaining on the other side.

The helicopters, refueled and rearmed, are now on standby, only minutes from the fight. Fighter jets have also been refueling and taking off in small groups. Ensuring that they can provide heavy air support at a moment's notice.

"This is going to be a long day," a sniper says to his spotter. "Let's call for a relie -"

Before he finishes his sentence, an invisible blade punctures through his bulletproof vest and his chest. Plunging into the ground under him. His spotter's eyes grow wide with shock as his brain tries to figure out exactly what is happening.

Unable to scream or move his head, confusion turns to panic. In his last moments, the spotter sees his own blood, dripping off another invisible blade. The tip, protruding about a foot out of his gaping mouth. He never even felt it enter the back of his skull. As his vision fades, the spotter falls over onto the sniper's back.

This scene repeats hundreds of times, all at once, down the length of the entire kill zone perimeter. Infantry teams, observe streams of blood gushing from the backs of snipers, as well as the mouths and throats of their respective spotters. Yet, no one can see let alone identify, the assailants responsible for the carnage.

Clearly caught off guard, the complacent infantry squads scramble for their weapons and take cover in what were supposed to be fall-back positions. They begin blindly firing in the general direction of the now-dead sniper teams. Whom they were assigned to protect.

"Contact! Contact!" Horrified voices of men and women come across various radios in the command center.

" - stealth!"

" - are shielded!"

" - invisible!"

Are the few words that can be discerned from among the dozens of voices that overlap one another's radio transmissions. Each, followed by gurgled screams and groans, before cutting out completely.

"What the hell is happening?" A lieutenant in charge of radio communications demands. "How did they get through? I thought we had thermal cameras; we should have been able to see any stealth units."

"You assumed that they didn't have the technology to cloak their heat signatures," replies General Adams in frustration, as he grabs his radio. "All teams! All teams! The enemy is using stealth! It is not visible to our thermals! I say again, thermal imaging is unreliable!"

As though on demand, hundreds of Elves positioned around the perimeter spread their arms and begin to channel ambient energy into spheres of light. Within seconds, the glowing orbs are launched into the air, where they hover steadily. The dark night that had previously only been disrupted by flashes from explosions, is now dispelled by the combined glow of hundreds of light spheres. Illuminated by the Elven light, the battlefield comes into focus.

Staring at the screen, everyone in the command center and around the world gasps at the carnage. Corpses line almost every square foot of the kill zone. They are piled on top of each other, having been flung there by massive explosions from the artillery rounds. Red, orange, blue, green, and purple streams of blood seep away from the piles of dismembered bodies. Pooling together into a brown slush that soaks the two-mile standoff distance.

Thousands of AGI troops, continue to pour through the crystal, taking refuge behind their shields and piles of bodies. Each artillery strike seems to kill fewer and fewer enemies, but creating new paths for others to follow without direct exposure to the blasts.

As leaders around the world observe the carnage, each one falls to his or her own religious solace. Some trace the points of a cross across their chests, others begin to pray out loud. Even those who have deemed religion as a weakness, pray silently for fear of appearing weak in front of their staff. However, the soldiers on the front lines have no such luxury, as they realize that thousands of stealth units are already upon them.

Countless translucent ghosts, rush across the bodies of the fallen. Like a swarm of ants, spreading away from the crystal, they pass over and between the piles of the dead. Although not a single regular AGI soldier has made it past the 500-yard mark alive, the stealth units penetrated deep into the ranks of the Earth's army. Even under the light of day created by the Elves, they are difficult to see. Their specialized armor warping light even as they move.

The infantry fires wildly at the fast-moving, nearly invisible assailants. However, most of the bullets are deflected by protective shields. Even after their shields fail, the armor absorbs much of the damage from the small arms fire. Energy blades extended from their gauntlets, slice through squads of men and women, as though they are weeds being hacked apart by machetes.

The fighter jets begin to drop their bombs and fire missiles at the streams of illuminated stealth units. Soon, the entire kill zone is crisscrossed with walls of fire from newly formulated napalm bombs. Flame throwers set help set the nearby enemies ablaze. Turning the stealth units into flaming monsters. All grounded helicopters and reserve planes are quickly scrambled for takeoff.

The stealth units that made it even further, behind the front lines, begin to attack the tanks. Using their blades to cut the barrels off every vehicle they come across. As the crews emerge to fight back, most are cut down without ever firing a single shot. The tanks in the back begin targeting those in front of them. Using flechette rounds and machine-gun fire, they aim to kill the enemy without blowing up their friends.

With the crystal's energy once again permeating the world, the Evolved begin to realize their full potential. Elves draw their bows, charging their arrows with fire, electricity, or ice. As they let loose, the arrows fly at seemingly impossible speeds piercing through the enemy's shields and armor alike.

Some electrified arrows release bolts of lightning severely damaging or shorting out the shields and stealth of nearby units. Stunning them and leaving them susceptible to attack. While those imbued with fire and ice cause devastating explosions or shatter into razor-sharp crystals. Each one killing multiple enemies at once.

Behemoths swing wildly with massive clubs. Smashing the enemy into the ground or sending their broken bodies flying across the battlefield, until they crash into armored vehicles or defensive structures. Valkyries take to the skies and dive like falcons. Delivering devastating blows or decapitating their targets with blades and hammers, charged with Elven energy.

Like the cavalry of old times, the Centaurs charge into the fray. Wherever they see an AGI soldier, they spray the area with a barrage of bullets from their mini-guns. Hitting the one they were aiming for, along with several cloaked units.

The Valkyries, having killed all the units that were attacking the tanks, take to the skies to identify where they're needed next. As she leads their formation, an energy blast nearly misses Julia. It passes so close to her face that she can feel its energy as it zooms by. For a brief instant, everything seems to grind to a halt.

The bullets appear frozen in mid-air. On the ground, the blood of the AGI's troops mixes with that of humans and Evolved alike. Thick mud now coats everything as though it had been raining for days. Many die before their bodies ever hit the ground. Piles of dead create mounds and trenches throughout a previously flat landscape.

Massive fireballs and arcs of lightning stream into the kill zone from the Evolved who managed to beat back the stealth units around them; and are now focusing all their efforts on preventing more from reaching the front line.

The death toll is incalculable... Julia thinks to herself as she banks hard and dives towards another group of embattled soldiers.

Other Valkyries follow her lead. Like massive falcons, they dive from high above, delivering killing blows to the AGI's troops. Then picking up any that were not hit and flinging them back into the kill zone, or flying them high above the battlefield and dropping them to their death.

The rearmed and refueled helicopters return to the fight and take aim at pockets of enemies streaming through the paths made by piles of the dead... Suddenly, several dozen AGI troops stop and take aim at the helicopters. Just moments before the next artillery round lands on them, a volley of energy blasts is released from their gauntlets, in an almost perfectly synchronized attack...

As the energy from each shot courses through the steel frames, the fuel tanks and unfired rockets aboard each helicopter explode. Most of the helicopters blow up in midair. Their burning shells crashing down onto the troops below. A few lose all power, stall, and begin spiraling out of control. The pilots and gunners can only watch, as the swirling ground gets closer and closer, powerless to prevent the impact.

"They just took out all the fucking choppers!" A panicked voice is heard yelling over the radio, in the command center.

General Adams and several other officers collapse into the chairs behind them.

"That..." A Russian General struggles to find words in English. "That was over one-hundred-fifty helicopters, destroyed in less than ten seconds... Three. Hundred. Men! How?"

"Shit!" General Adams utters in disbelief, as he buries his head in his hands. "I thought we were beating them back..."

The room falls silent, as all the officers seem to struggle for words. Each one of them quickly comes to the realization that the 300 helicopter crew members are only a drop in the bucket, compared to the thousands of men and women who have been killed on the ground.

"Send an order to the jets," General Adams breaks the silence, as he pulls his head from his hands. "Have them time their strikes between the artillery blasts. They should be fast and far enough to avoid being targeted. Tell the tanks to only fire at the fringe groups that make it past all the rest. We must hold until the reinforcements arrive!"

Chapter XXXIV

The sun has come and gone and the Elves have sent up new spheres to light up the night. General Adams' plan to time the air strikes in between artillery volleys, rather than continuous bombardment, proved to be very effective. It made a significant impact on the enemy's ability to advance. Affording the ground forces the chance to defeat the troops who had made it out of the kill zone.

However, the enemy continues to pour in through the crystal. Any break in bombardment affords thousands of AGI troops an opportunity to charge the front line. Exhaustion and hunger make every minute feel like hours. Even fighting in groups to allow for short periods of rest and relief, is helping less and less.

The Centaurs have run out of ammo long ago. Shedding the massive ammo drums and mini-guns. They now fight with swords and hammers. Even the seemingly inexhaustible Behemoths are staggering under the weight of their massive weapons and succumbing to the enemy's energy blasts that previously had little effect.

Reinforcements that were staged miles away have been brought in. However, even they are starting to falter to the exhaustion of the incessant firefight. The artillery and tanks continue to pepper the kill zone. Still taking out massive amounts of enemy troops, but making it almost impossible to rest.

In the face of the enemy's relentlessness, the Russian government quickly allowed any and all countries to bring in aircraft, tanks, infantry, and supplies. Anything to help bolster the Earth's defenses. However, those forces are hundreds of miles away.

Only the aircraft - fighter jets and bombers have been able to make it in any reasonable amount of time. Affording a brief reprieve to those pilots whose only breaks consisted of refueling and rearming. A few supply planes from China have landed, bringing more ammo and food. Some lighter vehicles trickle in for support, but the heavy guns are still days away.

"We need to increase rotation times," General Adams says wearily. "Our men and women need to sleep."

"As do you General," responds Colonel Zhukov, who just got back from a lengthy two-hour nap. "You have not slept since well before the fighting began. This puts you at over fifty hours, with no sleep. It is time to step back. The reinforcements are on their way, we have been resupplied. At this rate, little will change in a couple of hours."

"You are right..." General Adams admits in a defeated tone. "The coffee isn't doing shit anymore. Though if we make it through this, I want a pallet of it sent to the US quarterly."

"I am glad to see you still have your sense of humor, General," Zhukov replies with a sincere smile.

General Adams stumbles out of the command room and towards an elevator. Which, serves as the only way to get to the sleeping quarters. Deep below the surface and miles away from the kill zone, he finds an empty cot. The others are filled with officers from almost every country in Europe.

As he lays down, onto what most would consider an incredibly uncomfortable, styrofoam mattress, his exhausted body feels like it is on a cloud. The nearby artillery batteries continue to fire. This deep underground their consistent thuds now have an almost hypnotic effect. He closes his eyes and fades off into the darkness.

His rest is short-lived, however, as he is snapped awake by a blaring siren and strobing red light. General Adams opens his eyes and stumbles back into the elevator, without waiting for anyone else. As he exits, a Russian Lieutenant rushes past him, without so much as a word.

Although normally this would seem disrespectful, as the elevator doors close between them, General Adams notices that the Lieutenant's eyes are filled with tears.

"What the fuck is going on?" He demands as he bursts through the doors into the command room.

The handful of Russian officers and enlisted sit at various computers in an adjacent room, visible through a sound-dampening glass. The men and women shout back and forth in Russian, while frantically typing on their keyboards. Colonel Zhukov and the Russian General, stare at a single screen that reads 'No Signal' in various languages.

"What the fuck is happening, Colonel?" General Adams demands, physically shaking Colonel Zhukov, to get his attention.

"It hacked us…" The Colonel responds with dismay.

"Hacked us how?" General Adams asks in confusion.

"Some of their stealth units," Colonel Zhukov responds. "They must have gotten through and hacked into our satellite and communication arrays. Our systems are down, and we are completely cut off from the other command centers."

"All right," General Adams says decisively. "How long will it take to get everything back?"

"It does not matter," the Russian General standing next to Zhukov, interjects in a thick accent. "We are lost…"

"What? Why?" General Adams demands in confusion and frustration, at the despair in the men's tones.

"Because," responds the Russian General, "a few years ago we took a note from the Israelis. Their tanks can be guided by satellite. To bring them back to base in case the crew is killed."

"We put this technology into all our planes." Colonel Zhukov takes over the conversation, to help the General who is struggling to explain the situation in English. "It would prevent the planes from being stolen. More importantly, it would give us a back door into those that we sell to other nations. So, if they tried to attack us with our own aircraft, we could just take the plane over and turn it against them."

"Wow," General Adams responds, shocked by the brazen idea. "So, what does this mean? Can't your pilots override the system?"

"No," Zhukov responds. "We took our system to the next level. We wanted to make sure that if a pilot decided to defect, we can lock them out of the plane's controls. This also gave us the ability to turn all our planes into drones -"

"Fuck..." General Adams cuts him off, as he realizes the implication. "So the AGI can use the weapon systems."

"Yes," the Russian General interjects, with despair.

As they speak, the Russian pilots lose all control of their planes. Some target the artillery batteries, and others, lock onto allied jets and fire their missiles. From the ground, the night sky is instantly filled with explosions.

Hundreds of planes explode in mid-air. Within minutes, the AGI has taken down the greatest, international air combat fleet ever assembled. The air-to-ground missiles and bombs, take out a majority of artillery units. Once out of ammo, each Russian fighter jet sets a collision course for a supply depot, barracks, runway, or any other strategic target.

As the final artillery round falls in front of the crystal, it becomes evident how the AGI managed to accomplish its hack. A small group of AGI infantry linked hands through the crystal, with a group on the Millanthean side.

The two to three million remaining units diverted their energy to supply continuous power to the shields of the small group in front of the crystal on Earth. Affording them the ability to withstand the constant bombardment. More importantly, it also gave the AGI an uninterrupted data link to Earth.

It only took a single stealth unit to get to the satellite communications tower. Then, the AGI hacked all the firewalls and took control of the Russian satellites and computer systems, within the command center. Giving it total control of all Russian aircraft.

Far from the kill zone and the Elven lights, the command center is shrouded in darkness. Running only on backup generators, the only source of illumination is a few flickering emergency lights and whatever is left of the burning artillery batteries. As the guards for the command center search for the location of the infiltrator, they are mercilessly cut down by the seemingly invisible foe.

"We don't have a choice," says Colonel Zhukov. "We must use the emergency fallback protocol."

"What protocol?" Demands General Adams.

The Russian General looks at the Colonel as though condemning him for speaking out of turn or revealing something that General Adams was clearly not supposed to know about.

"What fucking plan?" General Adams yells in a commanding voice.

"We have buried fifty nuclear warheads, leading away from the crystal," Colonel Zhukov responds reluctantly. "Once we detonate the one that is next to this command center, control moves to the Kremlin. From there, they will detonate them as the enemy advances further and further from the crystal."

"Have you lost your fucking minds?" General Adams yells out in bewilderment. "We're sitting on top of a nuke? Our men and women are out there! Even if your government doesn't give a shit about foreigners, there are over 100,000 Russian souls out there!"

"It was a measure of last resort," the Russian General responds. "At the rate that the enemy has been coming in, they will have a million soldiers out there within an hour. Our troops will not survive for much longer. This would be a mercy to them."

"No!" General Adams says sternly. "I have at least one-hundred-and-fifty C-17, aircraft, heading this way with reinforcements. All the special teams of humans and Evolved who have been training for almost a year. Their abilities, my gunships, and the troops who are already here will be enough to hold off the AGI's forces until reinforcements from the other nations arrive."

"I am sorry about your men and women," the Russian General responds. "I too wanted to come home a hero. Unfortunately, my orders are clear - if it becomes obvious that this command center is going to fall, I must detonate the first nuke."

"My own daughter is on one of those planes!" General Adams says with furious desperation. "She is coming here to fight! I will not let your orders or your cowardice, be the end of her. If either of you so much as move towards trying to detonate this nuke I will kill you where you stand. Even if it means spending the rest of my life rotting in some Russian prison!"

With those words, he pulls his pistol out of its holster and takes aim at the Russian General.

Fuck! General Adams thinks to himself. That is why that Lieutenant rushed passed me! He wasn't going downstairs to sleep. He stopped the elevator from going back down. They trapped everyone else downstairs so that no one else would interfere!

"I understand," the Russian General says calmly with his heavy accent. "My son is here as well. I think you passed him on your way from the elevator. You think I wish for him to die?"

"Your son," General Adams retorts, "is the only thing keeping some of the world's top officers from helping us! We just need to buy a little time. Last I heard, they were an hour away! At this point, it's minutes! Just wait!"

Unfazed, the Russian General closes his eyes and nods his head, as though sending a signal. Before General Adams has a moment to figure out what it means, he is hit in the back of the head with a heavy object... As he comes to his senses, he finds himself handcuffed to a metal chair. Next to him, are two officers from the adjacent room.

Fucking bastard General Adams thinks. As soon as I pulled my pistol, he saw them coming. That's why he was so calm! He kept me talking to give them time to sneak up on me.

"I truly am sorry General," Colonel Zhukov says solemnly. "We had no intention of hurting you, nor do any of us wish to die here. However, this is our country, not yours. We must protect her and the rest of our people."

"Damn you all!" General Adams cries out, struggling to break free. "Give my people a chance! All of them are coming here, prepared to fight and die to protect our planet. Including your fucking country!"

As though he can no longer hear him, the Russian General turns the key to activate his manual link to the nuke buried just outside the command center. The red button to detonate begins to flash and a robotic voice announces something in Russian over the intercom.

"Please! Don't do this!" General Adams continues to plead with the Russian officers.

The Russian General stands at attention, to him, General Adams' pleas sound distant and muffled. Colonel Zhukov reaches into his pocket and takes out his cell phone. After a few taps on the screen, the Russian national anthem begins to play through the phone's speaker. Both he and the Russian General turn to salute their flag, as the anthem plays.

Tears roll down their faces, as they realize that these are their last moments. Both men think about their wives, whom they will never see again. Their children who, if they survive this invasion, will have to live life without them. They can imagine the horrors the men and women on the front line are witnessing. All of whom will soon perish in a single instant.

As the anthem comes to an end, the Russian General and Colonel Zhukov wipe their tears. They turn to one another and express the honor they felt serving by each other's side. Then as the Russian General moves his hand to detonate the nuke, a deep vibration gives him pause. Then another, and another. As wave after wave of massive aircraft flies over the command center and towards the kill zone.

"They're here!" General Adams cries out. "Please! Don't kill my little girl…"

Chapter XXXV

The Childhood Crush

Those eyes... I remember when they were the color of a cloudless summer sky. Like two blue crystals that refracted the light, almost as if toying with it. I could gaze into those eyes for hours. Perhaps it's cliché, but there is something to the idea that eyes are the windows to the soul. If that is so, then Sam had the purest soul of anyone I've ever known.

I know full well that those eyes, which are now black and devoid of any light, will never shine again. As I continue to examine, that which my childhood friend has become, I cannot help but feel a lump forming in my throat. What does the world look like through them? It must be so dark... We've been through so much together this past year, yet I haven't really taken the time to fully accept what is happening to the world... or to us.

I think back to the days when we were teens. Our only concern in life was getting into clubs. It doesn't feel like that long ago, that Sam was fending off all the creepy guys who would hit on me night after night. I never gave it much thought back then. Even if I had, what would it matter? I doubt that the attraction was reciprocal.

Sam was always something else - fearless, but not reckless; strong, yet gentle; simple, yet beautiful in so many ways. I should have been honest... Why have I been lying to myself for all these years? What have I been so afraid of?

The deafening roar of the engines is muffled by the military-grade headsets. I turn my head and peer into the dim green corridor, that is the body of the plane. I don't even remember what normal flights feel like anymore. There are no rows or seat numbers. No flight attendants shuffling down the aisle, providing customer service to grumpy passengers. All of whom are crammed into seats that are spaced for maximum occupancy, rather than humans.

Instead, the walls and center of the plane are lined with flip-down benches that run the length of the fuselage. No one is wearing the typical 'comfy clothes' or business attire that has become the norm for air travel. There are no crying babies, no stranger drooling on my shoulder because he fell asleep watching an inflight movie.

The passengers of this flight all look the same. Their uniforms, their hair, everyone is the same. As I look closer, I see the faces of students, interns, office workers, and kids who should be taking orders at a drive-through from annoying customers, not from military commanders. Many of them are now battle-hardened. Some, have had to watch their friends torn from life and most have been forced to make choices that no one should have to at their age.

They should be bitching about first-world problems and posting pictures of their crappy dinners and over-exaggerated social life on the latest social media platform - eagerly awaiting to see how many 'likes' and comments they'll receive. All in order to feel validated, in a seemingly pointless race of 'keeping up with the Joneses.'

Instead, they've stepped up, faced horrors, and now share the looks of those who have come before them. Whenever I looked at old war photos, I never gave much thought to the fact that the faces did not belong to men and women who were raised to fight; but to kids who found themselves in the throes of death and were forced to grow up, or to die trying. Some might say that it is a horrible thing to endure. Yet, here they are, ready to jump into the belly of the beast...

Sam's scales reflect the green overhead light in the most amazing way. I try not to stare, but I can't help myself. My friend sits silently, with sadness about what is to come. It is somehow blatantly visible in those black eyes. The scales resemble tiny, grey crystals, fitted ever so perfectly. They form fascinating patterns, that mesmerize the imagination. In some strange way, it is beautiful.

I feel like a child, staring at something so absurd. Trying to describe what I see to someone who hadn't seen Sam or another evolved would sound crazy. Perhaps, the listener would think that I spend too much time playing video games or that I need to stop reading all that fantasy stuff. Yet, this is real. Half-human and half-dragon, that is what my life-long friend has become.

The light above us turns red, indicating that we are about to jump. I reach over and squeeze Sam's hand. In part, because I am scared, but I'm also curious. In all this time, although we've hugged, I haven't felt Sam's skin.

"Holy, shit!" I exclaim. I thought it... I thought it would be like -"

"Like when you touched that snake, at the petting zoo?" Sam interrupts.

"Yes," I admit and probably turn every shade of red. "I didn't really know what to expect. But it feels like... silk. I don't get it. How are you bulletproof?"

"Sometimes, I wish I wasn't..." Sam replies with a certain sadness. "Perhaps then you would not have to see me this way..."

"How dare you?" I yell out in frustration. "I should slap y-"

"Here we go!" A female voice announces over the plane's communication system, as the ramp in the back begins to open.

We're almost there. My knees begin to shake a little. It's always a bit unnerving before we jump. But this time, the enemy is not like us. It is no longer just another Evolved nor is it human. Who knows what nightmares await us below?

We aren't children anymore... The thought hits me as though all this time we were playing a game.

I cannot help but think about the fact that some, maybe even all of us won't make it. I guess I was so lost in thought that I didn't realize I was next to jump. Sam, right behind me, ready as always.

I am not sure if it is the uncertainty about what we are headed into or fear of the possibility that I may never get another opportunity... but for a split second, I feel a rush of whimsical courage. The kind that affords one a moment to break through inhibitions and forget about society's judging gaze.

I spin around on my heels. My hands lunge forward and grasp Sam's uniform. Our eyes lock and a chill runs down my spine. I don't know what this means, but it feels perfect.

"I know you hate it..." I shout, but my words are barely audible. "But I've always preferred your full name... Samantha."

Through a sincere smile, I lean in and kiss her, more passionately than I have ever kissed anyone before... Then I let go. Fearlessly stepping off the ramp and into the abyss. I can feel a stupid grin forming on my face, as I plummet toward the battle below and likely some twisted death.

At least now she knows.

THE STORY CONTINUES...

IN

HELIX MYSTERIES:
THE SECOND SUNS

A special thanks:

Dear Reader, I want to sincerely thank you for joining me and my characters on this crazy journey. I've been working on this book for over ten years. So, I hope you had some laughs, enjoyed the twists, found some inspiration, and are excited to see what comes next. I know I am.

Thank you for reading…

Sincerely,

- Daniel

Get Involved in Helix Mysteries!

If you love this story and want to learn more, show support, contribute to the Helix Mysteries Universe, or want to connect with Daniel, please visit: www.endisherenews.com

Find him on Twitter: @castlewrite

Made in the USA
Columbia, SC
06 February 2023

11189573R00193